MW00586741

BLOOD RUBIES

BLOOD RUBIES

MAILAN DOQUANG

THE MYSTERIOUS PRESS
NEW YORK

BLOOD RUBIES

Mysterious Press
An Imprint of Penzler Publishers
58 Warren Street
New York, N.Y. 10007

First Mysterious Press edition

Interior design by Maria Fernandez

Library of Congress Control Number: 2023922768

Cloth ISBN: 978-1-61316-521-8
ebook ISBN: 978-1-61316-522-5

10 9 8 7 6 5 4 3 2 1

Printed in the United States of America
Distributed by W. W. Norton & Company

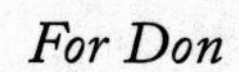

For Don

DAY 7

Upper Manhattan

Ten thousand and eighty sounds like a lot. Imagine someone handing you a check for over ten thousand dollars, or ten thousand kittens running loose inside your house. What if, by some anomaly of nature or science, you were ten thousand times stronger than everyone else? Ten thousand times faster? An honest-to-god superhero. Ten thousand may seem like a lot, but Rune Sarasin—clever fox that she was—knew better. Her eyes darted around the pitch-black room. A ragged breath escaped her lips. She pulled hard at her restraints, rattling the metal chair. Ten thousand and eighty minutes. A hundred and sixty-eight hours. Seven measly days. That was all it took for her life to derail.

Her head snapped sideways at the low creaking coming from outside the room. The sound was ominous. And it was close. Just how close, she couldn't be sure. The darkness was disorienting. The oppressive heat didn't help, nor did the blows she took to the head and torso. She sat immobile—her breath shallow, her ears tuned in to the silence. A twinge of panic jabbed at her as she waited for the creaking to return. *No*, she pleaded silently when she felt it swell inside her chest. She had to keep her wits about her, otherwise she would never get out of this room. She squeezed her eyes shut and counted down slowly.

Five . . . four . . . three . . . two . . . one . . .

Her eyes sprang open. The measured ritual did not have its usual calming effect. If anything, it made her hyperaware of the passing time. Every molecule in her body told her that the longer she stayed in this room, the worse things would be.

Another creak hoisted Rune's head straight up. The sound was closer this time, so close the hairs on her body stood at attention. Her heart thundered against her ribs. She took an unsteady breath to force it back into a normal rhythm. Her cheeks puffed when she let the air out, dislodging the auburn locks plastered against her skin. She wanted to scream when the synthetic strands settled at the base of her neck. Fear magnified every sensation—the scratchiness of her wig, the gritty film coating her tinted contacts, the starched cotton of the prim navy-blue dress she picked up earlier that day. She had changed her appearance for a particularly tricky job—one that involved ripping off a powerful gemstone collector. What she did was wrong, there was no question, but she was paying for it a hundred times over now.

A bead of sweat rolled off Rune's brow, snaking its way down her temple until it reached the tip of her earlobe. It slithered past a trio of jade studs, dangling perilously for a moment before dripping onto her neck. It was the smallest of things, but it was the proverbial last straw. A feral growl rose from her throat as her willpower faltered and slipped away. She bucked ferociously against her bindings. The plastic zip ties bit into her wrists. Her back spasmed as she flailed from side to side, flopping uselessly like a fish in its death throes.

Most people would give up hope in these circumstances. They would close their eyes and pray to God or Vishnu or whoever to spare them any more pain. They would beg for death to come quickly. But Rune wasn't like most people. Her name meant "happy" in Thai, but there had always been a darkness about her. At least that's what her dapper Asian father and whey-haired American mother used to say.

We've given you the world. How much more is it going to take?

Smile sweetheart. Those lines will become permanent.

Maybe it was Rune's nature. Or maybe it was something else. All she knew was that life's horrors found her early—in places where she was supposed to be safe. She had quashed her guilt and anger. Pieced herself back together. Left that weak girl behind. Or so she thought. The weight of the memories prompted her to wrench her feet so hard it sent electric shocks all the way up her legs. Her face contorted in a soundless scream. The pain was terrible. Excruciating, even. But it had an unexpected effect. It cut through her terror and fueled her determination. She gave another wrench. *Yessss!* she howled silently as her legs pulsed and ached. Pain was good. Pain was useful. She wanted to feel every bit of it.

The wrist cuffs were too tight to slip out of, but that didn't stop Rune from trying. She struggled for several long minutes, twisting her hands until the plastic was slippery with her blood. When that failed, she tugged with all her might to rip them from the frame of the chair. Her efforts left her panting from exertion, but no closer to freedom. Undeterred, she tried again, chomping on her lip to keep from crying out as her joints strained in their sockets. This time, the bindings gave ever so slightly. It was all the encouragement she needed. She redoubled her efforts, madly pulling her arms until every bit of energy was drained from her. She paused to catch her breath.

You can do this. You can do this, she repeated silently, trying to summon the strength to continue. Failing was not an option. Not after what she had been through.

Creak . . . creak . . .

Rune's eyes flicked sideways, wide and panicked. The sound was louder and more regular than before. She knew what it meant. Her captor was out there, pacing just outside the door—preparing for the next round of beatings, preparing to kill her. She angled her head to listen for the slightest change in his rhythm. The wait stretched on so long it was almost a relief when the creaking finally stopped. She let out a thin breath, but her relief was short-lived. Fear soon took its place. It started slowly—a twinge in the pit of her stomach, a metallic taste at the back of her throat. Then came the avalanche of terror at the thought of what was coming next. A high-pitched ringing filled her ears. Her muscles twitched uncontrollably. She released her bladder, soaking herself and her new dress. She whimpered as she felt what little control she had slip from her grasp.

Five . . . four . . . three . . . two . . . one . . . Five . . . four . . . three . . . two . . . one . . .

She counted down methodically. Obsessively. Bodily autonomy was no longer hers, but she still had her mind. That he could never take away from her.

Long seconds passed. The seconds turned to minutes, but still the door remained closed. Maybe this was his ploy all along—to terrify her to death. The fear was a manacle around her chest, constricting her breathing until she was gasping for air.

"Open the door, you bastard!" she shouted when she couldn't stand the silence a moment longer. She had meant the words to come out defiantly, but her voice shook with angry terror. She tried again, more forcefully this time. "Did you hear me? I said open the goddamned door!" An eerie stillness greeted her words, but she knew he was out there. She had never been more certain of anything in her life.

With no other course of action, Rune resumed her compulsive counting. She was in the middle of her fifth set when she first noticed the rising temperature. New York in the summer was always a sloppy mess, but this was something different. The room felt hotter than it did even moments before. The drops of sweat that dotted her forehead were now steady rivulets. Her breathing was more labored.

It's all in your head, Rune chastised herself silently. She had almost convinced herself when an acrid smell crept into her nostrils. Then her eyes started to burn, and it wasn't the wretched contacts.

"No!" Rune croaked. The realization of what he had done came crashing down on her. All that creaking—it wasn't him pacing outside the door. It was the sound of wood being transformed—at a molecular level—by heat. The building was on fire, and she was trapped inside.

"Help!" she cried out, even though there was no one around to hear her. "Somebody! Please, help me!"

She redoubled her efforts to free herself, roaring with fear and rage as smoke poured into the room. She didn't want to die this way—alone in the dark. She didn't want to die at all. A fit of coughing wracked her body, but still Rune struggled, rocking wildly as she fought to free herself from her restraints. "Let me out!" she screamed, thrashing and pulling with more strength than she knew she possessed.

It wasn't just the prospect of an excruciating death that drove Rune to shred her skin and sprain her own wrist. It was knowing that her dying would doom the only people she loved in the world—Kit, her boyfriend of nearly a year, and Madee, the precocious kid sister he'd been raising for over a decade. Without her, Kit was as good as dead. And with both of them gone, there would be no one left to look for Madee. Spunky, gapped-toothed Madee—all of fifteen years old. Rune choked back a sob. The cost of her failures filled her with profound sadness. The feeling washed over her. It blotted out fear. It blotted out everything.

The smoke in the room thickened, caressing Rune's body and slithering into her orifices. Her movements slowed as her energy began to wane. A rattled gasp slipped from her lips. Tears streamed down her face. She wondered, as she had repeatedly over the past seven days, just how it had come to this. She opened her mouth to call for help one last time, but the words stayed lodged in her throat.

So this is how it ends, she said silently as she felt herself start to let go. All the tension and gut-knotting fear that had gripped her began to seep from her body. Her eyelids fluttered shut. Her body went slack. There was nothing left to do but to accept the inevitable. And so, with a final labored breath, she did.

DAY 1

1

The Mandarin Oriental, Bangkok

"You need to relaaaaax," Rune murmured as she glanced at Kit's latest text. It was the third he had sent in thirty minutes, each more urgent than the last. She didn't bother responding. Kit was a worrywart. Besides, all would be forgiven when he saw their haul.

She closed the safe and gave the dial a quick spin, watching as the numbers dissolved into a quivering white halo. She waited for the digits to reappear before turning to scan the luxury suite one last time. Her lips curled in a satisfied smile. Everything was as it should be. The iridescent silk cushions and polished teak furnishings were exactly as she found them when she arrived. The bed was made, the bathroom towels undisturbed. The only sign of her presence was the room service tray outside the door. The mid-job pick-me-up was an indulgence, to be sure, but Rune forgave herself the small transgression. After all, the Mandarin Oriental was renowned for its fine dining and it would have been a shame to miss out. The room's rightful guest, an American gemstone trafficker named Charles Lemaire, would undoubtedly notice the tray, but Rune was willing to bet he would dismiss it as a housekeeping hiccup or otherwise explain it away. She had learned long ago that making excuses was one of the things people did best, no matter the circumstances. By the time the American put two and two together, she would be long gone. And so would his blood rubies.

Rune fixed her gaze on the sun as it disappeared over the Chao Phraya River sixteen stories below. She was, by any conceivable measure, unusual, an arresting synthesis of her Asian and white parents. Her cheekbones were high, her lips the color of Bing cherries—her signature shade. She kept her dark hair sheared almost to the scalp, with a chevron pattern etched at the nape of her neck. To say that her hazel eyes were the size of an anime character's was only a slight exaggeration. She stepped closer to the window, her golden skin taking on an even warmer hue under the variegated shades of orange and purple streaking the smog-filled sky. She closed her eyes and let her mind float to a different time—a darker time—when freedom was just a word on a page. A pained expression crossed her face, only to fade an instant later. Those days were long past. She was in control now.

9-1-1!

The phone buzzing in Rune's hand jerked her back to the present. The American was on his way up. It was her cue to move. She grabbed her motorcycle helmet from the coffee table and slipped it on before stepping into the well-lit hallway.

A uniformed maid pushing a cart of soiled linens shot her a curious look just as she closed the door. Rune lowered her tinted visor and made her way to the bank of elevators, her sneaker-clad feet gliding silently over the marble floor. She passed a middle-aged blond couple on the way, both looking worse for wear after long hours of sightseeing. Neither adhered to the Mandarin Oriental's strict evening dress code. Then again, neither did she. The woman's face was bright red, but whether it was from sun exposure or exertion, Rune couldn't be sure. Sweat stains marred the man's white linen button-down. He ogled her lithe body unabashedly, his eyes lingering on her paper-thin muscle tank and faded black jeans. On any other day, Rune might have called out the boorish behavior, but she was in a hurry. Besides, if the wife didn't speak up, why should she?

The elevator dinged. Rune stepped inside and punched the button for the lobby. She kept her eyes trained forward and her back straight as the doors closed, the familiar sound of Vivaldi's *Four Seasons* filling the empty cab. It stopped midway through its descent for a harried couple and their three children, the youngest of whom was a fussy infant. The doors closed. The middle child, a toddler with an enviable head of red hair, wobbled when the elevator began to move, bracing himself against Rune's thigh with a sticky hand. She winced behind her helmet and exited on the following floor.

She was waiting for the next elevator when she heard the crackle of a radio to her left. If it hadn't been for her dark visor, the two security guards at the end of the hallway would have seen her mottled eyes narrow ever so slightly.

"Come on, come on, come on," she muttered, punctuating her words with firm jabs of the elevator button. The guards gestured in her direction. Rune swore under her breath. She was made. It was an unfortunate development, but not entirely unexpected. The fact was, this was the fourth luxury hotel she and Kit had hit in as many weeks. Word had clearly gotten around. Without so much as a look back, she turned on her heel and strode away.

"Yut!" one of the guards called out. *Stop!*

Rune quickened her pace. The guards' footsteps rang out behind her. She caught sight of an exit sign up ahead and hurried to close the distance. She was about to disappear down the stairwell when another idea came to mind. She spun to face her pursuers. Her hand shot up to the fire alarm. It was a peculiar hand adorned with pure black nail polish and rings on every finger, even on her thumb. She grabbed the lever. The men froze.

"Yaa tham!" they shouted in unison. *Don't!*

It was too late. The clanging sliced through the hotel's meditative atmosphere, luring well-heeled guests from their rooms.

"Bomb!" Rune yelled with just the right amount of urgency in her voice. "Everybody, get out! There's a bomb in the hotel!" Her panic was contagious. Before she knew it, she was engulfed by jittery masses teetering on the edge of a stampede. A mischievous smile played on her lips as she slipped down the stairs and melted into the crowd.

The situation escalated in the time it took Rune to reach the lobby. Unnerved guests jostled to flee the building. Their screams bounced off the marble-clad walls and the lofty coffered ceiling. The normally sweet-dispositioned staff showed signs of strain as their directions went unheeded amid the deafening cries and the trample of footfalls. The frenzied hordes charged toward the hotel's main entrance as if their lives depended on it, because for all they knew, it did. Furniture toppled in the frantic effort to escape the building. Trapped behind slow-moving bodies, one group lost patience and smashed an armchair through a window leading to the hotel's manicured grounds, sending shards of glass in every direction. A fight broke out beneath a multi-tiered floral arrangement that hung like a chandelier at the center of the room. Fists flew until one man threw another headfirst into a fountain filled with pale pink lotus flowers. It overflowed the moment his body hit the water, making the floor dangerously slippery.

If Rune felt any remorse about the mayhem she had caused, it certainly didn't show. Property damage was not her concern, nor was the physical and mental well-being of the guests. She elbowed her way through the mob disgorging from the hotel and cast a final look back. Unbelievably, the two guards she'd encountered on the upper level still had her in their sights. She silently cursed the sticky-handed ginger who put her in this mess before ramming her shoulder into an oversized plant potter.

Crack!

"Gun!" Rune screamed. "Get back inside! He has a gun!"

The guests went to pieces, pushing and pulling in opposing directions as they were forced to choose between an active shooter and a fiery death. Rune congratulated herself for her quick-thinking and sprinted toward the vintage Ducati Scrambler idling in the street.

"What happened?" Kit asked as she swung her leg over the bike. His English was heavily accented. His black outfit matched hers almost exactly, save the red stripe on his helmet.

"Not now, love," Rune said tightly. Her heart raced inside her chest. Her skin prickled uncomfortably. She had been outside less than a minute, but beads of sweat were already forming all over her body. Going from blasting air-conditioning to the great outdoors was never an easy transition in Bangkok—a city that held the dubious honor of being one of the world's hottest—but it was particularly challenging during monsoon season, when the humidity was so high as to be nearly suffocating.

"We have to talk," said Kit.

"Not now," Rune repeated.

As if on cue, the guards emerged from the crowd and zeroed in on them. "Thang nan!" one of them shouted, gesturing madly in their direction. *Over there!*

"Drive!"

Kit didn't need to be told twice. The engine came to life. The Ducati lurched forward. Rune cast a glance over her shoulder just as they were about to make their first turn. One of the guards looked to be tearing his hair out at the roots. The other was spitting instructions into a cellphone the size of an Etch A Sketch. She threw her head back and laughed so loudly the sound cut through the rumble of rush hour traffic.

2

Central Bangkok

If making a quick getaway without drawing attention was an art, Kit was an undisputed maestro. He drove neither too quickly nor too slowly along Charoen Krung Road, the oldest paved street in Bangkok. He did not obey traffic laws. No self-respecting local did. Instead, he split lanes and wove between cars whenever it was convenient, like every other motorcyclist on the road. Rune's breath caught when he cut in front of a blue and white city bus. In her native New York, such an infraction would have led to a barrage of honking or even a shouting match, but the people of Bangkok were positively genteel about such matters.

Traffic ground to a halt at a red light. The Ducati stopped behind a motorcycle taxi carrying a schoolgirl riding sidesaddle—sans helmet—with one hand on the back of the seat and a cellphone in the other. Beside them was a family of four crammed inside a tuk-tuk, a motorized rickshaw and unofficial Thai emblem. The mother fanned herself listlessly with a guidebook, while the father kept his eyes firmly on the darkened road. Sandwiched between them were two squabbling tweens whose voices twisted and tangled so gratingly Rune was of a mind to intervene. She was spared from the task when the light turned green and the motorcycle sprang forward, leaving the schoolgirl with the death wish and the miserable family behind.

They had barely made it one block when Rune spied two Royal Thai Police officers on Yamaha FZ1 motorbikes whizzing between lanes from the other direction. She held her breath and counted down slowly.

Five . . . four . . . three . . . two . . . one . . .

The wail of sirens cut through the night air just when she thought they were in the clear. A quick look back confirmed what she already knew. The cops had made a U-turn and were flying toward them. She gave Kit a firm tap on the thigh, but he was already a step ahead of her, edging the bike well past the speed limit. They both knew that the Ducati was no match for the Yamahas. Brains, not brawn, was their only way out of this.

Rune issued rapid-fire directions over the roar of the engine. Kit's driving became more reckless in response. They reached a fork in the road and hung left, zipping across a canal faster than road conditions warranted. A light turned red up ahead.

"Go!" Rune shouted.

Kit gunned the motor, taking aim at the rapidly closing gap between two cars traveling in opposite directions. The drivers leaned on their horns and slammed on their brakes, their screeching tires leaving ugly skid marks on the road. Rune shrieked as they sped through, not out of fear, but out of the sheer exhilaration that came with living on the precipice. She was a thrill-seeker and an adrenaline addict, always had been.

Kit's maneuver didn't spare them for long. The cops were behind them again and steadily making up ground. Rune's senses sharpened when she spotted the traffic circle marking the entrance to Chinatown up ahead. The neighborhood's warren of streets was an ideal place to lose a tail. She leaned with the motorcycle as they thundered through the roundabout, the golden spires of the famed Wat Traimit a mere blur in her peripheral vision. She pointed to the right. Kit understood her meaning immediately and veered onto a one-way street heading in the wrong direction. Car horns blared as they dodged a flatbed truck hauling racks of untreated lumber. The driver of a black Mercedes sedan hurled profanities at them as they narrowly avoided a head-on collision.

Kit took a hard turn across three lanes of heavy traffic. He jumped the curb, earning vociferous protests from pedestrians as he maneuvered the Ducati along the crowded sidewalk, storefronts on one side, temporary food stalls on the other. The pungent smell of fish sauce wafted from a popular noodle stand where a young woman with unexpectedly muscular forearms toiled over a collection of smoking woks. A flame burst from a blackened grill layered with savory moo ping skewers. The heat was even more oppressive here, held in place by tarps erected to shelter shoppers from Bangkok's torrential rains and scorching sun.

A strident sound rang out from behind, followed milliseconds later by a long plaintive cry. Rune turned in time to see the two Yamahas speeding away from an upended fruit cart and its elderly minder. The decent thing would have been to stop and lend a hand, but the officers had other priorities.

Kit steered the Ducati off the sidewalk and made a sharp turn on Maha Chak road, a cramped side street and favorite parking spot for motorcycle and scooter aficionados. A deliveryman pushing a hand truck piled high with plastic soda crates stepped out from between two idling cars. Kit swerved to avoid mowing him down, slamming straight into a parked BMW sports bike. It toppled to one side, knocking over the adjacent bike, which in turn knocked the next one over. The domino effect ran all the way down the length of the street, coming to an end with a metallic clunk. Startled bystanders were briefly left speechless, but their surprise quickly turned to fury as the scope of the damage set in. They poured into the street, forming a barrier that threatened to block traffic. The Ducati growled as they closed in. Kit was an adept Muay Thai fighter, and after nearly a year of training, Rune was not half bad herself, but the two of them combined were no match for a rankled crowd.

"Get us out of here," she murmured nervously. "To the ferry."

Kit immediately complied, picking up speed until they blew through the intersection at the end of the block. Meanwhile, the crowd behind them grew thicker and more vocal. The first cop needled his way through their ranks, but his partner was not so fortunate. He was besieged the moment he skidded to a stop.

The remaining Yamaha continued to give chase, closing in on the Ducati at a speed that surprised even its driver. The neighborhood grew emptier and more dilapidated the further they rode. Kit made a series of hard turns. Rune tightened her grip around his waist. Within moments, the Ratchawong Ferry Terminal came into view. Rune's jaw clenched as they barreled toward it. Right on schedule, a river crossing boat was pulling away from the dock, ready to make the five-minute journey to the opposite bank of the Chao Phraya.

Kit hit the brakes. The bike careened to a halt. They jumped off in tandem, sprinting past the ticket booth and down a metal ramp, their eyes fixed on the rapidly growing gap between the pier and the boat. By the time they reached it, it seemed impossibly wide. They took the leap in unison, flying through the air as the murky water sloshed beneath them. Their feet hit the ferry with a heavy thud, earning them bewildered stares from fellow passengers. Rune turned just in time to see the cop stop short at the end of the pier. She watched him for several long seconds. When she reached a safe distance, she took off her helmet and locked eyes with him. Her shirt flapped in the night breeze. Her chest rose and fell as she fought to catch her breath.

"We need to talk," Kit said, his breathing ragged and shallow.

Rune directed her gaze at him. He, too, had removed his helmet, revealing a shock of bubblegum-pink hair and luminous skin that was the color of raw honey. *God, he's beautiful*, she thought. His eyes were so dark they were nearly black, his cheekbones so high he looked like he'd gone under the knife. The only imperfection on his face was a small scar by his right temple, a memento of the car wreck that had made orphans out of him and Madee. She leaned in for a kiss.

"Don't be cross," she said when he turned away. She pulled a soft pouch from her pocket and poured the contents into her hand, revealing two dozen AAA rubies that glittered beneath the boat's swaying lights. Then she flashed him a victorious smile and said, "There's plenty here for a new bike."

"Forget the damn bike."

Rune's elation faltered. There was an edge in Kit's voice. It was her first inkling that something serious was wrong. His next words brought her world to a screeching halt.

"It's Madee. She's missing."

3

Sky Bar, Bangkok

A crisis of a different sort was unfolding simultaneously a few miles away, on the rooftop of the State Tower, one of Bangkok's tallest skyscrapers. Charles Lemaire—known to everyone simply by his surname—strode into the photogenic Sky Bar like a man accustomed to wielding power. He had the posture of someone who had served in the military. Not a strand of brown hair was out of place. There was a small scab on his chin where he had nicked himself shaving. The rest of his angular face shone like polished glass. He ignored the hostess with the insinuating smile and made his way to the crowded bar. The view from the open-air venue was unbeatable, but Lemaire paid it no heed. He was angry. No, it was worse than that. He was raging, but his command of his emotions was such that only those closest to him would have noticed. His security chief, a mountain of a man named Michael Anderson, was one such person. Lemaire waited until they were both seated before quietly taking Michael to task. "My rubies are gone," he said in a deliberately even tone. His pale eyes bore into Michael's. "Explain to me how that happened."

"I don't know, sir," Michael replied with a flap of his arms. His cherubic features wrinkled with uncertainty. His jacket strained heroically across his broad chest.

"It's your job to know."

"I reached out to my contact at the hotel. He's working on it."

"For your sake, he better work fast."

The bartender arrived just in time to stop Lemaire from laying into Michael. It didn't much matter. The man had worked for him long enough to take even his most opaque threats seriously. Top-shelf bourbon and a club soda with a twist of lime appeared in front of them moments later.

"The police are sweeping the hotel. It will be a few hours before they let us back in," Michael said after taking a sip of his club soda.

Lemaire adjusted his glass so that it was precisely centered on its coaster. His perfectionism was not a quirk, but a barometer of his mental state. The more pressure he was under, the more exacting he became. His temporal vein thumped as he thought about his stolen rubies. If he didn't recoup them, he would be out a quarter of a million dollars. The thought made him reach for his bourbon and down it in one go.

"Another!" Michael called out to the bartender.

Lemaire's lips formed a tight line. He knew Michael was overcompensating. The minion probably thought he could salvage the situation, but forgiveness wasn't Lemaire's style, not when it came to money. He brushed an invisible piece of lint off his dress shirt and wondered if some clever outsider had somehow gotten wind of his operation, or if he had a traitor in his midst. He was keenly aware that smuggling rubies into Thailand—a global hub for the illegal gemstone trade—depended heavily on loyalty.

Maybe it was one of the miners. Or perhaps a courier, Lemaire said to himself before nixing the idea. People at the bottom of the food chain didn't even know who he was, much less where he was staying. The same could not be said for the customs officials on his payroll. There were three of them in total, all stationed in Mae Sai, a sprawling town straddling the border of Thailand and Myanmar.

Lemaire's head twisted upward at the distant sound of thunder. *Goddamn monsoons*, he thought. He loathed traveling to Thailand from his home base in the States, but Bangkok was the epicenter of a lucrative gemstone market and close to the world's primary source of high-grade rubies—Mogok in central Myanmar. The Mogok stone tract was home to hundreds of mining operations that sourced Burmese rubies—also known as pigeon blood rubies—gems valued for their incredible clarity and deeply saturated hue. Most rubies from Mogok reached global markets through licensed dealers, with annual exports nearing half a billion dollars, but an increasingly significant portion bypassed official channels entirely. Lemaire's gemstones were among these. Ironically, it was the growing demand for ethical gemstones that fueled the black market. Concerned about human rights violations, international retailers large and small were refusing to do business with the Myanmar Gems Enterprise, the government body tasked with regulating the country's gemstone industry. Genocide gems, activists called them. Blood rubies, the selling of which propped up a repressive military regime. Conscientious buyers were catching on, prompting retailers to seek out responsibly sourced rubies, or rather, rubies that could be passed off as such. Consequently, more and more gems coming out of Mogok's mines were exported outside the formal system and then received a more palatable provenance.

Lemaire had been capitalizing on these developments over the past decade, with an end-to-end business he built from the ground up. He recruited men, women, and children to mine illegally in Mogok, hired mules to transport the ill-gotten rubies to Bangkok, and paid skilled lapidaries to cut and polish the stones on the down-low. He then sold the gems on the legitimate market, alongside expertly forged certificates of origin attesting to their Thai origin. Ethical buyers around the world were none the wiser.

A roll of thunder sounded, closer and louder than before. Lemaire huffed before he could catch himself. He had every reason to be upset and not just about the impending rain. Losing a shipment of rubies was not a mere setback but a disaster of the highest order. Half the stolen gems were already earmarked for specific buyers. Worse, the shipment included a particularly large ruby that could easily fetch six figures. Lemaire was calculating how to make up for the loss when he heard Michael's phone emit a soft ping.

"We have a lead, boss."

Lemaire inclined his head as if to say, *Continue.*

"My contact got his hands on the surveillance footage from the hotel. We can access it as soon as the authorities clear the building."

"Show me."

Michael handed over his phone without hesitation. He didn't think twice when Lemaire slipped it into the pocket of his perfectly pressed trousers, nor was he concerned when his boss stepped away from the bar to make a call. He took a sip of his club soda and watched Lemaire disappear into the crowd. The cold liquid felt good as it slid down his throat. He took another sip and surveyed the room with attentive eyes.

The first sign that something was off came a few minutes later, when two men from Lemaire's local entourage showed up. One was tall and lanky with bloodless skin and thinning black hair. The other was short and powerfully built. They had names, but for the life of him, Michael couldn't remember what they were.

"Come with us," the tall man said.

"What's this about? Where's Lemaire?"

"That's not your concern anymore."

"The hell it isn't!" Michael knew what was happening. Lemaire was blaming him for the theft and kicking him to the curb. Acid pooled inside his stomach. He had given up everything for this job—his wife, his twin daughters, the house he renovated with his own bare hands. For what? To get fired for something that wasn't even his fault. Lemaire should have kept a tighter lid on his whereabouts, and the Mandarin Oriental should have invested in better safes. "This is bullshit," he said so loudly that other bar patrons turned to stare. "You can tell the boss I said as much."

"Take it easy," said the short man. "There's no need to make a scene."

Michael rose to his full height. He puffed his chest out so far the middle button popped off his shirt. Then he felt a gun press against his ribcage and his bravado melted away.

"Come with us," the tall man repeated.

This time, Michael acquiesced. He suddenly understood that more than just his job was at stake. A lot more. He seemed to shrink as he allowed himself to be led away from the crowd to a deserted corner of the bar, far from the tipsy patrons and well-trained staff. *So this is it*, he thought. The words played in his mind like a soundtrack on a continuous loop, but Michael didn't truly believe it would happen until he found himself standing on the ledge of the building. He glanced at the traffic zooming below and felt a surge of vertigo. His oversized body swayed. He raised his eyes until he found himself staring down the end of the tall man's pistol.

"Go on," the man said.

Michael shook his head.

"Do it, and your family will live."

Michael knew he was serious. He had helped Lemaire make dozens of people disappear over the years, some of them innocents. Still, he couldn't bring himself to step over the edge. "Give me a minute," he begged. "Just one minute."

"No," the short man said. He took a step forward. His eyes were devoid of mercy.

"Wait!"

But it was too late. The man gave him a hard shove. Michael's face registered his surprise. His enormous body swayed as he fought—and failed—to keep his balance.

At first he felt weightless. Then he felt nothing at all.

4

Khlong Toei Slum, Bangkok

The Land of Smiles. The City of Angels. These pithy catchphrases helped draw roughly twenty million tourists to the Thai capital each year, making it the single most visited city in the world. Critics pointed to rampant corruption and soaring crime rates, and to the country's antiquated lèse-majesté laws and military strongmen, but nothing could stanch the flow of visitors to the thriving metropolis. They came for the street food and the nightlife. The Grand Palace, the Temple of Dawn, and the Chatuchak Weekend Market were at the top of every itinerary. Sightseeing took them to every corner of the city. Every corner, that is, except the notorious Khlong Toei slum.

Rune and Kit climbed out of their tuk-tuk to the deafening sound of traffic. They were on the outer edge of the slum, under the perpetually busy Chalerm Maha Nakhon Expressway. They could have done without the walk, but their driver refused to take them any further, even declining a generous tip. Given Khlong Toei's maze of unpaved alleys and dead ends, Rune couldn't say she blamed him.

"Madee was here this afternoon!" Kit said loudly, trying to be heard over the cars zooming above.

"What?" Rune shouted back.

"This way!" He inclined his head and started toward the defunct rail line marking the slum's northern edge.

Rune hesitated before following. She wasn't normally skittish, but it was dark, and she was the boob about to enter Bangkok's sketchiest neighborhood with a fortune's worth of rubies in her pocket. A lump formed at the back of her throat. "This has to be a mistake," she said when the din of traffic finally receded.

"Not according to the app," Kit replied. "I tracked Madee's phone when she didn't check in after school." He brushed his pink bangs away from his eyes and held up his phone for Rune to see. Sure enough, it showed the Khlong Toei Youth Center as Madee's last location.

"That was three hours ago."

"Her phone went dead after that."

No phone. No help. The lump in Rune's throat grew. "Isn't the Youth Center a place for street kids? What was Madee doing there?"

Kit shook his head and averted his eyes. Rune didn't push the issue. She could tell he didn't want to talk. He got that way sometimes—quiet and distant. Taking care of his sister weighed on him, even on the best of days.

He never lets me do anything!

He loves you. He's just trying to protect you.

He's ruining my life!

Madee was a good kid, but like all fifteen-year-olds, she knew how to push her brother's buttons. She was mouthy. She spent more time online than Kit liked. And she flat out refused to abide by her curfew. The fact that Kit was a teenager himself when their father drove into a pole with the family in the car only complicated matters. Madee was too young to remember, but Kit's world went dark after that. He told Rune all about it the night they met. How he'd spent months in the hospital and four hellish years in foster care. How he'd visited Madee in secret every day. How he'd petitioned the court for legal custody as soon as he reached the age of majority. He never spoke about the accident after that first night. He coped alone and Rune didn't press him. When you lived through one catastrophe, you spent the rest of your life girding yourself for the next.

Rune was still thinking about the accident when they turned a corner and found themselves in the slum proper. Her shoulders stiffened. She had braced for the worst, but nothing could have prepared her for the labyrinthine alleys of Khlong Toei. Rows of shacks made of decaying wood and corroded metal unfolded before them. The ground was unpaved and littered with all manner of debris. Packs of mangy dogs scavenged through festering mountains of trash. The squalor was disturbing. The noise even more so. To their left, teenaged boys argued over a soccer ball that was visibly soft. To their right, amped-up men gathered around a makeshift enclosure to watch a cockfight. Women and girls were conspicuously absent, probably for good reason. A sweet, sickly smell wafted through the air. Rune's throat tightened when she realized that what she was smelling was crystal meth. "We need to get out of here," she said, unable to keep the tremor out of her voice.

"You're nuts if you think I'm leaving without Madee."

It wasn't just Kit's tone that momentarily stunned Rune, it was the cold glint in his eyes. He had never looked at her like that before. Anyone else would have gotten an earful, but Kit was The One. Rune knew it the moment they met. She spoke her next words slowly. "I don't think you meant to speak to me that way."

Kit stopped and faced her. He looked contrite. Ashamed even. He leaned down and gently pressed his nose against hers, like a Māori performing the traditional hongi.

Rune closed her eyes. This was what he had done when they first met on a crowded Skytrain nearly a year ago to the day.

I know you, he had said with a startled look.

We've never met.

Yes, but I know you.

It was the way he had stressed the word "know" that moved Rune. That, and his behavior. Getting in a stranger's face on public transit could go sideways in a hurry, but she had a soft spot for quirky guys, especially when they looked like Kit. They got off the train that night and had drinks in a converted tobacco factory. Drinks led to dinner. Dinner to sex. They'd been inseparable ever since.

Rune breathed deeply. Kit was her everything. The love of her life. The antidote to her pain. She didn't need him to apologize for snapping at her. She knew better than anyone that fear made people say and do things they otherwise wouldn't.

Kit pulled away, sensing he'd been forgiven. "Come on," he said, giving her hand a gentle tug. "The Youth Center is this way."

Rune tightened her grip as Kit led them deeper into the slum. Every step added to the feeling of encroaching dread. Madee was here, alone in this strange place—this *bad* place—with no way of contacting anyone for help. She struggled to understand why Madee would willingly come here. Unless, of course, she didn't.

A muffled grunt pulled Rune away from her dark thoughts. Her eyes zeroed in on the source—a club-footed man dragging himself forward, inch by painful inch, on the hard ground. An ugly rash marred his otherwise handsome face. His bare torso was crisscrossed with keloid scars of varying shapes and sizes. Rune reached into her pocket and fingered the rubies she had stolen only hours before. The thrill of the job at the Mandarin Oriental seemed distant, like it happened in another life.

"Don't even think about it," Kit said, as if he were reading her mind.

"We don't need all of them," Rune replied. "A small one could get him a decent place to live. And a wheelchair."

"It could also get him killed."

Rune's brow furrowed.

"You'd be putting a target on his back. People die over a lot less in Khlong Toei."

Kit's words stirred a mix of emotions in Rune—sympathy for the man, frustration at her helplessness, anger that some people had so much, while others had nothing at all. The feelings collided with her growing fear for Madee's safety, bubbling just beneath the surface until she forced herself to stuff them away.

"How is it that you know your way around this place?" she asked, not because she was curious but only to distract herself.

"I hung out here after my parents died."

"Strange place for a kid."

"It was better than foster care." A frown clouded his features. "Looking back, it's hard to believe nothing bad ever happened."

Rune grew pensive. She had grown up in vastly different circumstances, but bad things still found her. Her mind wandered to her parents' cozy co-op on the far west side of Manhattan, near the scenic Riverside Park. A dream home for people like them. A perfect place to raise a child. Until everything changed.

"Over there."

Kit's voice intruded on her memories. She followed his gaze to a sprawling complex surrounded by whitewashed walls. "This is it?"

He nodded and led the way to the gated entrance.

The Youth Center was bigger and more modern than Rune had imagined, comprising a number of well-kept buildings scattered around recreational spaces. It was also deserted. The playground was entirely free of children. So was the crystalline pool. A solitary ball lay abandoned on the basketball court. Rows of empty swings creaked in the night breeze. Kit jiggled the handle and gave the gate a firm push. It was locked.

"We're too late," he said with frustration. "It's closed." Dejected, he started to walk away.

"But Madee was here. The least we can do is look around."

"The door's locked."

"So what? Give me a boost."

Kit looked at her with uncertainty.

"What are you waiting for? No one will even know."

He managed a crooked smile. Sometimes Rune's complete disregard for the rules was exactly the right thing. He lifted her by the waist until she was able to grab the top of the gate and hoist herself to other side. He followed with ease.

"Where do you want to start?" Rune asked after he landed soundlessly beside her.

"At the beginning."

5

Khlong Toei Youth Center, Bangkok

The moon was high over Khlong Toei when Rune and Kit finally called off their search. They had left no stone unturned, poking through every bush and peering through every window of the Youth Center. Madee was nowhere to be found. Tensions were high but the mercury mercifully lowered as they retraced their steps to the gate and climbed over, kicking up dust on the other side. They walked to the main road slowly. Wordlessly. There was nothing to say. There was nothing left to do here.

"Where to next?" Rune asked when she couldn't stand the silence any longer.

Kit shook his head to indicate he wasn't sure.

"I think it's time to go to the police." Rune didn't make the suggestion lightly. Any interaction with the cops was risky for people neck deep in the illegal gemstone trade. Her hand unconsciously found the rubies in her pocket.

"The police won't do anything," Kit scoffed.

"But Madee's a minor."

"And?"

"*And* she's been missing for hours."

"You don't understand how things work in Thailand," Kit said with a cursory wave of his hand.

And there it was. *Farang*. Foreigner. *Luk khrueng*. Half child—a colloquial term for people of mixed Thai and non-Thai origin. Her white mother, her American upbringing, and her shaky grasp of the local language made her as alien here as her Thai half made her in the US. It was more subtle, but also more constant back home, a kind of white noise that wouldn't go away, no matter how hard she tried to block it out. People weren't malicious for the most part. Just clueless. Like the girl at school who insisted they were in the same boat because her surname—Hristova—was hard to pronounce, and the teacher who seemed shocked when she proved, over and over again, that she was terrible at math. Reminders that she was different were everywhere and nowhere. Subtle looks. Pregnant silences. Being asked where she was *really* from. What was the saying? A thousand little cuts? A loud sigh came out of her mouth.

"What was that for?" Kit asked, stopping dead in his tracks.

"Do you really have to ask?" Rune replied with the exasperation of someone who was used to being dismissed.

He shot her a perplexed glance.

"Look Kit, I may not have grown up here, but that doesn't mean I'm stupid."

"Whoa, what are we talking about here?"

"The police."

"What about them?"

"We should call them. No cop on this planet looks the other way when a fifteen-year-old child goes missing. It's ridiculous."

"You can't possibly be this naïve."

Rune's eyes flashed. Her exasperation was on the edge of turning into something substantially more volatile.

"Countless kids go missing in Thailand every year. Do you really think the cops care about one girl? Do you?"

Rune found herself at a loss for words. The intensity of Kit's tone took her off guard, as did the look of ire on his face.

"They end up in sweatshops making things people throw away a month after buying, or in private homes working themselves to death as nannies and housekeepers. The truly unlucky ones are sold to sickos who do unspeakable things . . ." Kit paused, overcome by the mere thought of Madee falling prey to traffickers. He took a breath, then continued, "Human trafficking is a multibillion-dollar industry in this country. The networks are global. Everyone is on the take, including the cops. That's why we can't go to them."

Rune suddenly felt very foolish. Kit was right. She *was* an outsider and she didn't know the first thing about police corruption in Thailand. But knowing he was right and admitting it were two entirely different things. A discomfiting silence fell over them.

Only when Kit's shoulders drooped slightly did Rune feel herself soften. "It's going to be okay," she said, her tone on the cusp of conciliatory.

Kit looked up as he fought to regain control of his emotions.

Rune's annoyance evaporated fully when she saw his lips press together. He was hurting. Now wasn't the moment to give him a hard time. "It's going to be okay," she said again. "We'll find Madee. I promise."

"This is all my fault."

"Let's not imagine the worst."

"I should have kept a closer eye on her."

"Seriously, we don't even know that anything's happened. You said so yourself, you used to come here with your friends."

"Madee's nothing like I was at her age. She's book smart, not street smart."

Rune couldn't argue there. School. Homework. Chores. That had been Madee's life since she had been in Kit's care. Only recently had she started rebelling.

You never let me do anything!

Someday you'll thank me, Madee.

It's not fair! I hate you!

Rune adored Kit, but she couldn't blame Madee for pushing back against his rules. She saw firsthand how his anxiety wore on her. That it came from a place of love didn't make it any easier to live with.

"I'll never forgive myself if something happens to her," said Kit.

"Let's just focus on finding her, okay?"

"Where? How?"

"We can start by tracking down Madee's friends. Someone has to know something."

A look of uncertainty shrouded Kit's face. Rune understood his apprehension. Leaving Khlong Toei felt a lot like abandoning Madee, but she knew in her gut it was the right move.

"Let's go," she said, giving his hand a gentle tug. "I know just where to start."

6

Khlong Toei Slum, Bangkok

The slum felt more menacing as Rune and Kit traversed it for the second time. The alleys were emptier, the smell of meth more pronounced. Each turn made Rune realize just how disoriented she really was. If Kit left her now, she would be hard pressed to find her way out. She glanced at her phone, but Google Maps was no match for Khlong Toei's jumble of alleys and dead ends.

Movement behind a pile of weathered cinder blocks caught Rune's attention. She peered through the darkness until two men grinding against each other came into focus. She turned her head, but not before seeing the dominant of the two spin his partner around and wrench his hair so hard his back arched. A gunshot went off in the distance. Somewhere nearby, a baby howled inconsolably. Rune picked up the pace.

"Stop," Kit said in a hushed voice.

She threw him a questioning look.

"Over there." He pointed to an emaciated man slumped in a plastic lawn chair. A threadbare shirt hung from his skeletal frame. There was a large stain on the front of his cargo shorts where he had soiled himself. Open sores lined his spindly arms. Rune dropped her gaze to stop from staring. They landed on a cigarette hanging loosely from the man's fingers. She lowered her eyes further until they found the rainbow-colored backpack at the man's feet. Seeing it was like having a bucket of ice water dumped on her. Her head snapped up. Her eyes found Kit's.

"The bag. It's Madee's," Kit said, confirming what she was thinking.

Rune's breathing grew more rapid. The blood rushed to her head. This was it. Their first tangible link to Madee. She lunged forward, ready to shake any and all information out of the man.

"Slow down," Kit whispered, pulling her back by the arm.

"But this guy might know where Madee is."

"You don't think I know that?"

"Then what are we waiting for?"

"Look at him."

Rune shot the man a quick glance. Kit had a point. The man was clearly high. The situation called for a light touch, not her usual bull-in-a-china-shop approach. *Quiet. Gentle*, she said silently as she considered how to proceed. Several seconds passed, then she called out, "Maa jaak nai?" *Where did you get that?* She spoke the words softly, like she was addressing a spooked animal.

The man looked up from his drug-induced state. His eyes were glassy, his gaze unsteady. She repeated the question. Louder this time.

"You just asked him where he got his horse," Kit said with more than a touch of annoyance in his voice.

Rune backed off. She was the first to admit that her grasp of Thai was questionable, at best. She had begged her father to teach her when she was young, but he was always too busy with work. He taught her other things as she got older, though. Like how to grade and appraise gemstones. It started quite by accident, when Rune showed up at his office in the Diamond District one afternoon after locking herself out of the house. She ignored the fractions and decimals on her worksheet and instead eavesdropped on his conversations. She learned about the four C's that day: color, clarity, cut, and carat. Her father was so impressed when she recited them on the subway ride home that he allowed her to return the next day. And every day after that. It wasn't that Rune had a particular fascination with gems. Like any child, she simply wanted her father's love and attention. He was happy to oblige, so long as their interactions revolved around his work.

Rune moved to Bangkok to capitalize on what amounted to a years-long apprenticeship in gemology, one of the few good things to come out of her fraught relationship with her father. She scoped out the city's gemstone district until she found what she was looking for—people involved in the black market. She and Kit planned their jobs meticulously. He kept an ear to the ground and identified potential targets. She turned their plans into action. She practiced cracking safes for hours on end. The money was nice, but more than anything, it was the high she was after. The jobs got more elaborate as she honed her skills. Soon she was breaking into hotel rooms, businesses, and even the odd mansion. She was the thief who stole from thieves. Like Robin Hood, only she and Kit kept the profits.

The sound of Kit's voice caught Rune's attention. He and the junkie were having an unexpectedly civil conversation, though half of it admittedly went over her head. The junkie spoke slowly, but his speech was slurred and indistinct, like he was under water. Rune strained to understand more of the exchange. Kit mentioned the Youth Center and asked about the backpack. The man claimed he found it near the Youth Center. Kit described Madee. The man shook his head and denied having seen her. His next words were unintelligible. Rune's unease grew as she tried to fill in the blanks.

The tenor of the conversation changed suddenly, like someone flipped a switch. It started with raised voices. Then the junkie sprang to his feet and charged forward. Kit sidestepped him with ease. He reached for Madee's bag, but the junkie put up an admirable fight given his condition. He drew the bag against his sunken chest, shielding it from Kit by hunching and twisting his torso. Kit reached around and grabbed the straps. Still the junkie held firm. Rune couldn't say she blamed him. The backpack alone would fetch a nice sum at the local market, and who knew what goodies Madee had stashed inside.

"Argh!" Kit cried out, cradling his hand.

The junkie had chomped down hard enough to break the skin. He followed up by driving his knee straight into Kit's groin. Kit's body folded in half before falling to ground.

Rune jumped in instinctively, delivering a kick to the man's torso that would have made her Muay Thai instructor proud. The junkie stumbled momentarily. Then he became angrier and more alert, lunging at Rune with brutal ferocity. Instead of backing down, she took a step forward and threw an elbow across his face. It connected with his nose with a sickening crack. She would have followed up with another strike, but the man was already on the ground, his body curled around the backpack.

"Get the bag," Kit coughed out, still writhing in pain.

Rune grabbed hold of the backpack and wrested it out of the man's grasp. The altercation might have ended there if she hadn't made a rookie mistake—she turned her back on her opponent. The junkie took advantage of her inattention, hooking her leg with both hands and pulling with all his strength. Rune's momentum worked against her. She fell hard—so hard it knocked the wind out of her. The junkie tightened his hands around her calf and pulled her toward him. She kicked with her free leg to shake him loose. When that didn't work, she pawed at the ground in search of something—anything—that might serve as a weapon. Her fists clenched around a squishy patch of dirt. The instant she got close enough, she twisted her body and threw the dirt into the junkie's eyes. He howled in protest, but still he got the upper hand. He spun her onto her back and straddled her torso. His weight bore down on her.

"Get off me!" Rune screamed as she clawed at his face. He silenced her with a well-placed jab to the throat. She opened her mouth, but the sound was trapped inside her chest. A soft wheeze came from her lips. She was still struggling to catch her breath when the heaviness on top of her abruptly disappeared. She raised her eyes in time to see Kit lift the man by the collar and unleash a series of ferocious punches to his head. She heard panting, then the unmistakable sound of bone and cartilage snapping. Blood jetted from the man's nose and flowed freely from a deep gash on his cheek. His bottom lip split open. His left eye swelled shut. Still the punches rained down.

"Kit!" Rune screamed. Her voice did nothing to stem the violence. Instead, Kit seized the man by the neck and started squeezing.

"Khao yuu tii nai?" he howled, his breath coming hard and fast. *Where is she?*

"Kit!"

"Khao yuu tii nai?" he repeated.

"You're going to kill him!"

"Khao yuu tii nai?"

"Please! Stop it!"

Rune's words finally cut through Kit's rage. He looked at the pulpy mess that was the man's face. His eyes moved down to the blood spreading on his tattered shirt. He loosened his grip. The man slid to the ground like a puppet with the strings cut.

"We have the bag," Rune said, slowly rising to her feet. She took a cautious step forward. "Let's get out of here."

Kit's gaze met hers. He gave a curt nod. They both knew that the junkie didn't have any answers. He simply had the misfortune of coming across Madee's backpack and then coming across them. Rune wanted to scream in frustration. Instead, she inspected Kit's bleeding hand. He winced and wrapped a protective arm around her. They started forward at a brisk pace, anxious to put as much distance between themselves and Khlong Toei as they could. As they hurried away, neither noticed that the pouch of rubies Rune had so carefully stashed in her pocket now lay abandoned in the dark alley.

7

The Mandarin Oriental, Bangkok

The mood in the room was tense. The air smelled stale, like hours-old coffee and anxious bodies. Only the *click, click, click* of the keyboard cut through the silence. The sound came from the table by the window, where Lemaire's two newly promoted lackeys were combing through the hotel's security footage. Meanwhile, Lemaire paced up and down the length of the suite, his spine straight, his hands crossed behind his back. He moved with automaton-like precision, walking past the king-sized bed, through the living room, and to the window, all the while imagining what he would do to the person who dared to steal his gemstones. *A bullet to the head*, he thought before quickly correcting himself. A bullet was too fast. Too clean. The person who did this deserved to suffer. Strangulation was nice and slow, but it seemed too gentle under the circumstances. It didn't capture his rage. A knife to the chest would be more appropriate. He nodded, pleased with his decision. Excitement rushed through his body as he envisioned driving a blade through the thief's skin, leaving his hand warm and sticky with blood.

The sound of yawning pulled Lemaire out of his dark reverie. He stopped pacing and directed his focus to the offender—the taller of the two men at the table. The man must have sensed he was being watched because his fingers froze above the keyboard for a moment before moving with renewed vigor, as if a mere glance from Lemaire was enough to shake away his fatigue.

Grainy screenshots of the thief entering and exiting the suite were scattered on the coffee table. Lemaire picked them up and stared at them as though they might offer more information than they did the previous times he looked. The camera angles were such that the photos were practically useless, almost comically so given the thief's motorcycle helmet. Lemaire leafed through the stack until he came across an image of a waitress dropping a room service tray outside the door about an hour after the thief arrived. His face grew hot at the thought of the eight-thousand-baht restaurant charge on his account, the equivalent of two hundred dollars. Being robbed of his rubies was bad enough, but he couldn't abide being taken for a fool. He flipped to the next picture hoping to distract himself from the feeling.

The screenshot was timestamped 6:45 P.M. and showed the thief closing the door to the suite. It seemed innocuous enough. Lemaire was about to set it aside when he noticed that the thief's head was angled ever so slightly to the left, as if he or she were looking at something, or someone, just outside the frame.

It's probably nothing, he said silently.

He was about to move on to the next photo when something made him stop. If there was one thing he trusted in life it was his intuition, and right now it was screaming at him to take another look at the security footage.

"Pull up the video from this floor," he said as he strode toward his men. "Start at quarter to seven."

"What are we looking for?" the tall man asked.

"I'll tell you when I see it."

The three men trained their eyes on the screen. The footage showed an empty hallway. The door opened at exactly 6:45. The thief stepped out and turned his or her head. Down came the visor. The thief disappeared. The tall man made a move to switch to the elevator camera to catch the thief's escape, as he did the first time they reviewed the video. Lemaire put up his hand to stop him. The two lackeys exchanged confused looks, unsure of what it was their boss expected to see. They didn't say anything, though. They were new to their positions, but already they knew that offering advice wasn't in their job description. They kept their mouths shut and fixed their eyes on the empty hallway.

"Stop!" said Lemaire when a housekeeper came into view some time later.

The tall man hit pause and waited for further instruction.

"Zoom in."

The image went from slightly pixelated to illegible.

"Get me the staff schedule."

The short man got on the phone to do Lemaire's bidding. Within moments, he had the hotel's general manager on the line. He relayed Lemaire's request, then covered the phone with his palm and said, "He wants fifty thousand baht."

"I'll give him half that," Lemaire replied without hesitation. Like it or not, haggling was a way of life in Thailand. Bribes were no exception.

"Thirty-five thousand baht," said the short man a few seconds later.

A thousand dollars, give or take. Lemaire could have lowered the price even more, but expediency mattered more than saving money in this situation. He gave the man a curt nod.

It didn't take long for the general manager's account details to appear on his phone. He transferred the funds at the click of a button. The staff schedule appeared in his inbox shortly thereafter. A quick scan revealed that there were only three housekeepers on duty at the time in question. "Bring them to me," he said. "*Now.*"

The two men quietly exited the room, leaving Lemaire alone for the first time since the robbery. He tugged at his shirt sleeves and smoothed his perfect hair. Then he made his way to the minibar and poured himself a bourbon. He downed it in one go. It barely took the edge off. He poured himself another and took it over to the window. Anyone else would have been enthralled by the view, but in this instance Bangkok's extraordinary skyline failed to work its magic.

Lemaire huffed unconsciously. He was in an unenviable position, there was no question about it. He wasn't confident he could identify the thief. And even if he could, his chances of recouping the rubies were slim, at best. The corners of his mouth turned downward as he let his mind drift to his clients. He could recover lost profits, but clients losing faith in his ability to deliver on what he promised, when he promised, was a very serious problem. He knew better than anyone that a good reputation could not be bought or sold. Like everything else that mattered, a good reputation was earned, and his was built on years of hard work. The thought of what he would have to do to regain their trust prompted him to take a long pull from his glass. The bourbon burned his throat, in a good way. It gave him the courage to face his problem head-on.

Who to call first? he asked himself as he scrolled through his contacts. His best client, an LA-based jeweler who worked for the rich and famous, was a fine place to start. He hit dial. The phone rang three times before someone answered.

"Mr. Di Angelo," Lemaire said, keeping his voice grave. There was a moment of silence. "Yes, I'm aware of the time." He paused, flicked his tongue over his dry lips, then took the plunge. "Sir, I'm afraid I have some bad news."

8

Central Bangkok

Rune once read that the first twenty-four hours after a child goes missing are the most crucial, with the chances of a positive outcome waning with every passing minute. The same study asserted that less than one percent of missing children cases enter the collective consciousness. Call it a gap in reporting. Or an unwillingness to listen. Whatever the case, Rune didn't blame the media for turning a blind eye, or the public for that matter. One set of distraught parents thrust before the microphones was barely tolerable every few months. A daily display of grief was unthinkable.

The tuk-tuk rattling over a pothole jarred Rune from her thoughts. Her shirt flapped about as the driver zipped through the muggy Bangkok night. Madee's backpack lay unopened on the seat between her and Kit. They each had an arm around it. It was an odd gesture, one that could trick inattentive onlookers into thinking they were two parents embracing a small child. The driver kept shooting them curious looks from the rearview mirror, but Rune didn't care. The bag was their last tangible link to Madee, not to mention their only clue in what was looking more and more like a suspicious disappearance.

They took a hard turn on South Sathon Road, speeding away from the decaying Khlong Toei slum. Soon they would arrive at the Omni, an abandoned warehouse turned techno club popular with locals and tourists alike. Madee and her best friend, Dara, were regulars there, at least that's what Dara's older sister had told them over the phone just minutes earlier.

How does a fifteen-year-old get into a nightclub? Kit demanded.

I lend her my ID.

And Madee?

Madee has her own.

What? Where did she get it?

I dunno. A guy she knows, I think.

The tuk-tuk hit another pothole, drawing a curse from Kit. Rune shot him a worried look. His face was locked in an expression of pained concern. Rune couldn't say she blamed him. Madee had been hiding things from him. Worse, she had been lying to him. That she had confided in Dara's sister made the situation even more rotten.

They like getting dressed up and dancing. What's the big deal?

They're fifteen years old!

All their friends do it.

Just thinking about those words made Rune nervous. Minors did not belong in night clubs, no matter what they thought. She knew that from experience.

A car backfired in front of them. The tuk-tuk slowed. Rune leaned her head out the side to see what the holdup was. She let out an impatient breath when she saw what appeared to be hundreds of cars crawling toward Sathon Bridge.

It took a good twenty minutes just to get to the ramp. Another ten to reach the bridge. Rune relaxed somewhat when traffic magically cleared midway across. Below them, lights from longtail boats glimmered on the Chao Phraya. Beside them, a Skytrain zoomed noiselessly on an elevated track.

The tuk-tuk driver changed lanes abruptly, forcing a taxi to slam on its breaks to avoid rear-ending them. The maneuver reminded Rune of Kit's three rules for driving in Bangkok. First, don't bother shoulder checking because, by the time you turn around again, everything will have changed. Second, nobody gives a rat's behind if you signal. And third, if you have to do something, just do it, everyone around you will adjust. The memory provided a much-needed distraction.

Rune glanced over at Kit. His eyes were fixed straight ahead. A morose expression crossed her face. Hard as she tried, she couldn't get the junkie's battered body out of her mind. She had always thought of Kit as a gentle soul—and kind to a fault—but the violence she witnessed in Khlong Toei raised uncomfortable questions. Love could fool you into thinking you knew a person intensely, completely even. But the fact was, flashes of their true self were the best you could hope for, and even those were hard to come by. Everybody had secrets. She knew that better than anyone.

Rune toyed with her rings, turning them around her fingers one at a time. Recognizing the nervous habit, Kit reached over and covered her hands with his. She relaxed the instant she felt his touch. She knew this man. Really *knew* him. What he did to the junkie was an aberration. Doing one bad thing didn't automatically make someone a bad person. If that were true, she was beyond redemption.

Reluctant to dwell on her own morality, Rune reached for the closest thing at hand—Madee's backpack. She looked to Kit for permission to open it. He gave her quick nod. She unclipped the front flap and loosened the drawstring to the main compartment. It contained everything one would expect to find in a teenager's schoolbag—a well-worn math reader, a see-through case filled with different colored pens, and a spiral notebook plastered with stickers of Madee's favorite band—a group called Big Thr3. Rune pulled the items out one at a time and gave them to Kit for inspection. He leafed through the notebook before his eyes came to rest on Madee's name on the front cover. He traced it slowly, letting his index finger linger on the final letter.

Rune busied herself with the backpack's side pockets. Seeing Kit in pain was more than she could bear. She squelched her disappointment when all she found were rumpled tissues. It seemed the junkie—or someone else—had helped themselves to Madee's valuables. She was about to give up when she noticed a slip pocket at the back of the bag. She reached in. Her fingers curled around something hard. Out came Madee's phone.

"Give it to me," Kit demanded.

Rune surrendered it wordlessly. She drew closer as he pressed the power button. The passcode screen appeared. Kit typed Madee's birthday into the numeric keypad. The phone vibrated but remained locked. 1234 produced the same result. Rune started fidgeting with impatience. It was clear to her that Kit understood absolutely nothing about fifteen-year-old girls. He punched in 0000.

"Try 2443," she blurted out, unable to hold her tongue any longer.

He threw her a skeptical look.

"Trust me."

Kit was stunned when the home screen flashed on. "How did you know?" he asked with a shake of his head.

"Big Thr3," she replied as if it were the most obvious thing in the world.

His bewilderment grew.

Rune pointed to the notebook. "It's a three-member band with an album called *Three*. Madee and I spent hours watching their videos. She substituted the letters for numbers."

The expression on Kit's face was somewhere between admiration and disbelief. "I didn't realize you were into that kind of thing."

"Really? But you look just like them."

His eyes found the stickers on Madee's notebook, all of which showed attractive Asian men with pastel-colored hair. He suddenly looked very self-conscious.

Rune leaned in as he started scrolling through Madee's phone. Her social media accounts showed no activity since her disappearance. Rune stared at Madee's last Instagram post—a selfie taken that morning with a girl she recognized as the neighbor's daughter. They looked like they could be sisters, mugging for the camera with their dark hair coiled in playful space buns. A two-day-old TikTok video captured her and Dara gyrating to the latest pop hit. Kit let out a soft tsk of disapproval before hitting the Gmail icon.

"Do kids her age even email?" Rune asked as she peered at the screen.

"It would seem not," Kit answered when he saw the last message in her inbox, a four-week-old birthday party invitation sent by the parent of a classmate. He moved on to Madee's text messages. There were over a dozen from him, each more urgent than the last. He scrolled down. Older exchanges between Madee and her friends raised no immediate red flags.

"What about her browser history?" Rune suggested.

"Good idea." Kit went to open Safari, but he hit the camera icon by mistake. The thumbnail on the lower left corner caught his attention. He tapped it open. A video started playing.

Rao pai nai? (Where are we going?)

Rune and Kit exchanged looks. It was Madee's voice. The picture jumped around erratically. It was apparent from the pavement shots that Madee had no idea she was filming. Whoever she was with spoke inaudibly, but it sounded like a man's voice. Their suspicions were confirmed when the camera panned up long enough for them to see a hairy leg with a distinctive S-shaped scar on the ankle. Madee's scuffed white sneakers came into the camera's frame.

Klai mai? (Is it far?)

Again, the response was incomprehensible.

Kha. (Okay.)

The image swung up again as Madee climbed into a parked vehicle. The screen went dark, but not before Rune and Kit could make out that she was in a taxi.

"Play it again," said Rune.

They watched in tense silence.

"Stop. What's that?" She pointed to a narrow canal lined with stone benches at the corner of the screen.

Kit paused the video and squinted. "I know this place," he said softly, as if to himself. "It's the park near Madee's school."

"You're sure?"

"I'm sure." His raised his eyes to hers. "You know what this means, don't you?"

Rune knew but she was afraid to answer, as if saying the words out loud would somehow make them more real.

Kit didn't share her reticence. He spelled it out loud and clear. "Madee was taken in broad daylight."

The tuk-tuk jerked violently. Rune braced herself against the back of the driver's seat. She couldn't bear to look at Kit, so she stared out at the dark city instead. The tension grew with every passing second. Only when she couldn't stand it any longer did she turn toward Kit. His grim expression mirrored hers. He didn't speak. He didn't have to. They hadn't found Madee. Worse, the last few hours had left them with more questions than answers. Who was the man with the scar? Why did Madee get in a cab with him? And where the hell had they gone?

9

The Mandarin Oriental, Bangkok

They looked like children who had been called to the principal's office. Anxious. Vulnerable. Their bodies swallowed by the plush couch. There were three of them in total. One was young and new to the job. The other two were career housekeepers with long histories at the hotel. They sat side by side in strained silence, their eyes cast down, their shoulders and knees grazing. They had every reason to be nervous. Lemaire was a regular at the hotel and a wealthy one at that. A single word from him could cost them their livelihoods, a fact not lost on them when they were rounded up and escorted to this room.

Lemaire sat in an armchair across from the couch with his two henchmen standing to either side. His posture was relaxed, but his pale eyes told a different story. They were sharp, bordering on scary. He wanted to intimidate the housekeepers, but not so much that they feared speaking up. To that end, he turned to one of his men—the taller of the two—and instructed him to bring refreshments.

"Right away, sir," the man said.

Lemaire directed his gaze at the women as sparkling water and four glasses were deposited on the coffee table. He reached for the bottle.

It hissed when he opened it. Next came the glugging as he filled each glass to the precise halfway mark. He screwed the cap back on and set the bottle down with a clink. Then he leaned back in his chair and crossed his legs. "Which one of you worked on this floor today?"

The short henchman repeated the question in Thai. The housekeepers shifted in their seats. An uncomfortable silence followed.

Lemaire pulled his lips to approximate a smile. He spoke his next words slowly. "You're not in any trouble. I just want to know who cleaned the rooms on this floor."

The youngest of the group, a diminutive woman with radiant skin and almond-shaped eyes, slowly raised her hand.

"Do you speak English?"

She gave a weak nod and timidly swept her bangs away from her forehead.

"You and I are going to have a chat, okay?"

Another nod.

Lemaire signaled to his men to escort the other two housekeepers to the door. "Give them something for their time," he said, knowing that money would buy their discretion. He waited until he heard the door latch before reaching across the table to hand the remaining housekeeper a glass of water. Her hand shook as she accepted it. He assumed a sympathetic expression and said, "What's your name?"

"They call me Mart."

"How long have you been working at the hotel, Mart?"

"Two months."

"Do you like your job?"

"Yes, sir, very much."

"So, you wouldn't want to jeopardize it by lying to a guest, would you?"

"No, sir."

He slid the screenshot of the thief exiting his suite across the table. "Have you seen this person?"

Mart chewed on her lower lip. Her chin began to quiver. She looked like she was going to cry.

Lemaire was by her side in an instant. "Hush, now," he said, patting her shoulder like he would a pet or a small child. "There's no need for that."

It took her a moment to get her emotions under control. Then she brushed her bangs aside again and picked up the picture.

"Look carefully," said Lemaire. "Do you know who this is?"

"I saw her outside this room."

Her! Lemaire thought triumphantly. Between the motorcycle helmet and the grainy surveillance footage, he hadn't known the thief was a woman until now. Questioning Mart was already paying off. "What can you tell me about her?"

"I only saw her for a few seconds."

"I'm sure you know more than you realize." It took some effort for Lemaire to keep the impatience out of his voice. He could tell Mart was on the verge of losing it. A hysterical woman was of no use to him. He forced another smile. "What do you remember about her appearance?"

"Nothing. She was wearing a helmet."

"Think." The word came out more firmly than Lemaire intended. Mart reacted as if he had slapped her. It was just the jolt she needed.

"She was taller than me, but not by much," she said, speaking so quickly she nearly stumbled over the words. "She wore all black, even her shoes."

"And?"

"Her hands. She had a lot of rings."

"What kind of rings?"

"Gold ones—one on all her fingers. I remember thinking it was strange." She paused, then added, "And her eyes. I saw her eyes."

Lemaire remained silent. Mart was on a roll now.

"They were mixed—green, gold, and brown. I've never seen eyes like hers. I'll never forget them."

Lemaire waited a beat to make sure she was finished before saying, "You did very well, Mart."

"I can go now?"

"Not just yet."

She deflated visibly.

"Do you see the computer over there?" Lemaire gestured to the laptop on the table by the window.

She nodded.

"You and I are going to use it to identify the woman in the picture."

"I . . . I don't know if I can."

"Finding her is very important. You see, she broke into this room and stole something very valuable from me. She got in and out without anyone noticing. Do you understand what that means?"

Mart thought for a moment. "It means she was here before and she knew the room would be empty. She knew my schedule. And yours, too."

"Very good." Lemaire gave a nod of approval. Mart was astute. That would come in handy when they started reviewing the security footage. He knew she was on board, but as an added incentive, he pulled four crisp thousand-baht notes from his wallet and placed them on the coffee table. It was a pittance—a mere hundred dollars—but it was a fortune to someone like Mart. "Go ahead," he said encouragingly. "They're yours."

Mart stared at the money. It was more than what she made in a week at the hotel. Her fingers hovered over the bills. She blinked hard several times. Then her shoulders squared, as if she had come to an important decision. She reached for the bills and tucked them into the pocket of her uniform. Then she turned to Lemaire and said, "Show me the video."

A half hour later, Lemaire was congratulating himself for recruiting Mart. It was her idea to start their search in the basement of the hotel, in an area reserved for service staff. She reasoned that the thief had used a master key to get into the suite—the kind housekeepers carried. They worked their way backwards from the time of the break-in, speeding through footage of staff going about their daily tasks. Mart was new to the job, but she had been around long enough to know who belonged and who didn't.

Their breakthrough came during the shift-change right after lunch, when Mart spied a woman she didn't recognize. She was dressed as a front desk clerk, with a collarless jacket and a calf-length skirt, but she lacked the purple orchid receptionists were required to pin to their uniforms. There was something off about her hair—like she was wearing extensions or a cheap wig. Her footwear was noticeably more casual than that of her colleagues. But it wasn't just the woman's appearance that drew Mart's attention, it was the way she carried herself. Her movements were swift and smooth. She kept her face angled down, away from the observing eye of the camera.

"There!" Mart said when the woman collided with a housekeeper.

Lemaire hit pause. The image wasn't great, but it was clear that the woman was palming the housekeeper's keycard. He zoomed in and leaned closer to the screen. The woman's features were fuzzy, but it was nothing good software couldn't fix.

"Can I have another thousand baht?" Mart asked, knowing she had provided valuable information.

Lemaire's brow rose. Mart was ballsier than he had given her credit for. He liked that about her. He handed her another thousand-baht bill and saw her out.

As soon as the door closed, Lemaire reached for his phone and called one of his contacts in the Royal Thai Police. Few foreigners knew that Thailand had one of the most sophisticated digital surveillance systems in Southeast Asia. The capital was equipped with thousands of AI-enhanced facial recognition cameras, provided courtesy of the Chinese government. The system allowed the authorities to track millions of people in real time—on streets, at tourist sites, and on mass transit. Lemaire's already erect posture straightened when he heard the phone click.

"Yes?" said a gravelly voice on the other end of the line.

"I need your help with something. I'm sending it to you now."

"Got it," came the voice a few seconds later.

An anticipatory smile spread across Lemaire's face. Soon he would know exactly who the mystery woman was. Once that happened, no place would be out of reach. She would have nowhere to hide.

10

Omni Techno Club, Bangkok

"Do you see her?" Rune shouted as Kit led them through the crowd at the Omni, a massive EDM club on the outskirts of the otherwise staid neighborhood of Thonburi. She peered around in search of Madee and Dara, but the dim lighting prevented her from seeing more than two feet in front of her. The music was cranked to ear-splitting level, making conversation impossible. It was just as well. No one went to the Omni to talk.

Kit cupped her ear and shouted, "It will go faster if we split up!"

Rune nodded and angled her head toward the passageway leading to the dance floor. Kit pointed in the opposite direction, indicating he was going to the bar.

The crowd grew thicker as Rune made her way down the hall. The deeper into the club she went, the darker and louder it became. The thumping bass enveloped her, filling her ears and beating in time with her heart.

She turned the corner. A sea of bodies swallowed her, pulling her toward the dance floor. Someone grabbed her waist. Her head whipped to the side. She squinted through the pulsing strobes, but all she saw were disjointed flashes of ecstatic faces and flailing limbs.

The room went black. A hypnotic drumming filled the air. A tense hush fell over the crowd. The anticipation grew as red LED lights slowly appeared on the opposite end of the dance floor. Rune looked up, fascinated by the spectacle unfolding before her. The lights illuminated an elevated DJ cage, casting a preternatural glow over its occupant—a rail-thin woman who could easily have passed for a prepubescent boy. She wore loose-fitting jeans slung low on her hips and a sleeveless black t-shirt with the word "speed" sprayed across the front in bold white letters. A twining cobra tattoo ran down the entire length of her left arm, from her bony shoulder to just past her knuckles. Her neon green hair was styled in a messy mohawk that seemed to defy gravity. Although Rune was instantly drawn to the DJ's appearance, it was the woman's mastery at the turntable that had her mesmerized. One hand was glued to her headphones as her head bobbed to the electro-pop beat. Her other hand moved effortlessly from a wide-screen laptop to a two-deck controller. A look of extreme concentration played across her sharp features. She was in total command of the room and everyone at the Omni knew it.

The lightshow resumed as the music picked up. Blue lights suspended from steel rafters panned across the space, illuminating the slick bodies writhing on the dance floor below. The strobes pulsated in time with the music, while random words flashed on gigantic screens affixed to the concrete pillars lining the sides of the room. The raw atmosphere and carefree vibe were intoxicating. Rune understood why Madee was drawn to it. She also knew she would never find Madee or her BFF, not from this vantage point, anyway.

Crossing the dance floor proved more challenging than Rune anticipated. Drunken revelers stopped her every second step. Some wanted to dance with her. Others were so lost in their own pleasure that the rest of the world just fell away. It was hard to get around people in that state.

The metal staircase leading to the DJ cage beckoned. Rune elbowed her way to it and ducked under the chain. The muscular bouncer stationed nearby was too preoccupied with a belligerent customer to notice. Rune climbed the stairs quickly and grabbed hold of the bars. "Khaaw-thoot! Excuse me!" she called out. "Can you let me in?"

The DJ tore her eyes away from her laptop long enough to stare at Rune. It wasn't clear from her expression if she wanted to clock her for interrupting or if she admired her moxie. She looked her up and down. Then she pulled her headphones around her neck and unlocked the door.

Rune smiled at the small victory. Sometimes when you wanted something, all you had to do was ask. She brought her palms together and lowered her head. "Khawp khun kha," she said. *Thank you.*

"Your Thai sucks," the DJ replied.

Rune pulled a face. *Farang.* Foreigner. *Luk khrueng.* Half child. The words echoed in her mind.

"It's okay," said the DJ. "I won't hold it against you."

"Thanks."

"Turn around."

"Why?"

"Because I said so."

Rune spun around slowly, puzzled by the request.

"I get off at two. Come back then." The DJ pulled her headphones up and once again directed her attention to her laptop.

"Wait. What?"

"You thought we would hook up now? In front of all these people?" The DJ gestured to the packed dance floor.

"Uh, I'm not here to . . ."

The DJ shot her an irritated look.

"Not that I don't find you attractive," Rune added quickly. "I do . . . I mean . . . you are. But that's not why I'm here." Embarrassed, she pulled out her phone and showed the DJ a picture of Madee and Dara. "Have you seen these girls? They've been coming here for the past few months."

"A lot of girls come here."

"It's important. The one on the left is missing."

The DJ glanced at the screen. Then she sucked her teeth and said, "Yeah, I know those two."

"You do?" Rune felt a rush of hope.

"They're regulars. They come here with *farangs*."

Her hope vanished. Her eyes darkened. "White guys?'

"White *men*."

Her face crumbled. The thought of Madee and Dara hanging out with older men was disturbing, to say the least. The fact that they were tourists and probably used to getting their way made her all the more fearful. She couldn't speak for Dara, but Madee wasn't equipped for this kind of thing.

"You're wasting your time," the DJ said. "They're not here tonight."

"Are you sure?"

"No doubt. I would have heard about it."

Rune's confusion showed on her face.

"Look, I don't know who these girls are to you, but I suggest you stay far away from them."

"Why?"

"They're bad news."

"Really?"

"They've been ripping off customers. They're really good at it, too. Last week it was a Rolex. The time before it was a diamond necklace. The cops were all over this place. It's bad for business."

Rune received the news in silence. An uneasy feeling settled like a cloak around her. She and Madee were close. How could she have missed this? She turned her attention to the dance floor, half expecting to see Madee letting loose. But Madee wasn't there. And neither was Dara.

A flash of pink caught Rune's eye. It was Kit weaving his way through the crowded dance floor. Then she spotted something peculiar—two men who appeared to be trailing Kit. She leaned forward and followed them with her eyes, trying to convince herself that what she was seeing was something else. Both men had dark, cropped hair. One had the long, lean body of a runner. The other was short and stocky. Rune's eyes narrowed. The men were at least twice as old as everyone else at the Omni. Their ill-fitting jackets and wide-legged trousers stood out amid a sea of graphic tees and torn denim. The lights flashed for a split second, just long enough for Rune to see the bulge of a gun at the tall man's waist.

"Kit!" she screamed.

The tall man placed a hand on his weapon.

"Kit!" she screamed again, slamming her palms on the cage in a futile effort to get his attention. The music drowned out the sound. The men closed in. "Shit! Shit! Shit!"

"What the hell is wrong with you?" the DJ asked, stunned by the outburst.

Rune didn't bother answering. She charged down the stairs and hurled herself across the dance floor. By the time she reached Kit, she was in full panic mode. "Two of them," she gasped. "They're right behind you!"

Kit took one look at her face and knew they were in trouble. "This way!" he said, grabbing her hand and pulling her deeper into the club.

They pushed their way through the masses, drawing all kinds of protests along the way. A woman wearing a crown of magenta-colored flowers spilled her drink all over Kit. A scrawny man with skin like an orange peel screamed obscenities at them. Undeterred, Kit pressed forward. Rune shot a glance over her shoulder. "Faster!" she shouted when she saw the two men closing in. But it was too late. The tall one had her by the shirt. She felt the hem tear when she staggered forward in fear. The man dragged her back as she fought to get away, wrapping his free arm around her neck to subdue her. She took aim at his foot, driving her heel down as hard as she could. Then she chomped down savagely, sinking her teeth into the fleshy part of his forearm. He loosened his grip momentarily, only to tighten it before she could slip away.

Rune twisted her head and tried to scream, but she couldn't catch her breath. Her throat hurt. She felt like she was dying. *Not like this*, she thought wildly. She stomped her foot again in desperation. This time she connected just below his knee. It buckled backwards as her sole scraped down the length of his shin. He let out a sharp cry. She gathered all her energy and drove her elbow firmly into his ribcage. To her amazement, his grip loosened. His body folded in half. She spun around in time to see Kit punch the shorter man square in the jaw.

"Let's go!" he shouted, grabbing her hand and pulling her away.

The two stumbled through the club, elbowing their way through the darkness until they reached a hallway covered in decades old graffiti. Kit yanked the door to an emergency stairwell and shoved Rune inside. The door swung closed. They stared at each other wordlessly. The sound of their breathing filled the dank air. Music pulsated in the distance.

"Who the hell are those guys?" Rune whispered.

"I don't know."

"Does this have something to do with Madee?"

"I said I don't know!"

A noise outside the door caught their attention. They flattened themselves against the wall. Rune's eyes found Kit's. He raised his index finger to his lips.

They stayed that way for a long time, until their breathing returned to normal and they were certain the danger had passed. Only then did Kit crack the door open and steal a glance down the hallway. It was empty, save two drunken partygoers devouring each other's faces.

They slipped out of the stairwell and hurried down the hall, in the direction opposite the dance floor. A few minutes was all it took to find their way to the back of the club and locate the emergency exit. They burst through the door and into the alley behind the building. With relief coursing through them, they ran toward the main road—toward lights and people and safety. Rune nearly cried out when it became clear they were going to make it. She counted down silently in time with her stride. *Five . . . four . . . three . . . two . . .*

She never made it to one.

11

Thonburi District, Bangkok

It was the far-off sound of shouting that lured Rune back to the realm of consciousness. Her mouth was dry, like she had spent the last few hours sucking on cotton balls. The jackhammer in her head made it difficult to think. She opened her eyes and blinked against the light. Her vision came in and out of focus.

"Wake up!" Kit hissed.

First came the confusion. Then the sickening rush of terror. Kit was kneeling on the floor with his hands clasped behind his head. His pretty pink hair was crusted with dry blood. Looming over him was a man with a slick black handgun.

"Get on your knees," the man growled.

His voice was strange and unplaceable, his eyes unnervingly pale. There was something familiar about his aristocratic features and shiny brown hair, but in her current state, Rune simply couldn't remember. The man smoothed an invisible wrinkle in his shirt with his free hand. The gesture struck her as odd even as she lay motionless on the concrete floor.

"Do as I say!" he roared.

Rune regained her senses enough to scramble to her knees. Her eyes were wide now, shifting from side to side in desperate search of an escape route. She felt physically ill when she realized that the only exit was behind their captor. She and Kit were trapped. "What happened?" she mouthed when the man momentarily turned his gaze away from her.

Kit responded with an almost imperceptible shrug of his shoulders.

With a gun in play, fighting was off the table. That left only one option—negotiation. Rune willed her mind to function. She had no idea how she and Kit had gotten from the dark alley behind the Omni to this windowless room. All she knew was that there was a knot the size of an egg on the back of her head, presumably from the blow that knocked her out. The muscles in her back were sore and tight. There was a dull ache in her right knee. She shifted her weight to try to alleviate the pain, but all that did was send electric shocks down her leg. She tried to imagine what the two men at the club did to her to cause such damage. Then she thought better of it. What good could possibly come of knowing? She took an unsteady breath as she worked up the courage to speak.

"My wallet is in my back pocket," Kit said, beating her to the punch. "Take it. It's yours."

"You think I'm here for a few baht?" the pale-eyed man said with a mirthless chuckle.

"What do you want, then?"

"I'm the one asking the questions." The sharpness in his voice left no room for argument.

Kit clammed up. He and Rune exchanged worried glances.

"Here's what's going to happen. Either you hand over what you stole from me or I shoot you both, starting with you." He took a few steps forward and placed his gun directly against Rune's temple.

"Jesus," she whimpered softly.

"Do you recognize me now?"

She knew exactly who he was, but she couldn't bring herself to respond. This was Charles Lemaire, the American gemstone trafficker they had ripped off just a few hours earlier. The unthinkable had happened. He had come for his rubies. She took a shaky breath and whispered, "How did you find us?"

"I have my ways," Lemaire replied cryptically. Then he threw her a bone and added, "There are eyes everywhere in Bangkok. Anyone can be found. For a price."

Rune's mind went back to the hotel escapade. Who was on the trafficker's payroll? The housekeeper with the cart of dirty linens she encountered on her way out of the room? The disheveled blond couple she took for tourists? The two security guards who chased her through the hotel? A chilling look from Lemaire put a stop to the speculation.

"You stole something of great value to me. Now hand over my merchandise so we can all move on and forget this unpleasantness ever happened. Believe me, you won't like the alternative."

"This is all a misunderstanding," Kit said. "We're not thieves. I work as a maintenance man . . ."

Rune listened to Kit babble, knowing full well that it was all for show. He was trying to buy time. A loud knock at the door cut him off.

"Don't do anything stupid," Lemaire said, moving his gun from Rune to Kit with menacing precision. He sauntered to the other end of the room.

Rune lowered her hand to her pocket while Lemaire spoke to whoever was at the door. She fished around for the rubies. Discreetly at first, and then more frantically. The realization that the pouch was gone sent a fresh swell of panic through her. The feeling became more acute when she realized that handing over the rubies wouldn't get them out of this. Lemaire was not simply going to accept the gems and be on his merry way. He would kill them the second he got his hands on the stones, of that she was sure. Her pulse raced. She needed a plan. No, she needed a goddammed miracle.

"I can help you," she blurted out, interrupting Lemaire's conversation.

He twisted his neck. His pale eyes held hers while he waited for her to continue. Kit looked on in shocked silence.

"It was me. I took the rubies." The words came out with a calmness she was far from feeling.

"Give them to me."

"I can't."

"What do you mean, you can't?" Lemaire strode forward until he was almost on top of her.

"I don't have them on me."

He swung hard, striking her across the mouth with his gun. She fell to the floor. Blood seeped from her split lip. Kit lunged forward, but he was too slow. He found himself staring straight down the gun's barrel.

"Get. Down. Now," Lemaire said, clearly enunciating each word. His measured tone was more terrifying than if he had screamed. "Go on. Don't make me ask twice."

Kit lowered himself to the floor like an obedient puppy.

"You two are playing a very dangerous game. Now tell me where the stones are."

"They're not here, but I can take you to them," said Rune. She spoke quickly, without a firm plan in mind. All she knew was that she was to blame for all of this. Stealing gems for a living was her brainchild. To make matters worse, she was the one who lost the rubies. The guilt gnawed at her.

"What kind of fool do you take me for?"

The edge in Lemaire's voice was enough to snap Rune out of her pity party. She had created this mess, now it was up to her to clean it up. Kit had enough on his plate looking for his sister. She choked down her fear and stared the American straight in the eye. "I'm trying to give you what you want," she said with as much confidence as she could muster.

"Tell me where the rubies are, or I'll kill you and the pretty boy."

Rune stole a glance at Kit. He was above such insults but, for some reason, it hit a nerve with her. She reacted with a fierceness that was as surprising as it was sudden. "If you so much as touch him, you can kiss the rubies goodbye," she seethed. "I'll never tell you where they are. You'll lose, what, a quarter of a million dollars?"

Lemaire looked to be weighing her words.

Seeing they were having the desired effect, Rune pressed on. "I can't imagine your clients will be happy when they find out you lost their merchandise. I'm guessing they're not nice people. They'll come after you so fast you won't know what hit you."

Lemaire remained silent, but judging from the look on his face, he was more than a little ruffled. The silence dragged on. Finally, he sniffed loudly and said, "I have some arrangements to make. Try anything and you'll both regret it."

Rune kept her eyes on him until he was out of the room.

"Where the hell are the rubies?" Kit whispered.

Rune shook her head to indicate she didn't know.

"Jesus."

"I know."

"You'll never get him to leave with you."

"I know!"

"He'll send you out to get them. You'll have to retrace our steps."

"What if I can't find them?"

"You have to."

"Should I go to the cops?"

"And tell them what? That you lost a bunch of stolen gemstones?"

"What about Madee?"

"You're going to have to find her, too."

"I can't do all this alone!" Rune cried, her distress now on full display.

"Yes, you can. I know you can."

"No, it's too much."

"Listen to me, Rune. You can do this. You're the only person I trust. You're also the bravest person I know."

"I don't even know where to start or who to . . ."

"You," Lemaire barked as he strode back into the room.

Rune clammed up instantly.

"Get up."

She scrambled to her feet. Her injured knee screamed in protest.

"Get the rubies and bring them to me."

"I can take you to them," she said in a last-ditch effort to lure him away from Kit.

"I'm staying exactly where I am. Your friend is my insurance policy, in case you get any ideas."

"You can trust me. Just come with me and let him go."

"Trust you?" Lemaire echoed with a snort. "You must really think I'm stupid."

"How do I know you'll free us once you have the gems?"

"I guess you'll just have to trust *me*."

Rune fell silent. It was a bad deal, but she didn't see an alternative.

"Better get moving. You have an hour."

"That's not enough time! The rubies aren't even in Bangkok anymore!"

Lemaire eyed her for several long seconds before coming to a decision. "You have until six P.M. tomorrow. After that, things get ugly."

Rune found Kit's gaze.

He nodded soberly.

She averted her eyes and walked away before she could change her mind.

"Remember, tomorrow end of day," Lemaire called out.

She raised her hand to indicate she understood. The door opened with a loud squeak. She passed the two men who had chased them through the Omni.

"Tick-tock," the tall one said, tapping the face of his watch with his index finger.

Only after stumbling outside did Rune realize her entire body was clenched. Her breathing came in short, halting gulps. She thought she might be sick, but there was no time for that, there was no time for anything except finding Madee and those bloody rubies. *Where do I start?* she thought, overwhelmed by the knowledge that Kit and Madee's lives were in her hands. She whipped her head from side to side, wracked with indecision about where to go. She staggered into the dark street, teetering like a drunk. A motorcyclist honked angrily as he narrowly avoided colliding with her. A clap of thunder sounded. Then the sky opened and the downpour began.

DAY 2

12

Khlong Toei Slum, Bangkok

Bangkok between the hours of five and six in the morning was a marvel to behold. Golden spires and glass skyscrapers appeared as if by magic as the city shed its cloak of darkness, rising like stalagmites from a cave floor. Signs of life slowly materialized across the city as the last of the stars phased out of the sky. Industrious vendors hauled a dizzying array of food and wares in preparation for the day ahead, while Buddhist monks in saffron robes processed through the streets dispensing blessings in exchange for alms. The sight was captivating enough to move even the most jaded observer.

But glorious views and the nascent hum of urban life were not at the front of Rune's mind as she stumbled into Khlong Toei that morning wet and alone. She had never experienced fear like this before. It flooded her senses, making it hard for her to breathe. It was also paralyzing. What was she supposed to do first? Save Madee or save the only man she had ever loved? What if saving one meant losing the other? Rune blamed herself for being in this impossible position. It was irrational. Absurd even. But that didn't make an iota of difference.

Her decision to return to the slum was the only thing that made sense under the circumstances. The rubies were still in her possession when she arrived in Khlong Toei the night before. She guessed that they fell out of her pocket during her altercation with the junkie, or perhaps when she and Kit searched the Youth Center. The Youth Center was also Madee's last verifiable location. The GPS in her phone proved that, as did her backpack. Children did not just disappear without a trace, even in neighborhoods like Khlong Toei. Someone saw something.

Drawing information out of people was one of Rune's talents, but it was of little use to her that morning. Khlong Toei was empty—eerily so. The only sound was that of pelting rain. It echoed through the slum, amplified by the predawn silence. Rune briefly considered knocking on doors, then immediately thought better of it. Nothing good ever came from waking people up. She knew that for a fact. Besides, the residents of Khlong Toei would be rising without her help soon enough.

Having one task off the table allowed Rune to focus on the other—finding the rubies. The first order of business was retracing the route she took with Kit the night before. It sounded so simple. In point of fact, it was anything but. Rune turned a corner. Then another. Within minutes she was hopelessly lost. A whisper of panic flicked through her. All the alleys looked the same—narrow, trash-strewn, lined with shacks that broke every building code in the book. Still she pressed forward, her eyes searching for something—anything—that might help her get her bearings.

Her head swung sideways when a guttural howl rang out nearby. The sound was neither recognizably human nor animal. She quickened her pace. A second howl sent her sprinting down the alley. She took a hard right.

Thud!

Rune hit the ground like a felled tree. A stab of pain shot through her shoulder. Her cheek stung from the force of the impact. She lay in the wet dirt for a moment, shocked and winded. An expletive slipped from her lips as she pushed herself to her feet and tried to brush the filth off her clothes. She glanced back to see what she had tripped on. Her stomach contracted reflexively at the sight.

The body was hideously disfigured. It was so frightful that Rune pitched forward and hit the ground again. A scream built at the back of her throat. She opened her mouth to release it, but all that came out was a strangled gurgle.

Stand up! the voice inside her head shouted.

She tried to obey. She really did. But the combination of terror and revulsion made it impossible for her to move.

Get up before someone sees you!

She only made it as far as her hands and knees before promptly vomiting. She began to cough. Acid burned her mouth and throat. Tears spilled from her eyes, only to be washed away by the rain. Her reaction was hardly surprising. Corpses were not on the list of things Rune was accustomed to seeing. And this wasn't just any dead body. It was the junkie she and Kit had encountered the night before. She dared take another glimpse to make sure and instantly regretted it. In addition to the trauma Kit had inflicted, the man had been stabbed several times. The murder weapon was a large knife, if the size of the wounds was any indication. The man's threadbare shirt was slashed in at least three places. There was a pool of coagulated blood beneath his torso that seemed impervious to the rain. Rune's stomach threatened to rebel again. Kit's warning about the dangers of flashing gemstones in a place like Khlong Toei entered her mind. She wondered if the junkie had found her rubies, and if that's what had gotten him killed.

Rune's instinct was to run as far as possible, as fast as possible, but the image of Lemaire holding a gun to Kit's head kept her exactly where she was. She spit in an effort to expel the foul taste from her mouth. Then she wiped her lips with the back of her hand and got to her feet. Her eyes scanned the ground for the pouch she stole from Lemaire's safe. Not seeing it, she approached the body and nudged it with her foot. It was soft and pliable, much like it had been when the junkie was alive. Rigor mortis was just beginning to set in. Rune's nose twitched when she caught a whiff of decomposing flesh. The man's body had already begun to turn on itself. Bacteria was multiplying and leaking from his respiratory and gastrointestinal tracts. Gasses were accumulating in his abdomen. Soon the corpse would start to bloat. Shortly after that the gasses would escape into the environment through his natural orifices—mouth, nostrils, ears, anus. The pressure would increase until his skin could no longer contain it. Rupture would occur. Fluids would seep out. The maggots would follow. And of course, the stench would be god awful. Rune was grateful she would be long gone before any of that could happen.

She slid a tentative hand into the man's right pocket. It was empty. Her search of his left pocket also left her disappointed. She was rolling the body to check the back pockets when she sensed she wasn't alone. A low whine from behind confirmed her suspicions. She didn't have to look back to know that the sound came from one of the mangey strays that patrolled the slum. She turned toward it slowly. "Nice doggy," she whispered.

The dog stared at her with its black eyes and emitted a throaty growl. Rune took a step back. The dog reacted with an aggressive snap. It wasn't a particularly large animal, but a bite was a bite, and she needed a rabies shot about as much as she needed a hole in the head.

"Easy," Rune said with a noticeable waver in her voice. She raised her hands and took another step back. It was critical that she put as much distance between herself and the corpse as possible. After all, it wasn't her the dog wanted, but its meal. She spied a broom with well-worn bristles in a pile of trash just a few feet away. She inched toward it, keeping her eyes on the dog the entire time. She reached back and felt around until her fingers touched the handle.

The dog snarled. Its weight shifted to its hind legs.

"Down!" Rune yelled as it leapt up at her. She took a swing. The dog let out a sharp yelp when her broomstick made contact with its snout. It came after her a second time, teeth bared, saliva dripping from the sides of its mouth. She raised the stick over her head and brought it down hard and fast. The dog whimpered and scurried away.

Rune kept a tight grip on the broom until she was sure she was alone. Only after scanning the area for other threats did she finally toss it aside. Her heart still thumping double time, she lowered her gaze to the dead man. "Jesus," she said.

Addiction had ravaged his body. His face was deformed from his run-in with Kit. The stab wounds looked like something out of a horror movie. Still, it seemed wrong to let the animals get to him. Rune eyed him with something resembling pity. Then images of Kit and Madee appeared in her mind. Her posture straightened. "I'm sorry," she whispered. On any other day, she would have stood guard until the authorities arrived, but with everything else on her plate, decency just wasn't in the cards.

13

Khlong Toei Slum, Bangkok

The rain kept coming. Hard. Incessant. It was the reality of living in the tropics. But while locals took the diurnal rainfall in stride, for the uninitiated, it was a nuisance plain and simple. No umbrella on earth was up to the task. Flooded streets were par for the course. Those who wished to stay dry had no option but to seek shelter and wait it out. Wet clothes and soggy shoes were bad enough, but it was the unpredictability of the monsoon season that drove many foreigners mad. Clear skies gave way to Biblical storms in an instant. Adhering to a schedule under these circumstances was out of the question.

Incongruous as they were, these mundane thoughts ran through Rune's mind as she searched Khlong Toei for Lemaire's rubies. It was a hopeless task and she knew it. The rain had transformed the unpaved alleys into mini rapids. Even if she could locate the spot where she and Kit had confronted the junkie—and there was a big emphasis on the if—her chances of finding the gems were remote, at best. That didn't prevent her from scouring the ground for anything that vaguely resembled the pouch she stole from Lemaire. She nudged at dirt and debris with her feet as she walked, uncovering broken housewares, obsolete electronic devices, and all other manner of rubbish. She was so focused on her task that she failed to notice the woman who was rushing toward her until it was too late.

"Oh!" Rune exclaimed. She started to apologize, but her words tapered off. The woman could have been forty or eighty—it was impossible to tell. Her skin was taut and smooth, but it was covered with age spots. Her hair was jet black, yet cataracts formed a milky film over her eyes. Her teeth were rotting. There was a dark growth on her neck that was very likely cancerous. This was poverty laid bare. The sight made Rune so uncomfortable she wanted to run as far away from Khlong Toei as possible. Instead, she bowed deeply and offered the woman a proper apology. The woman leaned in and said something Rune didn't understand. Her voice was soft and uninflected. Each word bled into the next.

"Phuut iik thii na kha?" Rune asked. *Can you repeat that?*

"She wants to know if you made an offering today," came a voice from over her shoulder.

Rune spun around and founded herself facing a shirtless man whose entire body was covered in tattoos, save his gaunt visage. Adorning his chest were small dots arranged in a concentric pattern, like a multi-strand string of pearls. Foliate forms interspersed with bright red hibiscus flowers extended from his shoulders all the way to his wrists. Entwined serpents covered his bare legs below the knees, the only parts visible beneath his soaking wet shorts. Rune fought to keep the discomfort out of her voice. "An offering?" she asked, speaking an octave higher than usual.

"To the land guardians."

She followed his gaze to a spirit house perched atop a nearby pedestal. The shrine was the size of a large dollhouse and shaped like a traditional Thai temple, complete with gilded finials and spires. Her thoughts drifted to her father, who happily blended his Buddhist faith with animistic beliefs in spirits, like many people in Thailand. Visiting spirit houses was one of the few things they did together outside his work. Her memories of these visits were vivid, like they happened yesterday.

Take off your shoes, Rune, he would say as he held incense sticks and garlands spun from brilliant marigolds.

Yes, daddy.

Now kneel and repeat after me.

Rune didn't remember the Thai prayer—maybe she never knew it—but she recalled it was a plea to the spirits for protection and good fortune. After reciting it, her father would place the incense in a sand-filled bowl, hang the garlands on the spirit house, and leave an offering of food or drink for the resident guardians. Maybe it was because Rune grew up in the States, or because her mother was Catholic, but she never embraced her father's beliefs as her own. She didn't adopt her mother's faith either, unless receiving Communion a few times a year between the ages of seven and thirteen was enough to make her Christian.

A tug on her arm drew Rune's attention. The old woman was speaking again, this time in a highly animated tone. Rune tried her best to understand, but all she caught was the last word: *danger.*

"Have you ever heard of Phi Tai Hong?" the tattooed man said before she could ask the woman to repeat herself.

"They're ghosts of Thai folklore. My father told me stories about them."

"It's not just stories. They're real. I've seen them with my own eyes."

Rune received the words with profound skepticism.

"Phi Tai Hong are people who suffered violent, unexpected deaths. Their ghosts are angry and vengeful. Anyone who crosses their path is in danger."

Violent and unexpected. The words precisely described the junkie's death. Rune wasn't the least bit superstitious, but a frown passed over her face nonetheless. "Why are you telling me this?"

"I'm not telling you anything. It's all coming from her." He gestured to the old woman.

"Pai hai kon," the woman said. *Go away.* She jabbed an arthritic finger at Rune's chest.

Rune took a step back. Something resembling fear started to creep in. The alley felt like it was constricting around her.

"Pai hai kon! Pai hai kon!" *Go away! Go away!* The woman was shouting now.

"I'm not leaving," Rune said sharply. Scared or not, she wasn't going anywhere until she had answers about Madee and the rubies.

An argument broke out between the woman and the tattooed man. Their voices grew so loud people emerged from nearby shacks to see what was happening. The woman walked away, but not before making eye contact with Rune and giving a vigorous shake of the head. Rune didn't know whether the gesture was a warning, an expression of disapproval, or something else. A well-timed clap of thunder sounded. The rain started coming down more forcefully.

"She's right, you know," the tattooed man said.

Rune's eyes swung in his direction. He seemed unbothered by the storm.

"You don't belong here," he continued. "Khlong Toei is no place for a *farang*."

"I'm part Thai," Rune replied as if it wasn't a ridiculous thing to say. Never before had she felt more like an outsider.

"If you say so."

Rune ignored his condescending tone.

"And what brings you to Khlong Toei, *luk khrueng*?"

She resisted the urge to tell him off. Who did he think he was, calling her a half child?

"Well?"

Rune had a decision to make. She could walk away from this creepy man who seemed to enjoy taunting her, or she could swallow her pride and ask for his help. Under the circumstances, it was an easy choice. "I'm looking for something . . . someone . . ."

"Which is it? Something or someone?"

Rune wasn't prepared to tell the man about the lost rubies. The last thing she needed was for word to get out. It could cause a stampede, or worse. And if someone else found them, she would never get them back. Instead, she pulled up a picture of Madee on her phone and showed it to him. "Do you know this girl?"

The man squinted at the screen. "No, but I know someone who might."

"Who?"

"I'll take you to him."

Alarm bells sounded inside Rune's head. "That's ok. Just tell me where to go."

"You think you can find your way around Khlong Toei alone, *luk khrueng*?"

Hmmm. The man had a point.

"Don't worry. You can trust me."

Rune was sure she couldn't, but what choice did she have? She would walk through fire if it meant finding Madee. She hesitated, but only for a moment. She gave the man a firm nod, then said, "Fine, let's go."

14

Khlong Toei Slum, Bangkok

He took her to an abandoned house on a canal swollen by hours of heavy rain. It was bigger than the typical shacks of Khlong Toei, with a wide porch and a towering second story. The stilts of the substructure were decayed from years of exposure and neglect, causing the building to tilt significantly to one side. All the windows were boarded up. Water poured off the rusted metal roof. Rune's brow rose when she saw the word "paradise" written on the door in messy Thai script. She knew before entering that the place was anything but.

The tattooed man let himself in without knocking. Rune followed him inside, pausing for a moment to let her vision adjust to the darkness. The interior of the house was as bad as she had feared. Broken glass and cigarette butts littered the floor. The furnishings looked like they belonged in a junkyard. There was a large puddle in the middle of the room, clearly caused by a leak in the roof.

"What is this place?" Rune asked.

The tattooed man didn't answer. Instead, he led her to the back of the building and up a flight of stairs. The third and fourth steps sagged so badly Rune thought they might collapse under her weight.

The staircase opened onto a long hallway with doors on either side. The tattooed man knocked on the closest one. There was a metallic click when the lock unlatched. The door cracked open. The tattooed man spoke in a quiet voice with whoever was on the other side before stepping out of the way to allow Rune to pass. She turned to him with questions in her eyes, but he was already partway down the stairs.

"I understand you're looking for someone," came a voice from the doorway.

"Y-yes," Rune stammered, doing a poor job of concealing her surprise. The speaker was not at all what she had expected. He looked like a middle-aged, slightly out of shape tennis player, with snow-white shorts and a matching polo shirt. Even his socks and sneakers were white. How he kept his garments clean in this filthy environment was a mystery for the ages.

"You came to the right place. Nothing goes on in Khlong Toei without my knowledge."

Rune silently questioned the veracity of this claim.

"No one made you come here," said the man, as if reading her mind.

Rune realized that her body language was all wrong. She looked defensive, confrontational even. She forced herself to relax. "I'm looking for a girl. I was told you could help me."

"That's correct, but first I'll need something from you."

Rune pursed her lips. Nothing in Bangkok was ever free. "How much?"

"Four-thousand baht."

A hundred dollars. It was a small price to pay if it helped her find Madee, but she knew the man would lose all respect for her if she didn't haggle. This lack of respect would then give him free reign to lie to her. She didn't have time to waste on false leads, so she shook her head and said, "Two thousand."

The man's smile was all teeth and no sincerity. "I won't do it for less than three."

"I'll give you twenty-five hundred. Final offer."

The man nodded once. Rune counted out the bills and handed them over.

"So, tell me about this girl," he said after pocketing the money.

"Her name is Madee. She's fifteen years old. She went missing from Khlong Toei yesterday afternoon."

"And what makes you think this girl wants to be found?"

"Madee's not a runaway. She's a good girl." Rune realized the moment she said the words that they were untrue. *Bad news.* That was how the DJ at the Omni had described Madee and Dara.

"Many kids her age come here. You're welcome to look around." He stretched his hand toward the door.

"That's all I get for my money?"

His hand came down. His expression soured. "That's where we start."

Rune shot him an irritated look and walked into the hallway unable to shake the feeling that she had been scammed. She approached a closed door. A soft knock brought no answer. She pushed it open.

Paradise.

One look inside the room and the word scrawled outside the house suddenly made perfect sense. This was a drug den, and the washed-up tennis player was a dealer. Rune chided herself for not figuring it out sooner. Maybe Kit was right. Maybe she was naïve.

The room was more revolting than anything she could have imagined. Filthy. Rank. Crawling with roaches. There were eight people inside, most of them Madee's age, or perhaps a bit older. In one corner, a scrawny boy with jaundiced skin and a crooked nose tightened a tourniquet around his arm with his teeth. In another, three girls lay inert on a dirty mattress while a fourth took deep pulls from a hand-rolled cigarette. The remaining teens sat on the floor in semi-comatose states, their mouths slack, their gazes fixed and distant. Rune was instantly relieved not to see Madee. She approached the smoking girl even though it was the last thing she wanted to do. She crouched down and showed her a picture of Madee. The girl looked at her unsteadily and shook her head. Rune moved on to the boy who was shooting up and got the same response. The zombies on the floor didn't even acknowledge her presence. Visits to the other rooms yielded similar results. Disheartened, Rune went looking for the dealer about a half hour later. She found him on the back porch under an umbrella emblazoned with the Wimbledon logo.

"No luck?" he asked between puffs of mentholated cigarette.

Rune shook her head. The tumultuous storm seemed to mirror her emotions. The rain was coming down so hard it rattled the metal roof. Brown water swirled angrily in the canal below, straining the building's wood stilts.

"Khlong Toei is a big place," the man said by way of explanation.

"You said nothing went on in the slum without your knowledge."

"That's true."

"So, prove it."

The man took another drag from his cigarette and slowly blew the smoke out. "The girl you're looking for—where was she when she went missing?"

"At the Khlong Toei Youth Center. Her phone went dead after that. I looked for her there last night, but the gate was locked." Rune didn't want to admit that she and Kit had broken in. She didn't know why it mattered. Breaking and entering seemed harmless compared to dealing hard drugs.

"Hmmm," the man said, flicking his ashes onto the wet ground. "Your girl might be in serious trouble."

"What makes you say that?"

"Strange things happen at the Youth Center. They always have."

"What do you mean?"

"This girl of yours, she isn't the only one to go missing from that place."

Rune's face crumbled. The dealer's words confirmed her worst fears. Madee might already be lost.

"I'd take another look at the Center if I were you. A lot of kids go there. It's a perfect cover for a trafficking operation, don't you think?"

Fury replaced Rune's despair. Her face burned. The muscles in her jaw clenched and unclenched. Her fists tightened until her knuckles turned white. If the dealer was right, the people behind the Youth Center were the worst kind of scum—the ultimate wolves in sheep's clothing.

"You should hurry. From what I hear, they work fast."

Rune gave the man a brusque thank-you and practically ran out of the house. She slammed the door behind her, earning her a side-eye from a woman pushing an empty shopping cart. Then off she went to find the Youth Center. Questioning the workers would be her first order of business. She hoped, for their sake, that they were on the up-and-up. If not, she would tear their limbs off with her bare hands.

15

Khlong Toei Youth Center, Bangkok

"Open up! I know you're in there!" Rune yelled as she shook the Youth Center's metal gate. It rattled loudly under her efforts, scaring a one-legged pigeon from its perch. The rain pelted down on her so forcefully it blurred her vision. She squinted against the water in a pointless attempt to see more clearly. The Youth Center did not officially open for another hour, but there was a car parked just outside that hadn't been there the night before and Rune desperately wanted to speak to its driver. She raised her eyes to the torrents of windblown rain tumbling from the sky. She was sick of being wet and even sicker of being ignored. She slammed her hand against the bars again and shouted, "For the love of Christ! Open the gate!"

Relief washed over her when she caught sight of a distinguished woman striding toward her at a brisk pace. The rain was coming down on a diagonal, but the woman was inexplicably dry under her umbrella. She wore navy slacks and a matching polka-dot blouse tied at the neck with a perky bow. Her shiny black hair was styled in a low bun. She walked right up to Rune but stopped short of unlocking the gate.

"What's all this commotion?" the woman asked in considerably accented English. She was a head taller and fuller figured than Rune. Her features were sharp, like they were sculpted in stone. Her makeup was applied with a heavy hand, incongruously so given their surroundings.

"Please let me in," Rune begged. "I'm looking for a girl who went missing from this Center yesterday."

"A missing girl?" The woman's brown eyes widened. "I don't know anything about that."

"If I could just come in and ask you a few questions. It won't take long."

A look of distrust crossed the woman's face, like she was used to dealing with scammers. Rune must have passed the low-life test because the gate swung open suddenly. She wanted very badly to duck under the umbrella, but the woman didn't offer to share, and Rune wasn't going to beg. The woman's reticence was understandable. There was so much need in Khlong Toei that people would take the clothes off your back if you let them. Either you kept your guard up, or you ended up like the school teachers back home who dipped into their savings to buy pencils and glue sticks for their students. The system preyed on their empathy. The powers that be were just fine with that.

Rune circumvented lake-sized puddles as she followed the woman to the Youth Center's main office, a small, concrete building with sliding glass doors and a Thai flag perched at the top. They stepped inside. The woman shook her umbrella vigorously, spraying water all over the floor.

"Have a seat," she said, gesturing to a straight-backed chair that was either made for a child or a very small adult.

Rune surveyed the room looking for clues about potentially illicit activities. Posters of laughing children covered the walls, alongside framed newspaper clippings lauding the organization's positive impact on local families. A plaque on the desk identified Rune's host as Som Thongsi, the Youth Center's managing director. Displayed next to it was a picture of Som smiling broadly as she shook hands with the governor of Bangkok. Behind the desk hung a wood crucifix and, in a gilded frame, a bust-length portrait of the Thai monarch in full military regalia. Likenesses of the king appeared just about everywhere in Thailand. The Youth Center was no exception.

Som's wet shoes squelched against the floor as she walked to the other side of the desk and sank into an expensive-looking ergonomic chair. Rune shifted uncomfortably in her Lilliputian seat. A jar of hard candies caught her eye. She reached for one and popped it into her mouth.

"Those are for the children," Som informed her with an admonishing look.

"Sorry," Rune replied, even though she was not sorry at all. She was starving. She hadn't eaten anything since her fancy meal at the Mandarin Oriental the day before.

Som leaned forward and laced her fingers together. "So, what's this you say about a missing girl?"

"Her name is Madee. I'm certain she was here yesterday." Rune pulled up a picture on her phone and slid it across the desk.

"Dozens of children come through the Youth Center each day. We try our best to help them, but it's impossible to keep track of who comes and goes, much less what happens to them after they leave." Som said all this without deigning to look at the phone.

"She's only fifteen."

"What time did you say she was here?"

"After school. At around four o'clock."

"If that's the case, I really can't help you. I was at a meeting offsite yesterday afternoon."

"Is the Youth Center equipped with surveillance cameras?"

"Yes, but I can't let you see them. It's a question of privacy."

"This is an emergency."

"The rules are in place to protect the children."

"And I'm telling you that a child is in danger."

"I'm sorry, but my hands are tied."

Rune could no longer keep her frustration in check. Her world was collapsing, and all this woman was doing was tripping her up. It was hard not to see Som's actions as anything but deliberate. "What's wrong with you?" she demanded, her voice rising to the level of a shout. "The sole purpose of your organization is to help kids. A child is missing. Why won't you help me find her?" She looked unflinchingly at Som. The woman's features hardened. She clearly wasn't accustomed to being yelled at, especially not by an impertinent foreigner.

"I'm going to have to ask you to leave now."

Not one to back down from a fight, Rune pushed even harder. "I wonder what the press would say about your inaction. Imagine the headlines: *Youth Center Condones Child Abduction*. It would reflect very badly, not just on this organization, but on you personally. And on your benefactors." She lowered her eyes to the picture of Som shaking hands with the governor of Bangkok to ensure that the director understood what she meant.

An uncomfortable silence followed while Som appraised her coolly.

Rune held her breath and her tongue.

After what seemed like an eternity, Som placed her palms flat on the desk and said, "You'll have to speak to Thanu."

"Thanu?"

"He's in charge of security."

"Where can I find him?"

Som glanced at the sapphire-encrusted watch tucked beneath the cuff of her blouse. The extravagant accessory seemed grossly out of place. "I'm expecting him soon. You're welcome to wait for him in our security suite." She offered Rune a smile that did not reach her eyes.

Rune's mouth puckered. Soon could mean anywhere from five minutes to an hour in local parlance. Thai time, people called it. She wanted to scream. Instead, she nodded slowly and reached into the jar for another candy.

16

Khlong Toei Youth Center, Bangkok

F*ive . . . four . . . three . . . two . . . one . . .* Rune did not scream, and for that, she deserved a bloody medal. This was how she was spending her precious time, fighting not to lose it instead of looking for Madee and the rubies. *Goddammed rubies!* Kit had warned her about the potential risks of her operation, but as always, she had done exactly as she pleased. If only she had listened. Then she would only have one impossible problem to solve, and Kit would be right by her side to help. Instead, she was on her own, Kit had a gun to his head, and Madee was running out of time. The urge to scream returned. Rune breathed in deeply and resumed her deliberate counting. *Five . . . four . . . three . . . two . . . one . . .*

Rune lost track of how many times she had repeated the exercise, that was how long she had been waiting in what Som euphemistically described as the Youth Center's security suite. In reality, it was a glorified supply closet. A shelving unit stacked with office materials covered one wall. Boxes overflowing with outdated electronic equipment occupied another. Someone had taped a historic map of Bangkok behind the door, while a yellowing poster of Renoir's *Luncheon of the Boating*

Party hung above the small metal desk. These half-hearted attempts at decorating only emphasized the dismal character of the space. Most dismaying of all was the surveillance equipment, the sum total of which was a single computer monitor hooked up to two cameras—one at the entrance gate and the other near the rear of the complex. Rune wanted more than anything to review the stored footage, but the computer was password protected. She knew this because she had tried to access it. Repeatedly. To no avail. And so, she counted silently. Five-second increments were about all she could handle.

Rune was certain she was near madness when the elusive Thanu arrived sometime later. She sprang to her feet. His startled expression told her he didn't know she would be there. She was also taken aback. He looked too young to oversee security, or anything else of importance. If she had to guess, she would put him in his late teens or early twenties. He was tall and rail thin, with arms like pipe cleaners and peach fuzz on his hollow cheeks. Deeply set eyes and teashade glasses gave him a thoughtful appearance. His dark hair was pulled back in a man-bun, the style of choice for the young and woke. His wrinkled polo shirt was bone dry, revealing that the rain had stopped, at least for now.

As the younger of the two, social etiquette dictated that Thanu bow first. Rune waited a moment before losing patience and bringing her palms together. "Sawatdee kha," she said as she lowered her head. *Hello.*

"I speak English."

He wasn't kidding. His accent was that of a California surfer. It was clear he had spent time in the States. Either that, or he had wasted his youth watching a lot of American television. Whatever the case, Rune silently thanked her lucky stars.

"I need to review your security footage," she said, cutting straight to the chase. "I was told you could help me."

"I've never done that before."

Rune shot him a disbelieving look.

"Okay, okay. Give me a second."

She kept her eyes on him as he dumped his messenger bag on the floor and took a seat. She wanted to yell at him to hurry up as he adjusted the height of the chair and the angle of the backrest, but she bit her tongue. "If we could get started. This is an emergency."

"What do you want to see?"

"Footage from yesterday afternoon. From four o'clock onward."

"Both cameras?"

"Uh-huh." She leaned over his shoulder and drummed her fingers on the desk.

Thanu glanced nervously at her black nail polish and surfeit of gold rings. Rune stayed where she was. Making him comfortable wasn't her responsibility.

"Here you go," he said, ceding his chair after cueing up the footage. "You can speed up and slow down, if that helps."

Rune stared at the split-screen. Not surprisingly, the hour after school ended was a busy time at the Youth Center. Children streamed in and out of the front camera's frame, some accompanied by their parents, but most of them on their own. The camera at the back of the complex showed no activity. Rune directed her attention to the front camera and drew closer to the screen.

A young woman in a canary-yellow sundress caught her attention as she chased after two toddlers with a newborn strapped to her chest. It was like watching her try to herd a pair of recalcitrant cats. An adolescent boy in fluorescent orange swim trunks pursued a girl around the swimming pool with a plastic bucket of water. It was all fun and games until he tugged at her bathing suit strap. She rewarded him with a slap so forceful it left a handprint on his cheek. Rune was itching to speed up the footage, but the Youth Center was so crowded she was afraid she might miss something. Twenty minutes elapsed. Her attention remained on the screen while Thanu busied himself with his phone. Her vision grew blurry after thirty minutes, but still she kept at it. Hope started fading at the forty-five-minute mark. By the end of the hour, she knew it had all been for nothing. There wasn't a trace of Madee anywhere on the video. It was like she didn't exist. Rune dropped her head in her hands in frustration. It took all her willpower not to cry.

Thanu looked up from his phone long enough to notice her distress. "I take it you didn't find what you were looking for?"

Rune raised her eyes to his and shook her head. "A girl is missing. I thought the footage might help me find her."

"Missing? From the Youth Center?"

"Yes. She was here yesterday. At least I thought she was." Rune took out her phone and pulled up a picture of Madee. "Maybe you saw her? She was traveling with a man in a taxi."

Thanu glanced at the screen. "Oh!" He took a step back, visibly shaken.

"What is it?"

"Nothing."

"Clearly it's not nothing."

"It's just that . . . I think I . . ."

"For god's sake, spit it out!"

"I think I know this girl."

Rune thought she misheard him. "What?"

"Yeah. She comes here sometimes."

"You're sure?" Rune was not aware that Madee frequented the Youth Center. Kit was also in the dark, otherwise he would have put a stop to it.

"Madee something, right?"

Rune's heart leapt at the sound of Madee's name. "Did you see her yesterday? Who was she with? Where did they go?" The words came tumbling out of her mouth.

"Whoa," Thanu said, holding up his hands. "Slow down. She wasn't here yesterday. Not that I saw, anyway."

"I know she was here."

"Well, it's not like I was looking for her." His words came out somewhat defensively. He put his hands on his hips and thought for a moment. "Have you tried the Church of the Holy Redeemer next door? A lot of the kids hang out there. The priest knows everyone."

Rune's eyes lit up at the prospect of a new lead. "Where do I find this priest?"

"Go out the way you came. The church is on the right. You can't miss it."

Rune rushed out of the security suite without so much as thanking Thanu. A moist heat greeted her the moment she stepped foot outside. It sucked the air out of her lungs, but she ignored her discomfort as she hurried toward the front gate. Madee was all that mattered right now. The girl had been hiding things from her and Kit. If Thanu was to be believed, the priest might know something about it. Better yet, maybe he knew where to find her, and the lost rubies.

17

Church of the Holy Redeemer, Bangkok

Of all the houses of Christian worship in Bangkok, the Church of the Holy Redeemer in Khlong Toei stood out as the least church-like of the bunch. No lofty bell towers marked its facade, no flying buttresses or statues of saints articulated its flanks. There was no dome. The building did not even adhere to the ubiquitous cruciform layout. Architecturally, it had more in common with the neighborhood shacks than most churches Rune was familiar with. The small, boxy building consisted of an un-aisled vessel made of wood planks that were painted a funereal-gray hue. It was fronted by a sagging porch that looked to be on its last leg. The gable above it, while solid, was covered with mismatched shingles. Whoever was in charge obviously had no interest in outward appearances. In fact, the only sign that the building was even a place of worship was the simple wood cross affixed to the roof.

Rune bounded up the staircase and pulled on the door so hard it nearly came off its hinges. She strode inside. The door groaned closed behind her.

It was almost pitch black inside the church. The smell of damp wood and stale incense was everywhere. The sole source of light was an overhead fixture glowing like a beacon at the far end of the building.

A plank creaked. Rune's head spun to the side. She was fairly certain she was alone but the truth was, a serial killer could have been looking over her shoulder and she would have been none the wiser. She groped her way forward, advancing just a few steps before slamming straight into the collection box.

"Jesus Christ!" Her words carried through the empty space. She bent down to rub her bruised shin.

"Is there something I can help you with?" came a lilting voice from the rear of the building.

Rune winced at her poor choice of words. Then she gave a cursory shrug. It wasn't as if she could take them back. "I'm looking for the priest," she called out.

"You found him. I'm in the chancel. Join me."

That Rune made it to the back of the church without falling or knocking into anything else was nothing short of a miracle. Perhaps there was something to this Jesus thing after all. Once there, she encountered a man so small she might have mistaken him for a child had it not been for the deep crevices around his eyes and his shiny white hair. His facial features were downright elfin. Tortoiseshell glasses were perched precariously on the tip of his upturned nose. Behind them blinked a pair of intelligent blue eyes.

"I'm Father Bergdahl. Welcome to the Church of the Holy Redeemer," he said with a dimpled smile. His black cassock billowed mysteriously of its own accord.

Rune opened her mouth to respond, but Father Bergdahl launched into a well-practiced speech before she had the opportunity to speak.

"We offer morning and noonday prayer services on weekdays, in addition to afternoon Mass. There are two Masses on weekends, and confessions are heard on Saturday afternoons between three and four." He paused to take a breath. Then he cocked his head and said, "But I can see from your expression that you're not here for our worship schedule."

"I'm looking for a missing girl. I was told you might be able to help."

A look of resignation crossed Father Bergdahl's face. He let out a heavy breath. "Children go missing more often than they should in these parts. We do our best, but it's an unfortunate reality."

"She's a good kid from a nice family," Rune said. She didn't want the priest to dismiss Madee as a slum child. Not that it should make a difference where she was from. Missing children deserved concern and consideration, regardless of their circumstances.

"I can see you're upset. Why don't you come to my office? We can try to sort this out."

Rune gave a terse nod. She swallowed the lump in her throat and followed him to the back of the church, behind the area of the altar. How it was that he could see in the dark, she was at a loss to explain. Another miracle, she thought glibly. She breathed a silent sigh of relief when he stopped in front of an unassuming wood door. He slipped a hand inside his pocket and pulled out a large ring chock-full of keys. They jingled as he searched for the right one.

The door swung open. On came the lights, revealing an unexpectedly spacious room that looked like an office, a cloakroom, and a classroom rolled into one. A large desk dominated the back wall, directly across from the entrance. To the left was a wardrobe crammed with liturgical vestments that seemed to belong to a much bigger man. A wooden bench and an old-fashioned chalkboard covered with English words occupied the right side of the room, near the only window. The floor tiles were a distinctive shade of burnt cinnabar. Father Bergdahl gestured to a chair in front of the desk and settled on the other side. He looked even smaller from this vantage point.

"You're American?" he asked, leaning forward and interlacing his fingers in an inviting manner.

"From New York," Rune replied with a nod. Her eyes moved over the desk, taking inventory of everything that was on it. It was a short list: stacks of brochures, a jar of pens, and a desktop computer that was built like a tank. A tripod leaned against the back wall, next to a plastic cooler.

"Ah, New York. What a coincidence! I attended seminary school there. I have such fond memories of the city."

"Oh?" Her tone was meant to dissuade chitchat. She was there to find Madee, not to reminisce. Besides, there was a reason she had left New York.

Father Bergdahl somehow interpreted her lackluster response as an invitation to share. "I arrived in Bangkok over thirty years ago, at a time when people wanted nothing to do with Khlong Toei. It looked even worse back then, if you can believe it. The slum had grown unchecked for decades. No one paid attention—not the politicians, not even the grass-roots organizations." His face brightened. "Did you know that the Church was the first to establish charities in the neighborhood? The orphanage down the street was our flagship project. Then we opened an HIV clinic in the mid-nineties, at the height of the AIDS epidemic." He handed her an STI information pamphlet with a picture of a nursing mother on the cover.

Aware of the Catholic Church's historic stance on contraception, including its prohibition of condoms, Rune was sorely tempted to throw the pamphlet in the priest's face. Instead, she placed it on the desk unopened. She must have done an adequate job of masking her true feelings. That, or Father Bergdahl was awful at reading body language.

"The Youth Center is our most successful project. You must have seen it on your way here. The overarching goal of the Center is to give young people from poor families the semblance of a normal childhood."

Rune wondered what constituted normal. Her middle-class childhood looked good on paper, but scratch beneath the surface and a different story emerged.

"We've come a long way since the early days," Father Bergdahl continued with a note of pride in his voice. "Catholics now number three hundred and eighty thousand in Thailand, and we're over a hundred thousand strong in Bangkok. A growing number of Thais are converting, but, of course, our community is primarily international." He pawed around for more pamphlets. "Perhaps I could interest you in some of our volunteering opportunities? We offer language instruction, computer literacy programs for adults and children, addiction outreach . . ."

"About the Youth Center," Rune interjected, eager to put an end to the infomercial. "The girl I'm looking for was there yesterday afternoon. She arrived in a taxi with a man with a scar on his leg. I was told you might know something about it."

"Troubled children come through our doors every day. We try our best to help them. We provide food, guidance, and educational services. But the truth is, there are limits to what we can do. The need far outweighs our resources."

"I'm not asking about all the children in the slum. I'm asking about one specific girl. Maybe this will help." Rune held up her phone.

The priest grew reflective as he looked at the smiling picture of Madee. The corners of his mouth sank slightly. His eyes softened behind his glasses. "You have to understand," he said, raising his gaze to meet Rune's. "Even if I knew something—and I'm not saying I do—I couldn't tell you. The only reason we're able to help the children is because they trust us. They share things with us that they can't—or won't—share with anyone else. Not even their families. It's a special bond. If we break their confidence, everything falls apart."

Rune greeted his words with silent disbelief. She wondered why it was that Father Bergdahl had bothered to sit down with her if he wasn't planning to tell her anything. Her irritation roiled beneath the surface, but she held it in check when she realized he was still talking.

"The privacy and safety of the children are our primary concerns," he said.

"I can assure you I'm only interested in Madee's safety," Rune replied through gritted teeth.

The priest's eyes became quizzical. "Tell me, what's your relationship to this girl, if you don't mind me asking."

"She's my sister-in-law." It wasn't exactly true, but it was close enough.

Father Bergdahl leaned back in his chair and crossed his arms.

Two things were immediately clear to Rune: first, Father Bergdahl didn't believe her. Second, the conversation was over. His next words came as no surprise.

"I'm sorry, but my hands are tied."

Rune sized him up long enough for his placid expression to falter somewhat.

"Is there anything more I can do for you?"

"There's nothing else," she replied coolly. "Thank you for your time."

"Not at all."

Rune's chair scraped against the floor as she rose to her feet. She made her way to the exit, stopping short just before she reached it. The door had a deadbolt and a safety chain, neither of which she had noticed on her way in. It seemed excessive. Then again, they *were* in the middle of a slum. She was about to leave when she remembered she had one more question for the priest. She turned to face him. "Father, do you happen to know if anyone in the neighborhood has had a recent windfall?"

"I'm not sure what you mean."

"Has anyone come into something . . . *valuable*?" She chose the last word carefully, not wanting to give too much away.

"Like what?" Father Bergdahl asked with a perplexed look on his face.

It was all the answer Rune needed. It was obvious the priest didn't have a clue about the rubies. "Never mind," she said.

She felt his eyes on her as she left the room. The door latched shut behind her. She retraced her steps to the front door as quickly as she could without tripping over anything. As she walked, she focused on the sensation she'd had the instant she sat down with Father Bergdahl—the feeling that he knew more about Madee's disappearance than he was letting on. He confirmed her suspicions when he stonewalled her using exactly the same language as the director of the Youth Center. It was a question of privacy. They wanted to help, but their hands were tied. There was something off about these do-gooders, and Rune sensed it had everything to do with Madee.

18

Khlong Toei Youth Center, Bangkok

The first thing Rune noticed when she marched back to the Youth Center was that the sun was still out, promising another unbearably muggy afternoon. The second was the noise. She had only ever seen the complex empty—or nearly so—but children had arrived in droves in the short time she had spent inside the church and there was no reining them in. Squeals of delight could be heard from every direction. On one side, overexcited preschoolers chased after a soccer ball while older kids tried to impose a semblance of structure on the game. On the other side, a group of boys whose voices had only recently broken took turns dunking each other in the pool. Peals of laughter rang out from the playground as children dangled fearlessly from swing sets and monkey bars. Rune's ears perked at the tremulous sound of a boy crying. She watched as an adolescent girl pulled him to his feet and gently blew on his scraped knee.

He's lucky to have her, she thought. She turned slowly, scanning the area until she found what she was looking for.

The three girls were huddled in a far corner of the playground looking thick as thieves. They seemed to be about Madee's age, at once too old to be there, but too young to be left at home unsupervised without getting into mischief. They stole glances at the boys in the pool. In return, the boys doubled down on their antics, putting on a show for their captive audience. The boys grew rowdier, so rowdy they drew protests from other children as tsunami-like waves rolled over their heads and left them sputtering for air. The girls' giggles stopped abruptly. Their smiles turned into scowls. They averted their eyes. They went from hot to cold in an instant, all because a scrawny boy with a deep tan and the beginnings of a mustache had the temerity to wave to them. His buddies stared at him in disbelief. He looked upset and embarrassed. Rune watched the scene unfold with a roll of her eyes. It was like stumbling onto a bad afterschool special from the eighties, minus the crimped hair and shoulder pads.

The time had come to approach the girls. Rune did so cautiously, unsure of how they would react to her. It wasn't often that she regretted shearing her hair. This was one of those times.

As it turned out, Rune's reticence was way off base. The girls greeted her with shy smiles, the kind young people often get when they are around adults they don't know. They seemed not at all put off by her hair, or her hand adornments, for that matter. She pulled up a picture of Madee and asked if they had seen her in broken Thai. They shook their heads solemnly, like they understood the seriousness of the situation. Then she asked about the man with the scar on his leg. It was another dead end. She thanked them for their help and moved on to another group, and then another, until she had approached all the children—female and male—who were around Madee's age. No one knew her. It seemed that Thanu was mistaken when he said she frequented the Youth Center.

Rune was ready to throw in the towel when she noticed a wispy girl sitting alone at a picnic table with her eyes glued to her phone. She looked young. Perhaps eight. Nine at the most. Her hair was styled in pigtails held in place with bright yellow elastics. She wore a white bathing suit sprayed with palm leaves that brought to mind the local vegetation. There was a dark mark on the bench where the wood had absorbed the water dripping from her body. Rune caught the girl's eye and gestured to the bench. She slid in beside her after receiving a bashful nod. Then she showed her a picture of Madee and asked, "Kui hen ying khon nii ru?" *Have you seen this girl?*

"I know English."

Rune's eyebrows shot up. No other child at the Youth Center had been conversant in English, though some had leapt at the chance to practice, with varying degrees of success. "You speak English really well. Where did you learn?"

The girl looked in the direction of the Church of the Holy Redeemer. "Father Bergdahl teaches us."

The chalkboard in the priest's office—it was covered with English words. Rune bobbed her head knowingly. "Who else takes English classes?" she asked, hoping to gain the child's confidence with small talk.

"Malai, Kanya, and Preeda," the girl replied, counting on her stubby fingers. She pointed to the swings and said, "They're over there."

The scarlet polish on the girl's nails caught Rune's eye. The color was mature for a child, but its application was sloppy, like the girl had done it herself. "It's just the four of you who take classes?"

"Some boys, too."

Rune nodded encouragingly.

"Meow and Kanok used to come."

"Oh? Not anymore?"

The girl shook her head, causing water to drip from the tips of her pigtails.

"Where did they go?"

The girl stuck out her bottom lip and raised her shoulders to indicate she didn't know.

Rune held up a picture of Madee. "Was this girl in Father Bergdahl's English class with you?"

"Only the boys, Malai, Kanya, and Preeda," the girl said.

Right, Rune thought.

"Meow and Kanok used to come."

Like you said. This was a waste of time. The girl didn't know anything. Disappointed, Rune tucked the phone back into her pocket. The clock was ticking, and she was no closer to finding Madee or the rubies. She bid the girl goodbye with an artificially bright voice. Pretending wasn't normally Rune's style, but the kid seemed nice, and it wasn't her fault she didn't have any useful information.

Rune took a few steps forward before stopping suddenly. Something had been bothering her since she had set eyes on the girl, and she finally put her finger on what it was. Her phone. It was the latest Samsung Galaxy. The model retailed for nearly thirty thousand baht. That was more than the average monthly salary in Bangkok. What would a little girl from the slums be doing with such an expensive gadget? And come to think of it, where had those two other girls from Father Bergdahl's English class gone? What were their names again? She turned to ask the girl.

The words had not yet come out of her mouth when she felt a strong hand grip her forearm. She whipped her head to the side and found herself staring into the face of a Royal Thai Police officer. With his low center of gravity and implacable smile, he looked to Rune like a Buddha statue come to life. His liquid brown eyes glowered from beneath a pair of rebellious eyebrows. His shorn hair was barely visible under his visored cap. There was a large, amorphous spot on the front of his shirt where sweat had soaked through the fabric of his uniform.

"Maa kap phom!" he barked, squeezing her arm in a proprietary fashion. *Come with me!*

"Let go! You're hurting me!" Rune cried. She was far too spooked to say the words in Thai.

"Diaw nii!" *Now!*

"Let go!" she repeated, twisting her body and pulling away.

This proved to be a terrible mistake. The officer was not the sort to repeat himself. He emitted a low growl. Then he loosened his grip and smacked her hard with the back of his hand. The force was such that Rune instantly fell into unconsciousness.

19

Community Police Station 4, Bangkok

It was the overpowering stench hanging in the air that drew Rune out of her insensate state. Sweat was the best way to describe it. Not gym sweat, or the unholy mixture of perspiration and Drakkar Noir that permeated hotel bars and video game tournaments. No, this was something different. It was the smell of bodies confined in a small space for too long. Of bodies that had gone for days without bathing. Of bodies taxed by stress and fear.

Rune's eyelids fluttered open. It took a moment for her to get her bearings. She was on the floor of a windowless cell whose walls were covered with layers of institutional beige paint. Her arm was folded painfully under her body. Her cheek lay flat against the dingy concrete. A squat toilet, the kind best suited for Pilates masters, occupied one corner of the room. A metal bench lined the opposite wall.

The air in the room was stifling. A ceiling fan hummed overhead, but its blades were too sluggish to make a measurable difference in the ambient temperature. A trickle of perspiration inched its way down Rune's neck, disappearing in the soft fabric of her shirt.

Sharing the rank space on this steamy day were two dozen women in various states of mental distress. One kneeled down and brought her lips to Rune's ear, babbling nonsense as if they were real words. Another cracked her knuckles and eyed her with open hostility from across the cell. The rest were either too wrapped up in their own misery to notice her or too out of it to care.

Rune swatted the incoherent woman away. She raised her head, only to be rewarded with a searing jolt of pain. She reached up and realized the cop had left her temple tender to the touch. *Coward*, she said to herself when she remembered how he had struck her without warning. A fair fight would have ended very differently, that much she knew.

Rune's bravado ebbed somewhat after two failed attempts to get to her feet. *Third time's a charm*, she thought as she pushed herself up. She swept the sweat away from her face and, on shaky legs, staggered toward the cell door.

"Hello!" she called out hoarsely from between the metal bars. She cleared her throat and tried again. "Can anyone hear me? Let me out!"

A young, olive-skinned officer looked up from behind a desk at the end of the hallway, only to go back to the entertainment magazine she was reading seconds later.

"Please, let me out! I didn't do anything!"

This time the officer ignored her.

Splendid, Rune said to herself. She shook the door with as much force as she could muster. The metallic sound rang out through the cell like cannon fire. "I know you can hear me," Rune called out. "Let me out. I don't belong here. I'm begging you. I'm looking for a missing girl!" Her last words caught the officer's attention. Rune thought back to the conversation she'd had with Kit the day before. He had been so quick to dismiss the police, so convinced of their corruption, but this woman seemed to want to help. Rune felt hopeful for the first time since this ordeal began.

The officer slid out from behind her desk and approached the cell. She held herself with the erect carriage of a prima ballerina. Her uniform was spotless, like it had come straight from the dry cleaner. Her glossy black hair was pulled back in a compact bun and pomaded into place. She stopped in front of the door and pulled her lips into a Delphian smile.

Seeing she had the woman's ear, Rune moved closer and grabbed hold of the bars with both hands. Words came pouring out as fast as she could form them. "Please, you have to let me out. I'm an American. My sister-in-law went missing yesterday. Her name is . . ."

Whack!

The baton came down so fast it took a moment for Rune to register what had happened. A fraction of a second later came a burst of blinding pain. Tears filled her eyes as she doubled over and cradled her wrecked left hand. Her nails were throbbing. Some of her rings were bent. Her fingers were quickly ballooning to twice their normal size.

The officer barked at her in Thai.

"I don't understand!" Rune screamed back, still reeling from the blow.

The look in the woman's eyes was one of pure scorn. "Get back!" she spat, underscoring her words with a crack of the baton.

Rune retreated to an empty section of the cell and sank onto the floor. She couldn't believe the mess she had made of things. She had failed Madee, and she was no closer to finding the rubies. To make matters worse, now she was stuck in a Thai jail with no obvious way of getting out. She felt tears prick at her eyes. She held them back for as long as she could, but before she knew it, she was crying in earnest. She buried her face in her hands. Her shoulders shook with sobs. She stayed that way until the woman who spoke in tongues shuffled over and tried to comfort her. It was a kind gesture, but Rune shooed her away. "Get off me!" she screamed. The last thing she wanted was to be pitied by the pitiful.

20

Community Police Station 4, Bangkok

Time seemed to stand still inside the windowless holding cell of the Thai police station, and in the small corner Rune carved out for herself, she paced. Restlessly. Relentlessly. The longer she did, the more desperate she became. Her anxiety mounted until she was on the cusp of falling apart. Cleansing breaths and silly countdowns were not going to cut it. She was trapped, and the tide was coming in.

She was so stressed she felt ill when a stern-looking officer approaching retirement age finally unlocked the door and ordered her to follow him in fluent English. He was an important man by the looks of the multitude of pins and patches affixed to his military uniform. He had the stature of a former wrestler, with broad shoulders and a commanding build, even in old age. He wore his mostly white hair in a military buzz cut. His jaw formed a perfect ninety-degree angle, reinforcing his masculine air of authority. Rune took one look at him and knew that his words were not open for discussion. She scurried to his side. A chorus of complaints arose from inside the cell. The man ordered the women to quiet down. Then he set off down the hall at a brisk pace.

They stopped when they reached the woman who smashed her hand. Rune heard her warn the officer about the troublesome foreigner in his custody. He seemed wholly uninterested in the woman's opinion, much to Rune's relief.

The officer rummaged through the filing cabinets lining the hallway. Rune distracted herself by surveying the contents of the woman's desk. It held a desktop computer that was at least five generations out of date, a stack of reasonably well-organized folders, sticky notes and pens, and a ball of turquoise-colored yarn with knitting needles that looked like they could double as weapons. Why anyone in Bangkok had any need for woolens was beyond baffling. Rune caught the woman's eye and received an ugly smirk for her trouble. She looked away, bowing her head like a docile pet. She hated the woman, but she hated herself more for being intimidated.

The officer led Rune to a windowless interrogation room furnished with a table and two woven rattan chairs that would not have been out of place in a Parisian café. He gestured for her to sit. She acquiesced. He settled across from her and placed a recording device on the table between them. Then he opened his file folder and began reading from its contents.

"Rune Felicity Sarasin," he said, his diction clear and precise. He stopped long enough to shoot her a puzzled look.

Rune responded with a shrug. With hair like Bald Barbie and two names meaning "happy," looks were nothing she wasn't used to.

The officer gave a slow shake of the head and continued. "I see here that you're a citizen of the United States, and that you've been in the country since July of last year. Is this correct?" He raised his eyes and waited for her answer.

Rune nodded.

"Please answer out loud for the record."

"Yes, that's correct."

"I'm Colonel Panit Rattana of the Metropolitan Police Bureau, a unit of the Royal Thai Police. Do you know why you're here, Ms. Sarasin?"

Rune started to shrug before catching herself and saying, "I haven't the slightest idea." She wondered what she had done to warrant a high-ranking officer's attention. Then she realized she was probably getting special treatment because she was American. Sometimes it paid to be treated like a foreigner.

"We received complaints that you were trespassing and harassing children at the Khlong Toei Youth Center."

"That's a lie, I never . . ."

Colonel Rattana held up a hand to quiet her. "Several witnesses place you at the Youth Center this morning, and it says here that you were arrested on the premises. Do you dispute these claims?"

"Yes . . . I mean no. I was at the Youth Center, but I wasn't harassing children. I was looking for someone. A missing girl."

Rattana received the statement with a healthy dose of skepticism.

"All I was doing was asking questions when your colleague . . ." She paused and flexed her injured fingers under the table. "When your colleague arrested me." She wanted to file a complaint against the officer who knocked her out, and against the woman who bashed her hand, but she didn't know if police brutality was even a crime in Thailand. And even if it were, there was no reason to believe this man would do anything about it. Best to keep her mouth shut. She was in enough trouble as it was.

"We take safety very seriously in this country, Ms. Sarasin. Children's safety in particular."

"I can assure you, I'm no danger to children. Like I said, I was just looking for someone. My sister-in-law."

"You have family in Bangkok?"

"She's my boyfriend's sister," Rune conceded.

"And this girl you say is missing—did you file a report with officers at your local precinct?"

Rune shook her head and shifted in her seat.

"Would you care to explain why?"

"We—her family—thought it would be best to look for her ourselves."

"You think you can do police work better than we can?"

"No, of course not. What I meant was . . ."

Rattana didn't let her finish. "And where is her family now? That's to say, her *real* family."

The implication vexed Rune, but she was not inclined to explain her personal relationships to this man. She had a bigger problem on her hands, namely, how to account for Kit's absence. Different scenarios raced through her mind. All of them stretched credulity. "Her brother is out looking for her," she finally said. "Last I heard, he was heading to her school. We split up . . . for efficiency." The explanation wasn't great, but it was the best she could come up with on the fly.

Rattana seemed satisfied with the answer because his posture relaxed all of a sudden. He leaned forward in his chair, elbows on the table, fingers entwined. His face softened. When he spoke again, it was in an unexpectedly kind tone. "Ms. Sarasin, you're a visitor to this country and unfamiliar with our laws, so I'm going to let you off this time."

Relief washed over Rune.

"But consider yourself warned. You're to stay away from the Khlong Toei Youth Center, and from all places where children gather."

"Yes, of course, Colonel. Thank you. I promise to keep my distance." Rune would have promised him the moon if it meant getting out of there. She was getting ready to leap out of her chair when she noticed a dark look fall across Rattana's face. He pressed his lips together and exhaled audibly through his nose.

"A missing girl," he said.

Rune nodded somberly.

"It's a common occurrence in Bangkok. Too common."

"She's only fifteen."

Silence filled the room. It went on so long that Rune started to worry Rattana had changed his mind about releasing her.

"I'm retiring next month," he finally said.

"Oh?" Rune frowned, unsure of where the conversation was heading.

"I've spent my entire career trying to help people. I'd like to help you, too." He paused for a moment, as if to gauge Rune's reaction. "Since you're here, perhaps you'd like to file a missing person report?"

Rune's eyes widened. Rattana believed her. Not only that, he was offering to help. She thought again about Kit's warning. To his mind, local cops were worse than useless. They were complicit, if not outright corrupt. But Kit wasn't with her now. No one was. And Colonel Rattana's concern seemed genuine. It was up to her to make the call. She hesitated, but only for a moment. "I'd like that," she said softly.

Rattana nodded once. Then he picked up his pen and said, "Let's start at the beginning then, shall we?"

21

Community Police Station 4, Bangkok

They discussed the details of Madee's disappearance for almost an hour. Rune held nothing back. She told Colonel Rattana about the backpack and the junkie who found it in the middle of the slum. She also told him about the video of Madee getting into a taxi with the scarred man. She shared her suspicions about the Church of the Holy Redeemer and the Khlong Toei Youth Center, whose leaders used exactly the same language to dissuade her from asking uncomfortable questions. And lastly, she voiced her concern that the little girl she encountered by the Youth Center's pool was being wooed into doing who knows what with gifts that were both expensive and inappropriate for her age, stressing that two of her friends were possibly missing. Rune spoke quickly. Time was running short. But more than that, she needed to get the words out before she could change her mind.

Colonel Rattana listened to her attentively, interrupting only when he needed clarification. His no-nonsense disposition inspired confidence. It was a relief for Rune to unburden herself. If she had learned anything over the past few hours, it was that she was ill-equipped to handle Madee's disappearance on her own. She thought back to the picture hanging in the office of the Youth Center, which showed the director posing with the governor of Bangkok. She also thought of Father Bergdahl, who boasted about his church's international membership. In her effort to find one girl, she may have inadvertently stumbled upon a much larger problem, one that extended far beyond the confines of the slum.

"Is that everything?" Rattana asked when she finally grew silent.

Rune nodded. It wasn't exactly true. There was something else. Something big. She toyed with the idea of telling him the truth about Kit, but then she thought better of it. There was no telling what Lemaire would do if the police came storming in. And even if they managed to free Kit, there was still the small matter of the rubies. How could she explain the situation without also revealing why the gems were in their possession in the first place? Rune had a good feeling about the colonel, and honesty really was the best policy, but there was no sense in getting carried away.

"You're sure you have nothing else to add?" Rattana asked, as if reading her mind.

"I've told you everything," Rune replied with a perfectly straight face.

"Very well. You're free to go." He turned off the recorder and began gathering his things.

"Wait. That's it?"

"Yes. We're done here."

"But you haven't *done* anything." Rune could see from the colonel's expression that he was offended, but she didn't care. She had impossible problems to solve. Sparing his feelings wasn't high on her list.

"It's now an active case," Rattana explained with the patience of a man used to dealing with difficult personalities. "Rest assured, I'll be in touch if there are any developments."

"I thought you were going to investigate Madee's disappearance. How is filling out a stupid form going to help?"

“Hold on, now.”

“Hold on, what? You promised to help me, but all you’ve done is waste my time. This is bullshit.” Rune took a swipe at Rattana’s papers, scattering them across the table.

“Has anyone ever told you that you’re a very rude person?”

Rattana’s words silenced Rune. In her experience, Thai people did not tell foreigners what they really thought of them, not even in dire circumstances. After nearly a year of inscrutable smiles and equivocation, Rune found the colonel’s candor refreshing. He could be a real asset, if only she could convince him to help. She drew a deep breath and slowly let the air out. She was upset. Angry even. But not so much that she couldn’t take it down a notch. “My rudeness is neither here nor there,” she said, careful to calibrate her tone. “This is urgent. A girl is missing, and no one is lifting a finger to find her.”

“I understand, but what is it exactly that you want me to do?”

“I want you to do your job. I just told you that something is going on at the Youth Center and at that creepy church. Why don’t you start there?”

“Allow me to explain something, Ms. Sarasin. The Thai legal system is a lot like the American one. We have laws that prevent the police from barging into places of business, and places of worship, without cause.”

“I didn’t say you should take a battering ram to their doors. Just bring the director and priest to the station for questioning. Ask them about Madee and the other girls who have gone missing from the slum.”

“That’s simply not possible.”

“Why not? Who are you protecting?”

“I don’t know what you mean.”

“A cop showed up at the Youth Center and knocked me out just as I was starting to make headway. I don’t think that’s a coincidence, do you?”

“That’s a very serious allegation.”

"You're telling me that your department is free of corruption? That there's no quid pro quo? That no one is ever paid to look the other way?"

"Hmmm," was all Rattana managed to say. His broad shoulders drooped slightly. Clearly Rune's words hit their mark.

"So, are you going to help me or not?"

The colonel sat back in his chair. A pensive look fell over his face. He pressed his fingers together to form a steeple and closed his eyes, like he was meditating on something important.

A minute or so passed. Rune shifted in her seat when the silence stretched to two minutes. At the three-minute mark, she started to wonder if Rattana had forgotten about her, or worse, fallen asleep. That was a thing with old people, right? She thought about leaving. Instead, she cleared her throat loudly. She tried again a few seconds later. She was on the verge of walking out when Rattana's eyes sprang open.

"Here's what I can do," he said as if nothing had happened.

The incident was mystifying, but Rune decided to roll with it. She leaned closer, eager to hear what he had to say.

"I'll follow up with the officer who arrested you. Then I'll place a few calls to my contacts in Khlong Toei and ask them to keep an eye out for Madee." He gave a satisfied nod. "I trust that's acceptable?"

Rune felt her temper flare again, only this time, she didn't bother containing it. What Rattana was proposing was not nearly enough. She wanted him to search high and low for signs of a human trafficking ring in Khlong Toei. She wanted him to interrogate Som and Father Bergdahl about the strange happenings at their institutions. But most of all, she wanted him to tear down every door in the slum until he found Madee. Anger turned into rage. Rage to fury. It came from a place deep inside her, so deep it rarely saw the light of day. Rune had spent her entire adult life keeping that feeling in check. But now it swelled up. Relentless. Unstoppable. A wave crashing toward the rocks.

It happened the summer before high school, at a bucolic camp in Upstate New York. Her parents were reluctant to send her, but she begged for weeks until they relented. She was innocent for her age. She dreamed of horseback riding and kayaking and leaping into frigid lake waters with a bunch of new friends. What she got upon arrival was her first taste of bullying. It would not be the last.

All the girls knew each other. She was the only camper from New York City—an urban kid unfamiliar with the ways of her new milieu. She assumed that was the problem. It turned out there was more to it than that.

What kind of name is Rune? asked Sophie Hunter, an older girl with wide calves and arctic eyes.

It means "happy" in Thai.

Sophie erupted in a fit of laughter. Everything went downhill from there. The girls were merciless. They mocked her appearance—the clothes she wore, her pin-straight hair, the jade studs her father gave her on her twelfth birthday. They barked at her at every meal, a not-so-subtle reference to eating dog. Rune tried to explain that she had a terrier mix at home that she loved very much, and that consuming dog meat wasn't customary in Thailand, except maybe in the northeast. Nothing she said made a difference. Still, she kept trying. She wanted so badly to fit in.

Her breaking point came at the beginning of the second week, when she was invited to a camp initiation. Or so she thought. Her memories of that day were as clear as the day they happened. She had a theory that when traumatic events occurred, the brain didn't treat them like it did everything else. The memories went to a special place where they were stored in high definition, preserving every detail for posterity.

She was by an ancient pine tree deep within the Finger Lakes National Forest. A blindfold covered her eyes. Her socks were bunched around her ankles. Her legs were covered with red marks from where she had scratched at mosquito bites. It was the middle of July. The canopy was lush, so lush it blotted out daylight in some parts. She remembered a fly buzzing around her damp hairline. She wanted to swat it away, but she had been told in no uncertain terms that she was not to move. She didn't know how long she had been standing there when she finally heard rustling. It was distant at first, and then it grew closer. Her breath quickened in nervous anticipation.

Take off your shirt, a raspy voice whispered in her ear.

She remained frozen.

Take off your shirt, or it all ends right now.

She made a move to comply but changed her mind midway.

Come on, said Sophie, breaking out of character. *It's part of the ritual. We all did it.*

A chorus of young, female voices rang out in agreement.

She pulled off her t-shirt with clumsy hands. Many of the girls at camp had already hit puberty, but she was a late bloomer. She didn't even wear a bra yet, much to her embarrassment. She felt exposed, which was exactly the point.

The shorts, too.

She unzipped them and let them drop to the ground.

Now sit.

She obeyed and waited. Sharp stones and pine needles poked at her skin. She didn't like what she was being asked to do, but she was the new girl, and she was tired of eating every meal alone. Sophie, the ringleader, had promised that the initiation would open doors. And so, she sat on the ground and waited for the unknown.

There were more footsteps followed by muffled voices. She felt someone tug at her hair. It went on for a while—tug, release, tug, release. She didn't raise her hands to stop what was happening. She didn't raise her voice, either.

Lie down, Sophie said.

She did as she was told. Something warm was placed on her bare stomach. Her nostrils flared at the putrid smell. Whatever it was started to move with featherlike softness across her skin, tickling her abdomen. Then she felt liquid drip onto her face. She opened her mouth to protest and instantly realized her mistake. Her hands flew up to remove the blindfold. What she saw filled her with such anger she knew instantly she would never be free of it. Sophie and another girl were standing over her, grinning from ear-to-ear as they poured rancid milk on her face. She sprang up, sputtering in disgust. The movement sent the thing on her stomach sliding to the ground. Her expression turned to horror when she saw what it was—animal scat. From something big, by the looks of it. She heaved violently at the sight.

She had no recollection of how she got back to camp that day. All she remembered was Sophie and her gaggle of friends laughing so hard they nearly choked. They had planned it. They had even recorded it. And afterwards they had congratulated each other, as if debasing a kid was some great accomplishment. It wasn't until she got to the bathroom to wash the gunk off her body that she realized they had lopped off half her hair. She cried silently as she tried to fix it, cutting the rest off until all that remained was a choppy mess.

That might have been the end of it. It should have been, except she vowed to get back at Sophie. She waited until their last full day at camp. While everyone was at breakfast, she snuck into Sophie's cabin and stole her journal, a leather-bound notebook filled with disclosures that even the most self-assured person would find embarrassing. The older girl noticed it was missing at bedtime, and she knew exactly who had taken it. Enraged, Sophie chased her through the dark woods until they reached a twenty-foot gorge, the kind the area was famous for. There was a scuffle for the journal. Sophie slipped and fell into the churning water. When she awoke in the hospital the next day, she blamed everything on Rune.

She pushed me.

Those three words changed the course of her life.

She tried to tell the truth—that it was an accident and not retaliation for a prank gone too far—but no one believed her, not even her parents. It was a terrible betrayal. The betrayals continued for the next two years. First her parents sent her away to a psychiatric facility. Then they signed off on having her restrained. The meds were the last straw.

No one in her life noticed how angry she was after she got out. She should have said something, but by that point, she had become an expert at hiding her feelings. She grew impulsive. She acted out—stealing, partying, disappearing for days on end. Taking risks became her hobby. What did it matter if she self-destructed?

To this day, she never spoke to anyone about those two lost years. Not to her parents. Not even to Kit. The past was the past, at least that's what she told herself. A vicious bully had destroyed her life. What difference could it possibly make to say the words out loud?

Just this: if she started to scream, she might never stop.

And so, when Rune's pent-up anger reared its head in the cramped interrogation room of the Thai police station, no one was more surprised than she was when she surrendered herself to it. Fully. Without reservation. Her body shook as her molten rage erupted. Accusations flew. Furniture toppled over. She thrashed about fiercely, her fists leaving crescent-shaped dents in the drywall.

Colonel Rattana instinctively knew that her anger needed to burn itself out. He said nothing. He simply watched from the sidelines as the episode unfolded. When it was over, he picked her up off the floor and gently lowered her into a chair.

Her face was in her palms when the baton-happy officer who whacked her hand strode in some time later. The woman's smug expression froze when she saw the condition of the room. She opened her mouth to protest, only to be silenced by a dismissive wave of Rattana's hand. Her back straightened. Her mouth tightened with displeasure. She dropped the file she was holding onto the table and stalked out of the room without saying a single word.

Rune raised her head just as the officer was leaving. The sight of her slick bun cut through the haze in her brain. Her eyes cleared. Her self-restraint snapped back into place. She watched Colonel Rattana open the folder he had just received and scan its contents. A shadow passed over his face. The energy in the room shifted.

"What is it?" Rune asked with a slight tremor in her voice.

Rattana paused before answering, like he was looking for the right words to say.

"Well?"

"Officers responded to a call in Bang Na early this morning."

Rune's brow furrowed. Bang Na was a large manufacturing district on the eastern edge of the city. There was no reason to go there except to catch a show at the Bangkok International Trade and Exhibition Center. "And?"

"They found a body," he said somberly. His eyes darkened. The lines in his forehead deepened. "It matches Madee's description."

22

Samitivej Sukhumvit Hospital, Bangkok

It was late in the afternoon when Rune and Colonel Rattana pulled up to Samitivej Sukhumvit Hospital, a building that looked more like an international hotel than a healthcare center. A row of flags greeted them from the end of the driveway, directly behind a tiered fountain with at least thirty jets. Swaying palm trees lent the complex a resort-like atmosphere.

Colonel Rattana double-parked his silver Toyota hatchback and ushered Rune through the hospital's sliding glass doors. They crossed the spacious lobby to the elevator, watching in tense silence as its descent played out on the numbers above the door. They stepped inside. Rattana pushed the button to the basement, home to the hospital's morgue. Their expressions were somber as the elevator began to move. Identifying a corpse was a task neither of them looked forward to.

The doors dinged open. They stepped out. A black sign with white lettering directed them to the right. Rune walked half a step behind Rattana in a subconscious effort to delay the inevitable. The syncopated clatter of their shoes hitting the floor echoed though the bleak hallway. They stopped in front of an aluminum swing door with frosted windows designed to prevent passersby from inadvertently witnessing autopsies. Rattana pushed it open and moved aside.

Rune took a tentative step inside. The room smelled sterile, like someone had just doused it in industrial-strength cleaner. The air was dry and cold—unlike the air outside—reinforcing the strange otherness of the place. Goosebumps appeared on Rune's arms. She rubbed them away, unsure if they were a physiological response to the change in temperature or an emotional reaction to the circumstances.

There were four autopsy tables at the center of the room, all thankfully unoccupied. A stainless-steel counter with a built-in sink extended along one wall, across from a dozen or so mortuary refrigerators stacked on top of each other like building blocks. Rune's eyes lingered on them. A tremor passed through her body as she thought of Madee lying inside one of the airless compartments. She averted her eyes, focusing on the less morbid aspects of the room—the cheerful wall paint that went from deep violet to pale lilac, the desk lamp with a dolphin-shaped base, and the vintage travel poster of Koh Samui, a tropical island in the Andaman Sea. The promise of powdery sand and translucent water seemed out of place given the cold, clinical setting.

"How much longer?" Rune asked Rattana with a marked strain in her voice. She was simultaneously reluctant and desperate for the pathologist to arrive.

"She should be here any minute."

"Tell me again what she said."

"I've already told you everything."

Rune gave him a look that said, *Humor me.*

Rattana obliged. "Kids fishing off a pier in Bang Na found the body this morning. All I know is that it's a girl fitting Madee's age and height. The autopsy is scheduled for tomorrow morning."

"What's wrong with doing it now?"

"Do you know how many bodies came in today?"

Rune stared at him blankly.

"Three. And that's not counting the dead hospital patients."

"This place is full of doctors. Surely one of them could do it."

"We don't even know if it's Madee. There's no sense getting worked up prematurely."

Rattana's words did nothing to reassure Rune. Her eyes darted around the room like they couldn't find a comfortable place to land.

"Try to relax," Rattana said.

Rune counted down silently. The minutes ticked away.

A rush of nervous anticipation washed over her when a petite woman in light gray scrubs and a matching cap entered the room with an iPad tucked in the crook of her arm. Her face was flushed, like she had just come from the gym. There were flecks of gold in her warm brown eyes. They lit up visibly at the sight of Rattana, who greeted her like an old friend. He asked about her husband and two children, she congratulated him on his impending retirement. He extended a dinner invitation, she promised to check her calendar. The pleasantries dragged on.

Rune looked on in disbelief. She was there to identify a child's body, and they were carrying on like this was a social call. Her nails dug into her palms. She silently counted down again. Then she coughed loudly.

"Perhaps we should get started?" Colonel Rattana said, his eyes moving from the pathologist to Rune.

That's a terrific idea.

"Rune, let me introduce Doctor Sukhon Larsson."

Her married name, clearly.

"Doctor Larsson is the hospital's Chief Forensic Pathologist. She handles all police autopsies in Bangkok's eastern districts."

Rune put out her hand just as the doctor started to bow. She made a face. The doctor handled the awkwardness with more aplomb than she did.

"Did Colonel Rattana explain to you why you're here?" Doctor Larsson asked.

Rune pressed her lips together and nodded.

"This isn't typically how we conduct identifications, but I was told these are exceptional circumstances. Normally we take photos after the deceased has been cleaned. And we like to have a counselor on hand to . . ."

"I don't mean to be rude, Doctor Larsson, but if we could just get on with it."

"Of course." The doctor's expression became serious. "You should prepare yourself."

"I thought the body was only in the water for a few hours," said Rattana.

"That's correct, but there's severe trauma." She paused briefly to consult her iPad, then added, "And disfigurement."

Rune felt a shudder run down her spine. She knew from the slow deliberateness of the doctor's tone that what awaited was bad. "Was Madee murdered?" she asked in a throaty voice that sounded strange to her own ears.

"It might not be Madee," Rattana reminded her gently.

The doctor's face hardened further. "We won't know the official cause of death until I perform the autopsy tomorrow, but there's a strong likelihood her injuries contributed to her death."

"What kind of injuries are we talking about?" Rune's voice was almost inaudible now.

"According to the intake assessment, she suffered from blunt force trauma to the head and torso. There are superficial burns on her body, probably from cigarettes, and ligature marks on her neck."

Rune swallowed hard. "I'd like to see her now."

The doctor shot Rattana an uncertain look.

He gave a slight nod.

She walked to the wall of refrigerators, opened one of the units, and pulled out the tray. Then she called them over with a wave.

Rune inhaled sharply.

Rattana put his hand on her arm and coaxed her forward.

She shook her head to indicate that she had changed her mind. She didn't want to see what was on that metal slab. Someone else would have to do it.

He gave her arm a reassuring squeeze.

The doctor unzipped the bag. An unidentifiable smell filled the room—somewhere between sewage and spoiled fish.

Rune began her slow walk to the refrigerators. One step. Then another. And another, until she stood just inches away from the corpse. Still, she couldn't bring herself to look.

"It's okay," Rattana said softly.

Rune forced her eyes downward. She emitted a gargled cry and promptly fell to the floor. Rattana was by her side instantly. She watched his lips move, but his voice sounded faint, like it was coming from a different room. There was a loud ringing in her ears. It started to fade, but then it came back, louder than ever. She brought her hands to her head and squeezed in a futile effort to block out the sound. Her breaths came in short, labored spurts. The doctor looked on with concern.

"You're alright. Just breathe," said Rattana, squeezing her shoulders with both hands.

Rune's eyes found his—wide and panicked. She drew a big gulp of air, but her chest felt like it was filled with lead. She tried again. This time her lungs expanded.

It took many long minutes for her breathing to return to normal. It would be several more before the ringing in her ears stopped. Only when her heart rate slowed was she finally able to say, "It's not her, Rattana. It isn't Madee."

23
Central Bangkok

The stench of death stayed with Rune even after she left the morgue. It lingered in the air and settled into her clothes. It filled her nostrils and lodged itself in her throat. Worse, it left a residue on her skin that wouldn't go away, no matter how hard she scrubbed. Even when she held her breath, the foul smell remained. Its staying powers were incredible. Otherworldly even. That, or her mind was simply playing tricks on her.

She opened the passenger side window of Colonel Rattana's Toyota to try to catch a breath, only to be greeted by a sweltering tropical heat. The back of her neck began to tingle. Beads of perspiration formed on her skin. Still, she left it open. The hot air was better than the stink.

Colonel Rattana wordlessly cranked the AC—dying planet be damned. He pushed down harder on the gas pedal for good measure. The hospital shrank in his rearview mirror. Gradually it faded away.

"Where can I drop you?" he asked after merging onto Sukhumvit Road. The concrete tracks of the Skytrain hovered above them, casting shadows on the six-lane road. A train whizzed overhead. At ground level, traffic was congested, more so than usual.

Rune didn't answer. Instead, she closed her eyes and angled her face toward the window, letting the heat of the sun caress her skin. The stress leading up to identifying Madee's body—only to learn it wasn't her—left her emotionally spent. Her hand hurt. Her head ached. All she wanted to do was go home, crawl under the bedsheets, and forget that the last twenty-four hours had ever happened. One or three bottles of wine would help get her there. She licked her lips unconsciously.

Her eyes flew open when she heard a motorcycle roar past. The sound made her think of Kit. She pushed the image of sweating wine bottles out of her mind and glanced at her watch. Lemaire's deadline was fast approaching. Her stress level shot up. It was time to get back to Thonburi, with or without the rubies. What she would do when she got there was anybody's guess.

"You can let me out anywhere," she said, not wanting to waste more time with Rattana than she already had. It was abundantly clear that he would not—or could not—help her.

The colonel looked at her out of the corner of his eye. He changed lanes to pass a bus and said, "I can drop you anywhere. It's no problem."

"I heard you the first time," she replied. There was a distinct edge in her voice. Rattana was being nice because he felt bad about wasting her time and making her look at a dead child. It wasn't up to her to ease his guilty conscience.

"Are you alright?" he asked.

"Am I alright?" she repeated. Her tone was incredulous. She wore an expression to match.

"I can see that you're not."

"No, I'm not alright, Colonel. I'm light years away from alright."

"What can I do?"

"You can't *do* anything. I just saw the body of a mutilated child. Madee is still missing. And . . ."

"And what?"

"Nothing."

"I'm on your side. What aren't you telling me?"

Rune clammed up.

"You can trust me."

"Right," she said under her breath. She turned away from him and stared at the slow-moving cars.

An awkward silence descended between them. It was Rattana who eventually broke it. "Have you ever heard of the Ramakien?" he asked without taking his eyes off the road.

Rune swung her head toward him and knitted her brow, confused by his choice of topic. "It's a Thai epic. I saw paintings of it at the Temple of the Emerald Buddha."

"It's based on the Ramayana, an ancient text sacred to Hindus."

Rune wondered where Rattana was going with this.

"It tells the story of King Rama—the seventh avatar of Vishnu—and his wife Sita, who lived in exile in a forest. One day, Sita was kidnaped by an amorous demon king and taken to a faraway land called Lanka. Rama knew he couldn't rescue Sita on his own, so he enlisted the help of the monkeys and bears."

"Okaaay," Rune said. The expression on her face was one of utter bewilderment.

"The group set off on the long journey to Lanka, only to find it was an island in the middle of the ocean. The head monkey leapt over the water, found Sita, and told her she would be saved."

"Mm-hmm."

Rattana adjusted the AC again before continuing. "While the monkey was with Sita, the others built a bridge long enough to reach the island. Rama killed the demon king in battle, but instead of celebrating, he accused Sita of being unfaithful. To prove her innocence, she built a fire and walked through it. Not only was she not burned, but she transformed the flames into flowers. Afterwards, the group journeyed home with locals lighting the way with candles and lamps. The story is thought to have given rise to Diwali, the festival of lights Hindus celebrate every autumn."

"Why are you telling me this?" Rune asked after Rattana grew silent.

"There are some who see the Ramakien as an allegory about the quest for Nirvana, but at its core, it's a story about being able to ask for help, and about different groups cooperating to help someone in trouble."

"Just so I have this straight—am I Rama or the monkey in this scenario?"

Rattana opened his mouth to respond.

Rune silenced him with a withering look. "It's just another stupid story about a jealous husband and a princess who needs saving."

"It's an ancient epic," Rattana replied with exasperation.

"And that puts it above critical scrutiny? If anything, the fact that it's widely read should make people *more* critical of it, not less. What a load of crap."

Rattana looked like he was about to throw Rune out of his moving car. Then his posture softened, like he had just put himself in her shoes. "I want to help you," he said softly.

"Will you send officers to Khlong Toei? Will you bring Father Bergdahl and Som to the station for questioning?" Rune asked.

"I can't do that."

"Then your offer means nothing."

"This may be hard for you to believe, but not all police officers in Thailand are corrupt. We view human trafficking as a scourge. We have families. We care . . ." He adjusted his grip on the steering wheel and gave Rune a quick glance. "I'll be leaving the force soon. I want to do my part before that happens. I can help you, but you have to let me in."

Maybe it was the sincerity in his voice, or the fact that he had shown her kindness when she was at her lowest, but Rune believed him. As much as she wanted to trust him, though, she also knew that he wouldn't be so keen to help if he knew the truth about her. She was a thief, plain and simple. It was her fault Kit was in danger. And who knew? Maybe she was even to blame for Madee's disappearance. Confiding in Rattana would only complicate matters, she was willing to put money on that.

"I'm not your problem, Colonel. You can let yourself off the hook. Now stop the car."

The finality in her voice left no room for discussion.

Rattana pulled over.

Rune got out without a word.

"You're the type who doesn't like to rely on anyone for anything, aren't you?" Rattana said just as she was about to close the door.

Rune stooped down and locked eyes with him. "You don't know the first thing about me, Colonel."

"I think I do."

She snorted at his certitude.

"At least take my card."

She made no move for it.

"Just in case. What's the harm?"

She accepted it with an air of reluctance.

"You can call me anytime. I mean that."

"Don't hold your breath," she muttered. She straightened up, then bent down again and added, "You're wrong about me, you know."

Rattana tilted his head questioningly.

"I'm not afraid to ask for help. I choose my friends carefully. There's a difference." With those resounding last words, she slammed the door and walked away.

24

Central Bangkok

The drive to Thonburi was excruciatingly slow. Cars were backed up all the way to the Chalerm Maha Nakhon Expressway. By the time Rune's cab reached the ramp, traffic was at a full stop. She glanced at her watch. It was ten minutes to six. At this rate, there was no way she would make Lemaire's deadline. She was craning her neck in search of a way out of this rush hour nightmare when she spied a motorcycle taxi approaching from behind. She waved her hands through the window to catch the driver's attention. He stopped long enough for her to slide out of the car and hop onto the bike. Her legs tightened around the seat. She knew it was uncouth for a woman to straddle a stranger in Thailand, but she was in a hurry, and there wasn't a ghost of a chance she was riding sidesaddle.

"To Thonburi," she shouted over the sound of the engine. She threw a quick look over her shoulder as they pulled away. The cabbie was gesticulating behind the windshield, angry at losing his fare. Rune felt zero remorse.

Her driver wove between cars at a breakneck speed. The hot wind whipped at her face. The heat of the engine burned her legs. She tightened her hold on the back of the bike and reached for her phone with her free hand. She dialed Kit's cell, knowing it would be Lemaire who answered.

"You're cutting it rather close, don't you think?"

The American's words were chilling. Just hearing his voice was enough to rattle Rune. "I'm on the expressway," she yelled into the phone. "Traffic is terrible, I'll be there as soon as I can!"

"I'm not interested in your excuses."

"I'm telling the truth. Listen!" She held up the phone. Her driver chose that precise moment to rev the motor. She brought the phone back down to her ear. "I'll be there. I just need a little more time."

"Do you have my rubies?"

"Yes, I have them." Rune cringed as she said the words, but the fact was, she would lie, cheat, and steal—and probably do much worse—if it meant saving Kit. It wasn't like she had anything to lose.

"You'd better not be playing games with me."

"I'm not. I swear to you, I'm not. I have the rubies. I'm almost there."

"If you're lying, your boyfriend dies."

"How do I know you haven't killed him already?"

"You'll just have to take my word for it."

"No deal!" Rune spat. "I want to speak to Kit."

"You're in no position to be making demands."

"Oh no? Put Kit on, or I'll throw your rubies into the river!"

"You'd risk his life?"

"You'd risk losing the rubies?"

There was silence followed by the sound of footsteps. Seconds later, Kit came on the line. "Rune?"

She nearly wept with relief at the sound of his voice. "Kit, thank god! Are you okay? Please tell me you're okay!"

"I'm fine. Everything is fine." His voice sounded off, like he was speaking with difficulty.

"He hasn't hurt you, has he?"

"No, he hasn't hurt me."

"I'm on my way, my love. I'm almost there."

"Just tell me you found Madee."

Rune wanted to cry when she heard the words. She had failed Kit in the worst possible way, and now she had to tell him. He would never forgive her. How could he? She wouldn't if the situation were reversed. "I tried, Kit. I really did," she sobbed. "She's nowhere to be found."

"Listen to me very carefully, Rune," Kit said in a grave voice. "Don't come back here. Keep looking for Madee. Don't stop, don't ever stop . . ." A scuffle cut him off midsentence.

"Kit!"

He grunted unintelligibly.

"Kit! Talk to me!"

There was a long pause. Then Rune was treated to indistinct voices drowned out by static.

"For Christ's sake, Kit! Answer me!"

"He can't hear you," Lemaire responded seconds later. He sounded harried and out of breath.

Rune felt a chill, despite the muggy heat. "What did you do to him?"

"Nothing he didn't deserve."

"Don't you dare hurt him!"

"That's up to you."

"I just need a little more time."

"I've had enough of your lies. You have five minutes."

"No, wait!"

The line went dead.

"Dammit!" Rune screamed, her body rocking so abruptly her driver nearly lost control of the bike. Her tantrum spooked him. He started to slow, promoting her to lean in and yell, "Reo reo!" *Faster!* "For the love of god, go faster!"

Her mind went to a dark place in the hour it took to get to Thonburi. Had Madee fallen prey to human traffickers? Was Kit dead? What would Lemaire do to her when he found out she lost the rubies? Her entire body was shaking by the time her driver pulled up to Lemaire's safehouse. She tossed some bills at him and sprinted to the gate, opening it so forcefully it left a dent in the wall. She raced to the front door, her heart banging against her breastbone. It was locked. She gave the door a powerful kick. It held fast. She tried again and again. It finally gave on the fourth try. She tumbled inside, wild eyed and ready for anything.

First came the shock. Then the awful realization. Kit and Lemaire were gone.

DAY 3

25

Church of the Holy Redeemer, Bangkok

The sun was beginning its slow ascent on the horizon when Rune reached the Church of the Holy Redeemer in Klong Toei. After recovering from the initial shock of finding Lemaire's Thonburi house empty, she'd pulled herself together and done exactly what Kit asked of her—she set off to find Madee. She spent the previous night roaming the slum, showing Madee's picture to everyone she encountered. She did what Colonel Rattana couldn't or wouldn't do—she knocked on doors asking about the girl. She also kept her eyes on the ground in the unlikely event the rubies turned up. Most people would have given up by now. But coming up empty only fueled Rune's determination. She wanted to save Kit and Madee above all else. Exposing the nefarious activities in the slum was just icing on the cake.

A pall of smog hung over the neighborhood. The muted sounds of clinking utensils and distant conversations filled the sticky air. It was nearing breakfast time. The slum was calm, for the time being.

Rune found a discreet spot across the street from the church, one with a clear view of the entrance. She squatted next to a heap of discarded construction materials and pressed her back against a chain link fence. The workday was about to start. She wanted very badly to storm into the church but, for all she knew, the priest would be there any minute. She locked her gaze on the door and settled in for the long haul. *Watch. Wait*, she told herself. It was what Kit would have done. Her right eye started twitching almost instantly. Her knees began to ache within the hour. Concerned about drawing attention to herself, she made a conscious decision not to stretch. Getting caught lurking outside the church was not an option, that message had come through loud and clear at the police station.

Father Bergdahl arrived a short time later. Rune watched him unlock the metal gate and prop it open with a cinder block. She thought she heard him curse when his arm brushed against the concrete, leaving a white smudge on the sleeve of his cassock. He dusted it off with his hand, climbed up the porch, and disappeared inside the church.

Morning prayer service brought a steady stream of visitors. Rune took pictures in case any of them were mixed up in Madee's disappearance. She did the same thing before the lunchtime service, and again at afternoon Mass. Foreign nationals comprised most of the congregation. A few were repeat attendees. Rune paid particular attention to those people. In her opinion, anyone who went to church more than once a day was inherently untrustworthy.

Late afternoon brought children to the church, presumably for English class. Rune counted three boys and four girls, all of whom seemed to be between the ages of eight and ten. She grew more attentive when she saw the little girl from the Youth Center, the one with the expensive phone and the garish nail polish she had spoken to before the cop knocked her out. The girl's hair was pulled up in pigtails, just as it was the day before. Her red t-shirt was misshapen and faded from being dried in the sun too many times. The hem of her denim skirt was coming undone. Rune wanted nothing more than to run over to the girl and question her. She started to rise, then she got a hold of herself. Waiting to catch the girl alone was without question the smarter play.

Rune didn't move when the door to the church swung open forty-five minutes later. Two of the boys burst outside, followed almost immediately by three of the girls. They talked excitedly about their favorite cartoons as they skipped away from the church. Rune kept her eyes fastened on them until all that remained were their voices receding in the distance. Silence returned. It went on so long that Rune jumped when the door finally opened again. Her body relaxed when she saw a boy with a royal blue baseball cap emerge. She couldn't help but smile when he grabbed a dead branch off the ground and started brandishing it like a sword. *Go forth, brave warrior*, she thought as he walked away. Only Father Bergdahl and the little girl from the Youth Center remained inside.

The curtain of night descended. Rune flexed her cramped muscles. A soft groan rose from her lips as she rubbed the stiffness out of her shoulders and tilted her head from side to side to ease the tension in her neck. She wondered if the priest took the girl out the rear entrance. She considered leaving her hiding spot to investigate, but instinct told her to stay where she was. *Just a few more minutes*, she said to herself.

As it turned out, waiting was the right call. Not ten minutes passed when Father Bergdahl appeared at the front door. Rune squinted against the darkness in search of the girl, but the priest was alone. *Where did she go?* she wondered silently. Her forehead creased as she watched him lock up, make his way to the wrought iron gate, and secure it behind him. Moments later, he disappeared into the night.

Rune's concern for the girl deepened. Was she locked inside the church? Or had the priest smuggled her out the back door, never to be seen or heard from again? The waiting game was over. The time had come to act. *You've got this*, she said silently. *Remember who you are.* Her pupils dilated as adrenaline pumped through her body. The feeling was a familiar one, like muscle memory from her capers with Kit. She looked up and saw a cloud move in and obscure the moon. *Now!*

Her knees groaned when she sprang up and darted across the empty street. She came to an abrupt stop at the gate. It was nearly six feet high, with a row of decorative spikes along the top. She tried the handle. It jiggled, but the door didn't budge. With a quick look over her shoulder, she jumped up and grabbed hold of the top of the gate. Pain shot through her injured hand, but she managed to hold on. She grunted softly as she pulled herself up. Her feet flailed against the metal bars. Somewhere not far away, a car alarm screamed. She redoubled her efforts, throwing her leg over the top and heaving herself to the other side. She expected to drop to the ground, but her shirt got caught on one of the spikes, leaving her dangling helplessly in the air. It took several hard yanks for the spikes to release her. She fell to the ground with a painful thud—body intact, dignity not so much.

The entrance was in Rune's sights. She scrambled to her feet and ran toward the shadowy porch. She pulled at the doorknob and felt the resistance of the lock. Locked doors were nothing new to her, but she didn't have any of her usual tools. Her eyes swept the area for something to use to bash the knob. Finding nothing, she set off in search of another way in.

She jogged along the side of the church until she reached the back of the building. She spied a door, just as she suspected. "Terrific," she murmured when she realized that it, too, was locked. There was a window not far to the left. Rune decided to give it a try. It slid open, much to her surprise. She clambered through and lowered herself into the pitch-black room. She pulled out her phone and turned on the flashlight. "Yes!" she whispered with an edge of triumph in her voice. She was exactly where she wanted to be—inside Father Bergdahl's office.

Rune's sense of accomplishment diminished significantly when she realized the room was empty. The little girl was gone. She zeroed in on the next best thing—the desk. Surely it held the priest's secrets.

Disappointment set in soon after. The desk drawers contained nothing but papers related to the day-to-day operation of the church—drafts of sermons, orders for communion wafers, lists of institutional affiliates, and the schedule for something called Discussion and Discipleship. Rune turned on the computer and tried to guess the password. Jesus didn't work. Neither did Christ. Or Jesus Christ. She stopped after her third try.

The wardrobe was the next logical place to search. The door was ajar, just as it had been when she saw it the previous day. She dug through the rack without a clear sense of what it was she was looking for. Black shirts and cassocks occupied one section, waistcoats and capes another. An entire side was devoted to Mass vestments—purple for Advent, white for Christmas and Easter. She didn't know what the red and pink ones were for.

There was a drawer at the bottom of the wardrobe, the kind people used to store ugly sweaters they never wore but couldn't bring themselves to throw away. She pulled it open, wincing at the sound of wood squeaking against wood. She shone a light inside. It contained white clerical collars and, of all things, row upon row of black socks with the tags still on. The mere sight of them reminded Rune of how uncomfortably hot she was. Right on cue, a drop of sweat dripped down the nape of her neck, found the groove at the center of her back, and disappeared in the waistband of her jeans.

Rune's disappointment became more acute as she searched the rest of the office. There were boxes filled with outreach pamphlets next to the wardrobe, plastic crates with ESL materials near the door, and two filing cabinets containing financial documents by the desk. In other words, nothing out of the ordinary.

For the first time since this mess began, doubt began to creep into Rune's mind. Intuition told her that the priest was hiding something, but perhaps she was mistaken. Maybe her suspicions were just a figment of her imagination, brought on by too much stress and not enough food and sleep. She panned the room with her phone one more time to make sure she hadn't missed anything.

It was then that she noticed the tripod leaning against the wall behind the desk, next to a big cooler. She remembered seeing it when she sat down with Father Bergdahl a day earlier. Her pulse jumped. If the priest had a tripod, logic dictated he also had a camera.

Rune hurried over to the stand. It was large and heavy, the kind professional photographers used. Her eyes landed on the cooler. With a shiver of excitement, she opened the lid and lifted the removable tray.

Bingo!

Tucked inside was a digital camera with a telephoto lens, the kind the paparazzi carried. Rune took it out with care and closed the cooler. Then she sat cross-legged on the floor to inspect her discovery.

The camera had more bells and whistles than she knew what to do with. Turning it on was no problem, but it took an embarrassingly long time for her to locate the playback feature. In her defense, it was dark and she'd had a rough couple of days.

A picture of a small black and white bird flashed on the screen. Rune recognized it as an Oriental magpie-robin, a bird known for its melodious call and its ability to imitate other birds. She began scrolling through the images. A spotted owlet, a blue-tailed bee-eater, and a pink-necked green pigeon came on the screen, alongside dozens of other species. It seemed Father Bergdahl was an avid bird watcher. The images were taken all over Bangkok—in urban parks, on the banks of the Chao Phraya, and even in the gardens of Jim Thompson's house, the American spy who disappeared under mysterious circumstances, never to be seen or heard from again.

Rune's eyes took on a glassy sheen. She rubbed them with her fists in an attempt to clear her vision. A tired yawn passed through her lips. She was tempted to slip the camera around her neck and get out of dodge. She could make it look like a break-in simply by tossing the place and swiping a few valuables. No one would be the wiser. She went so far as to lift the strap over her head, but then she thought better of it. Why call attention to the fact that someone had been inside unless it was absolutely necessary?

She turned her attention back to the camera. The slideshow of exotic birds resumed—a cattle egret, a painted stork, a banded bay cuckoo—the pictures were taken in different places, and at different times of year. It was apparent that the priest took his hobby seriously.

Images of Chatuchak appeared on the screen. The chaotic weekend market on the northern edge of the city was the largest in Thailand. It was also a place where anything and everything under the sun was up for sale, including wildlife. The pictures showed row upon row of caged birds, most looking sick and injured. Rune's eyes lingered on a sad looking Oriental Bay Owl tethered to its cage. Someone once told her that the demand for pet owls skyrocketed after the release of the Harry Potter films, to the point where several wild species were now endangered. Who could resist having their very own Hedwig in the house? Rune briefly wondered if the novelty of owning an apex predator ever wore off, or if the owls died before that could happen.

The procession of birds continued. A caged cockatoo, a zebra dove, and a blue-rumped parrot appeared. The next picture flashed on the screen. Rune's breath caught. Her mouth opened involuntarily. One look was enough to dispel all other thoughts. It seemed she was right about Father Bergdahl after all. Birds weren't the only things he liked to photograph.

26

Church of the Holy Redeemer, Bangkok

The pictures set off all kinds of alarms. The first showed a bronze statue of Bodhisattva Avalokiteshvara, an enlightened being and embodiment of Buddhist compassion. The statue was over four feet tall according to the bar scale on the left-hand side of the photo. Depicted with four arms symbolizing the four immeasurables of Buddhism—loving kindness, compassion, empathetic joy, and equanimity—the svelte figure with a silvery sheen wore a plain skirt loosely belted at the waist. His torso was bare, save the sash across his chest. His coiffure could best be described as elaborate. Translucent black glass animated his wide-set eyes. Rune remembered seeing a similar sculpture on a school trip to the Met. Their guide, a graduate student who was so fidgety she undermined her own authority, told them that the eighth-century statue was from northeastern Thailand and that it was uniquely large. Rune stared at the picture and the accompanying scale. It seemed the guide was misinformed.

The next picture also showed a sculpture, this time of a stone Buddha. The figure sat cross-legged with his right hand raised as though taking an oath and his left hand resting on his lap, palm up. Next came pictures of simpler objects—stone reliefs, clay pots, bronze jewelry—all of which looked to be significantly older than the sculptures. Rune knew right away that what she was looking at were museum-quality artifacts—except the pictures were clearly not taken in a museum. She cast her eyes to the floor. The earthy red tiles of Father Bergdahl's office were the same as in the photos.

Rune was still pondering the significance of the pictures when the distant sound of footsteps caught her attention. She had almost convinced herself she had imagined them when they grew closer and louder. Alarm set in when she realized there was someone inside the church. She was madly looking for an escape route when she heard the doorknob jiggle. Rune launched herself under the desk and drew her knees to her chin just as the office door swung open.

The light flickered on. The scent of incense wafted into the room. Rune couldn't see who entered, but she assumed it was Father Bergdahl. She heard him moving around as though he was looking for something. He walked closer to the desk, so close she could see his feet poking out from beneath his cassock. A dew of fear covered her palms. Her grip on the camera became slippery. She tightened her hands around it and stifled a cry of panic. If he came around to the other side of the desk, it would all be over. She would be arrested again, and this time the cops would not let her off with a slap on the wrist. She held her breath as the priest moved things around directly above her head. His feet disappeared. The doors to the wardrobe squeaked open. Hangers raked across the wooden rod. Then the room went quiet. Rune squeezed her eyes shut and willed him to leave.

"It's me. I'm on my way."

Her eyes flew open at the sound of Father Bergdahl's voice. He spoke in a serious tone that was nothing like the singsong voice he had used with her.

"I forgot my wallet. I'll be there soon."

Rune held her breath.

"Hold on." His footsteps started moving toward the other end of the room.

The window! A shiver of fear ran through her. She had left the window open in her rush to get out of sight. Now her carelessness was coming back to bite her in a big way.

Father Bergdahl stood in front of the open window for several long seconds. Rune could almost hear the wheels in his head turning. Was something off, or had he simply forgotten to close it? She bit down on her lip hard enough for it to hurt. Her body began to shake. This was the end. It was all over. Kit and Madee were doomed, and she was going to spend the rest of her days in a filthy Thai prison. She dropped her forehead onto her knees and squeezed her arms around her legs.

Clack!

The window slamming shut made her jump. Her heart banged against her chest.

"Yes, I'm still here," Father Bergdahl was saying.

Her head rose.

"Yes, I understand."

Hope surged.

"I'll be there as soon as possible."

Father Bergdahl's footsteps receded. Darkness returned. The door closed. The lock latched shut. Rune waited until she was certain he was gone for good before scrambling out from her hiding spot. She turned off the camera and hastily dropped it into the cooler. She left the same way she had come in—through the window—making sure to close it behind her. She quickly made her way to the front of the church, jumped over the gate, and ran toward the street. It was deserted by the time she reached it, but she wasn't worried. The priest had a head start, but only just.

27
Central Bangkok

The tuk-tuk driver Rune flagged down simply smiled when she pointed at Father Bergdahl's disappearing taillights and demanded that he follow. She knew the drill. He wanted to haggle. She forced a smile of her own and thrust a five-hundred-baht note at him, hoping to close the deal. He didn't move. Social mores dictated they go back and forth a few more times, but in that moment, Rune cared not at all about etiquette. She shoved another five hundred baht into his hand and barked, "Pai! Pai!" *Go, go!*

The tuk-tuk took off like a spring unloading, raising a cloud of dust in the process. The wind lashed at Rune's face when she stuck her head out the side, peering through the darkness in an effort to locate the priest. It was just bad luck that he drove a black sedan identical to thousands of others trawling the capital.

"There!" she yelled, pointing down a side street to their right. The tuk-tuk took a sharp turn, sending her sliding across the leather seat. She anchored herself against the side and gave the driver an encouraging, "Reo reo!" *Faster!*

They caught up to the sedan just as it was taking the ramp to the expressway heading north. The tuk-tuk driver hung back. It clearly wasn't the first time he had tailed someone. Rune settled in for the ride.

Father Bergdahl signaled his exit around ten minutes later. The tuk-tuk driver followed suit, continuing west until Rune saw signs for the Victory Monument traffic circle, one of Bangkok's most famous landmarks. The towering obelisk at the center of the roundabout soon appeared in her sightline. The sedan circled it and took the second exit onto Ratchawithi Road. The tuk-tuk stayed close behind, speeding past a series of hospitals, pharmacies, and medical supply stores.

The neighborhood changed the moment they passed the Research Unit for Tropical Diseases of Mahidol University. Gone were the ultramodern healthcare buildings. Now they were in the posh Dusit District, home to Dusit Palace, a royal complex with residences and gardens covering an area larger than twelve football fields. Dusit was Bangkok's political nerve center. The official residence of the Thai monarch was there, as well as the National Assembly and the Government House, where the Prime Minister of Thailand and his cabinet ministers kept their offices. The political A-listers who called Dusit home enjoyed an architecture that was distinctly European, as well as squeaky-clean streets that were entirely free of food stalls and vendors, in contrast to the rest of the city. Rune wondered what business a priest who ministered in a slum might have in one of Bangkok's most exclusive neighborhoods.

They flew past the royal compound, made a few turns, and slowed when they reached a dead-end street boasting extra-large houses on well-kept lots. The sedan's taillights disappeared. The tuk-tuk pulled to a stop. The driver turned around, looking to Rune for direction. She drew her hands together and lowered her head. "Khawp khun kha," she said hastily before placing another five hundred baht in his hands. *Thank you.*

She advanced on foot under the dim glow of the streetlamps until she spotted the sedan at the end of the block. The car stood out in a neighborhood of Jaguars and Bentleys. It was parked in front of a three-story house with a white stucco facade and clay roof tiles that would have fit right in on the French Riviera. The owner was rich, extremely rich if the size of the house was any indication. A painted brick wall fronted the expansive property, providing the owner with security and privacy. The heart-shaped leaves of a young bodhi tree were visible directly behind it on the left. On the right, abutting the wall and facing away from the street, Rune could make out the top of a spirit house shaped like a traditional Thai temple.

The house was a fortress, but Rune was good at getting into places she wasn't supposed to. She slipped into the shadows and walked the length of the property, quickly determining that the easiest point of entry was the front gate. It was slightly lower than the flanking walls, and the bars would offer a better grip. The problem was, it was also terribly exposed. A halogen lamp swarming with mosquitos illuminated the porch. Lights were also on in one of the rooms on the ground floor.

The back of the house will offer better cover, she reasoned silently.

Two police officers appeared at the end of the block just as she was about to make her move. She ducked behind Father Bergdahl's car just in time to avoid detection. Most people would have called the whole thing off at the mere sight of cops, but Rune saw it as a challenge. The pair smoked cigarettes and chatted amiably as they meandered down the street and back again. Rune waited until they turned the corner before making her way to the rear of the property.

The backyard was dark. That was a checkmark in the pro column. Instead of a wall, it was enclosed by a wood fence—the kind that was easy to climb. Another check. That was all the convincing Rune needed. With a quick look behind her, she grabbed the top of the fence and pulled herself over.

She landed softly on the other side, right next to a cluster of water jasmine shrubs whose white blossoms gave off a heady scent. She crouched low and took a moment to get her bearings. The cool light of the moon illuminated a stone path that wove around gnarled trees and flowering plants. Birds of paradise and red ginger bloomed in the landscaped garden. A rectangular pond filled with orange and white koi—the centerpiece of the yard—extended the entire length of the covered patio. Beyond it, in shadows, lay the back of the house.

Rune moved swiftly, skirting the fence until she reached the side of the property. Then she made a break for the house, running so quickly she nearly lost her footing. A twig cracked under her foot as she flattened herself against the wall. She cringed. Then she scolded herself for being a ninny. *Calm down. You've done this a million times.*

Rune hugged the wall until she reached the front of the house. A quick glance around the corner told her that the coast was clear. She advanced to the first window and peered inside. The lights were out, but she could see it was a living room—spacious and well-appointed, from the looks of it. It was also empty. She scurried to the next window. This one emitted a warm light that spilled onto the front yard through gossamer curtains. She inched closer to the edge and stole a glance inside.

There were three people in the study. Father Bergdahl and another man sat on a black leather chesterfield across from a woman who occupied a matching armchair. Rune squinted. The priest's body obscured her view of the man seated next to him, but he looked to be wearing a police uniform. The woman's face was turned away from the window, but even from this vantage point, she fit Rune's image of the kind of person who would live in Dusit District. She wore a white blouse, conservative navy-blue slacks, and patent leather pumps. Her posture was excellent. Her shiny black hair was styled just right. She and the two men seemed to be having an animated discussion. Rune strained to hear them through the window, but their words were garbled and distant.

There was only one solution—she had to get inside. She started back the way she came, holding perfectly still when she heard a neighbor getting into his car. She waited until he drove off before retracing her steps to the rear of the house.

The back door was unlocked, much to Rune's surprise. Maybe burglars knew better than to rob the owner of this house. The thought made her question her plan, but only for a second. She stepped inside and found herself in a kitchen that was surprisingly rustic. The cabinetry was made of teak, the floor laid with terracotta. A collection of scratched pots and pans hung from a wrought iron ceiling rack. Two woks, blackened from years of use, were stacked on top of the counter next to an industrial-sized fan. Clearly this was the domain of the hired help and not of the woman of the house.

Rune pressed forward, passing a formal dining room with a crystal chandelier, a bathroom fitted with a Western-style toilet, and a hallway lined with nineteenth-century European paintings, including a luminous landscape that was signed by Pissarro. She became aware of faint voices coming from the far reaches of the house. They grew louder and more distinct the further she walked.

The door to the study beckoned. It was open, but only just. Rune drew closer until she was in a position to see through the crack. A sliver of the woman's face came into view. Rune immediately recognized her as Som Thongsi, the director of the Khlong Toei Youth Center. The picture-perfect house belonged to her. Rune's eyes moved to the two men sharing the leather chesterfield. Her breath caught in her throat. Her lips formed a silent O. She could hardly believe her eyes. Across from the director were Father Bergdahl and Colonel Panit Rattana, her purported ally at the Metropolitan Police Bureau.

28

Dusit District, Bangkok

Spying came naturally to Rune. When she was just seven years old, her father took her to a company gathering in a townhouse in Sutton Place, an affluent enclave on the far east side of Manhattan. Bored with the adult chitchat, she snuck away from the party and found herself surreptitiously observing the help in the kitchen. She watched as two waiters swished in and out while balancing platters of canapés on their fingertips, but mostly it was the cook who captivated her attention. She was mesmerized by the physicality of the comely woman's work—the tension in her hands as she wielded her chef's knife, the strain in her forearms as she beat egg whites into stiff peaks, and her bulging biceps as she lifted a cast iron pan on and off the burner. Rune saw it all from her hiding spot inside the walk-in pantry, and she remembered every detail. She remembered steam rising from the array of pots on the stove and the potent combination of savory and sweet aromas that filled the room. She remembered the cook whistling Frank Churchill's *Whistle While You Work* in perfect pitch. But most of all, she remembered their host—the CEO of her father's company—striding in right after the waiters departed with their trays of food. He set his champagne flute on the counter right by the pantry. Then he unceremoniously unbuckled his pants and raised the cook's skirt for a mid-party quickie. No words were exchanged, but their moaning was so loud Rune could hear it even after she covered her ears.

No one would ever have known she had been there if she hadn't made off with the freshly baked angel food cake. Not just a slice. The whole thing, which she blithely carried to one of the guest bedrooms. She had already pounded down half of it when the woman of the house discovered her with her hand in the proverbial cookie jar. One look at her face and Rune knew she was in big trouble. It was on their way back to the living room to find her father that Rune started to cry and told the woman what she saw. She was too young to know exactly what sex was, but old enough to understand that what the CEO and the cook did was wrong.

The woman's reaction was upsetting, to say the least. Instead of taking her to her father, she grabbed hold of her arms and squeezed.

Don't tell anyone! she hissed.

Rune yelped in surprise.

The woman's hands loosened. Her eyes became pleading. *My husband is a good man*, she said, more for her own sake than for Rune's. *He has a very stressful job. I don't want to hear another word about this, okay?*

The excuse was thin, and Rune knew it, even at the age of seven. As she scampered back to the party, her fingers sticky with icing, she vowed never to take anything anyone said at face value. The ugly episode was a turning point for her. Her parents had taught her to tell the truth—always—but at that moment, she understood that truth didn't matter one bit. People only saw what they wanted to see, especially those with something to lose. Everyone had something to lose.

Rune's days of spying at parties were far behind her, but old habits died hard. Trailing a mark without getting caught was part of every heist she and Kit had ever planned. In fact, it was her favorite part. *Plus ça change,* she said to herself at the start of each new job. As creepy as it sounded, Rune loved watching people who didn't know they were being observed. It was a power trip, certainly, but that wasn't what kept her interested. No. It was the honesty she was after. The sense that she was getting to know a real person, not the mask they put on every morning for the world to see.

Given Rune's background, it was not at all surprising that she managed to sneak into Som Thongsi's sumptuous house in Dusit District completely unnoticed. She hardly dared breathe as she stood outside the study, her face pressed against the crack in the door. She knew right away that the three people in the room were up to something, though it was unclear exactly what that something could be. Missing girls. Photographs of antiquities. An after-hours meeting between a youth center director, a priest, and a cop. A picture was starting to take shape in Rune's mind, but she couldn't make sense of all the pieces. She leaned closer at the sound of Father Bergdahl's voice.

"What you're asking will take a week to arrange, at minimum," he was saying. There was an edge to his voice.

"We don't have a week," Som replied in English as accented as Rune remembered. She crossed her legs and clasped her hands casually on her lap. Her posture was relaxed, but there was a finality in her tone. Her attitude was that of a powerful woman accustomed to getting her way. She added, "It has to happen now. Tonight."

"That's impossible," the priest said flatly.

"Let me make something perfectly clear. I decide what is or isn't possible. You do as I say. Is that understood?"

Father Bergdahl squirmed in his seat and looked down at the floor. "Yes, naturally, but . . ."

"I don't need to remind you that you're paid handsomely for your services. If memory serves, you received enough in the last year to break ground on your new clinic. A prenatal center, isn't that right?"

The priest nodded glumly. "Forgive me, Som. I appreciate everything you've done for the Church. You know I do. I'll try my best to speed up the timetable, but realistically, what you're asking isn't feasible. I need time to organize transportation, there's the issue of manpower . . ."

"I'm not interested in excuses."

Father Bergdahl shot Colonel Rattana a pleading look, silently asking if he could talk some sense into Som.

"It was settled," Rattana said. He spoke with just the right balance of firmness and deference, like he knew he had to tread lightly with Som. "Everything was arranged. Why change course now, if you don't mind me asking?"

"There's no need to concern yourself with that," she replied.

"With all due respect, if I'm going to call in favors and stick my neck out for you, I'd at least like to know why."

The director remained silent.

"I'm less than a year from retirement. You're asking me to risk my pension—my freedom—to rush a job that's been on the books for months."

Som leaned back in her chair. Her dark eyes landed on the colorful still-life hanging on the opposite end of the room. She gazed at it as she considered Rattana's words. After a drawn out wait, she spread her palms and said, "There's a hold-up with another shipment. We have to move up our timetable to compensate. Otherwise, we're going to have some very unhappy clients."

"What's the reason for the delay?"

"I'm not at liberty to discuss that."

"Can you at least say if there might be blowback on us?"

"That's not likely."

Rattana seemed far from satisfied with the director's cryptic answers, but he didn't voice his displeasure. Instead, he turned to Father

Bergdahl with a solution. "I know people who can help with transportation. We can trust them."

The priest looked apoplectic. "You can't just send me any old person. The work requires knowhow. I need men with experience."

Rattana's sigh indicated he was tired of the priest's can't-do attitude. The director's next words echoed the sentiment.

"Tell me, what's it going to take?" she asked, the pleasantness drained from her voice.

"We'll need at least five hundred thousand baht for the workers. And a rental truck—a large one," Father Bergdahl said.

"Done. Anything else?"

"Where am I unloading the cargo?"

"At the port, exactly as we planned. Nothing has changed except the schedule. Is that understood?"

Father Bergdahl mumbled an assent.

Rattana gave a curt nod.

"Well, now that that's settled . . ." The director's words tapered off. She offered them a smile that could only be interpreted as a dismissal.

Rune jumped when the three of them rose to their feet. Her eyes scoured the hallway for an appropriate place to hide. Seeing no alternatives, she slipped into a large armoire. There was a slight chemical smell inside, like a mixture of wood cleaner and mothballs. She closed the louvered doors just as the trio emerged from the study. She held her breath as they said their goodbyes.

Som began stripping off her clothes as soon as the front door closed, leaving a trail of garments in her wake. By the time she walked by the armoire, she was shadow boxing in the buff. Rune raised her eyes skyward and let out a long-suffering sigh. What no one told you about spying was that, more often than not, you saw things you sincerely wish you hadn't.

29

Port of Bangkok

The Port of Bangkok in Khlong Toei was one of the busiest container ports in the world, and if the Thai government got its way, it would soon get even busier. Their ambitious plan aimed to increase the port's footprint more than twofold. In addition to modernizing the terminals, updating the container yards and freight stations, and creating an entirely new maritime business center, the plan called for the total demolition of Khlong Toei's residential areas, including the infamous slum. On deck to replace them was the much-anticipated Modern Port City, complete with office spaces and condos, designer boutiques, and a department store with a high-end food court on the top floor. Also in the works was a new monorail to connect the port to the rest of the city. The express goal of the project was to create another landmark in the capital, one that offered convenient links to river-based tourism. In other words, the government was after the all-important cruise ship dollars.

Renderings of the new port project showed sleek buildings and clean, well-lit streets that were smoothly paved and easy to navigate. What Rune encountered when she hopped out of her tuk-tuk near the west quay was just the opposite. A crumbling stone wall topped with barbed wiring enclosed the yard proper. Beyond was a massive lot filled to the brim with steel containers stacked three high.

Rune skirted the perimeter for some time before concluding that it was impenetrable. She then set off in search of an easier point of access, only to learn that the sole unwalled area was the official checkpoint, which was manned by armed customs agents. She watched from the shadows as an endless procession of tractor trailers entered and exited the gate. Each driver paused while Port Authority officials remotely verified their container identification number, checking it against the bill of lading.

Rune scanned the incoming vehicles in hopes of catching Colonel Rattana and Father Bergdahl. The problem was, the Port of Bangkok had two terminals with separate entrances, and she had no idea which one they were using. It was a gamble either way. *You're already here*, she reasoned silently. She settled in for the wait.

Her break came about an hour later. The makeshift caravan stood out in the midst of the semis pulling up to the gate for inspection. Colonel Rattana led the way in his silver Toyota hatchback, Father Bergdahl trailed behind in his black sedan, and a white box truck driven by a man Rune didn't recognize brought up the rear. She could make out the silhouettes of two other men beside the driver, one with spiky hair, the other with a baseball cap.

Rattana opened his window when he reached the front of the line. He rested his arm on the door and spent a few minutes chatting with a customs agent. It was clear from their body language that the two knew each other well. Rune watched as Rattana reached into his jacket pocket, pulled out an envelope, and slipped it to the agent. There was much nodding and bowing. Then all three vehicles were waved through.

Rune sprinted toward an idling tractor trailer, the last in a line of four waiting to enter the port. She ducked under the back, hooked her arms and legs around the underride bar, and held on for dear life. The truck grumbled. Rune instantly questioned the sanity of her decision. Her arms started shaking the moment the truck inched forward.

As it turned out, grabbing hold of the underride bar was the easy part, something Rune realized as soon as it came time to let go. The truck quickly gained speed after going through the checkpoint. The wheels spit gravel into the air, pummeling her exposed arms. The situation grew more dangerous with every passing second.

Five . . . four . . . three . . . two . . . one!

Rune grunted when she hit the ground, rolling several times before coming to a stop. She lay motionless for a moment, until she was sure all her parts were intact. Then she staggered to her feet and turned to survey the shipyard. The rows of containers seemed to go on forever. Finding Rattana and the priest would not be an easy task.

The sound of clanking metal rang out. The roar of truck engines filled the night air. Rune set off at a fast jog, only to find herself ducking behind a parked tractor trailer to avoid a pair of customs officials who were evidently on break. Cigarettes dangled from their lips. The smell of tobacco and a hard day's work lingered in their wake. Rune didn't move a muscle until their voices receded, then she pressed forward.

She caught sight of the box truck's taillights glowing in the distance. It appeared to be heading toward the bridge leading to the east quay. She inched past a dormant gantry crane, easily avoiding its portly operator, and then broke into a run.

Getting across the bridge without being seen posed a bigger problem. Rune was wondering what on earth to do when she came across an idling pickup truck. The young driver was having an animated phone conversation with his girlfriend, who was yelling so loudly that Rune could hear every word, even though she wasn't on speaker. Rune slipped into the truck's cargo bed and curled up beside a metal toolbox. There was more yelling, a lot more. Then the girlfriend hung up on the driver and the truck was on its way.

Rune hopped out as soon as they reached the other side of the bridge. She took a moment to orient herself. The east quay was smaller than its western counterpart, but searching it was still a daunting task. Near the riverbank on her right were tall yellow cranes loading containers onto waiting ships. Warehouses and transit sheds lay directly in front of her. Beyond was an open yard with stacks of containers. *Where to start*? she thought. Then she remembered what Kit always said when she asked that question: *At the beginning.*

She moved through the quay systematically, going from one building to the next in search of Rattana and the priest. Everything was going rather well until she turned a corner and came face-to-face with a security officer. He was short and had a muscular physique, like he spent all his free time at the gym. His dark hair was cropped short and shot with gray at the temples. His eyebrows were thick black circumflexes. It was obvious from his startled expression that she was the last person he expected to see there. Rune sized him up in a split second. There was a gun holstered on his right hip. A mean-looking baton hung on the other side. Fighting was not an option. Nor was fleeing. That left only one option: playing dumb.

"Excuse me," she called out. "Do you know where I can find Ali?"

The man clearly did not understand what she was saying. "Khun pen khrai? Tam arai?" *Who are you? What are you doing here?*

She took a step closer. "I'm looking for Ali. He works in the customs department. We have an appointment."

"Yuu tii nii mai dai. Ham khao." *You can't be here. This is a restricted area.* There was a marked shift in his demeanor, from confused to suspicious. He wasn't buying her act.

"Ali's not here?" she asked, doubling down. She took a few more steps until she was directly in front of him.

"Hai phom du bat prajamtua?" *Can I see some identification?*

"I don't understand. Mai khaojai," she said, purposely massacring the Thai. She widened her eyes for good measure.

His hand found the radio on his shoulder.

So much for not fighting, Rune thought. She took a final step forward. Her elbow swung up.

Crack!

The officer let out a short grunt. His hands flew to his face. Ropes of blood oozed between his fingers and splattered the front of his uniform.

Busting the man's nose was all well and good, but Rune didn't need him disabled, she needed to lay him out cold. With that in mind, she grabbed the back of his head with both hands and, in a single fluid motion, pulled it down as she raised her knee. She connected squarely across his nose again.

Two strikes to the schnoz should have done the trick, but the security officer caught Rune off-guard by recovering in record time. He threw a hard punch. Rune tried to duck, but she was too slow. Her head snapped back when his fist landed on her jaw. He swung a second time, hitting her temple so hard she actually saw stars. Her vision became blurry. She could taste blood on her lips. A well-aimed strike to the abdomen caused her to bend in half and left her gasping for air. Her body was a symphony of pain, but the guard wasn't done with her just yet. He grabbed her by the shoulders and threw her against a container so violently it sounded like thunder rolling through the shipping yard. Then he pulled his arm back to punch her again. She twisted out of the way right before he made contact. The howl that came out of his mouth when his knuckles hit the metal was inhuman. She tried to make a run for it, but he shoved her forcefully from behind. She hit the ground with a loud groan.

She was curled up on the pavement wheezing when she saw him reach for his radio again. Somehow, she found the strength to roll onto her side and push herself to her feet. She teetered slightly. Then she tucked her head to one side and crashed her shoulder straight into his midsection. He stumbled backwards, winded. She landed on top of him and drew her knee up hard and fast, but in her haste, she just missed his groin. He gained the upper hand once again, flipping her over and pinning her down with his superior weight.

Rune could see the rage on the guard's face. She no longer feared being reported, now she feared for her life. He wrapped his hands around her neck. A dribble of blood-tinged saliva fell from his mouth and landed on her cheek as he started squeezing. His thumbs pressed down on her larynx, sending pulses of pain to every corner of her body. She clawed at his hands, but he seemed inured to physical pain. Her skin turned red as her brain was deprived of oxygen. Her clawing slowed.

As Rune's mind started to float away, she was filled not just with fear, but with a deep sadness at the thought of those who were going to pay for her massive failures. She thought of Kit, who made the mistake of trusting her with his life. But most of all, she thought of Madee. She wondered if the girl felt as alone and scared as she did at that moment. She closed her eyes in an effort to summon what little strength she had. It was through sheer determination that she managed to lower her hand to the guard's hip. She pawed around clumsily. Her fingers grazed the grip of his gun. They tightened suddenly. Then, in one fell swoop, she drew the gun from the holster, aimed at his side, and squeeze the trigger.

His body convulsed spasmodically for a second before slumping on top of her. The gun slipped from her hand and landed silently on the ground. Rune pressed her palms against his chest and struggled to get out from under him. After three tries, she finally rolled him off. She scooted out of reach on her backside, terrified that he would come to and attack her again. Her lungs expanded and contracted in quick, panicked bursts. She wiped the blood from her mouth with the heel of her hand and kept her eyes on the guard.

He lay on his back, perfectly still, his lips slack and his face passive. Rune was certain she had killed him. Her mouth fell open in a silent cry. Her eyes welled with tears. She had wanted him out of the way, not dead. She was many things—some of them really bad—but she wasn't a killer.

It took a long time for Rune to muster the courage to check his pulse. It was faint but steady. It was then that she realized there was no blood on his body, save what was dripping from his broken nose. Her eyes found the gun, followed the paired wires coming out of the muzzle end, and came to a rest on the two probes embedded in his torso. Relief flooded her senses. It was a taser. The officer would live.

Rune rose unsteadily to her feet. She was safe now, but it was essential that she get the guard out of sight. She slowed her breathing and gathered her energy. Then she grabbed his ankles and started pulling. Inch by painful inch she dragged him until he was behind a container. A plastic tarp covering a stack of wood pallets caught her eye. She grabbed it and threw it on top of his body, leaving a gap near his face so he didn't suffocate. The only thing left to do was pray he remain unconscious. She wiped her hands on her jeans and peered through the darkness. Rows of warehouses and containers extended as far as the eye could see. Her expression became serious. She had taken care of one problem. Now all she had to do was find Rattana and the priest.

30

Port of Bangkok

Rune found them in a deserted part of the shipyard, beyond the transit sheds and warehouses on the edge of the Chao Phraya. There were five of them in total: Colonel Rattana, Father Bergdahl, and the three Thai men she recognized from the lorry. The workers wore blue jeans and sweat-soaked t-shirts. They busied themselves loading large wooden crates into a shipping container mounted on a chassis. In the meantime, the priest was flitting about issuing instructions that were largely going unheeded, while Colonel Rattana stood by wearing the expression of a man who would rather be anywhere else.

The sound of crane engines was everywhere, broken by the echoing boom of steel hitting steel. Occasional shouts rang out as workers loaded containers onto cargo ships moored just beyond Rune's sightline. There was no distinction between daytime and nighttime activity at the loading docks. The global economy demanded that the port operate at full capacity twenty-four-seven.

Rune zigzagged through the shadows until she ducked behind a container so close she could hear Rattana's workmen grunt under the weight of the crates. She stole a glance around the corner.

"Be careful with those!" Father Bergdahl cried out. He pressed his lips together when no one deigned to acknowledge his words, let alone respond to them.

Rune had caught them on the tail end of whatever it was they were doing. The box truck was empty except for an oversized crate tucked at the very back of the cargo hold. The three workmen exchanged unhappy looks before climbing inside to retrieve it. There was more grunting as they dragged it forward. Two of the men hopped out of the truck while the third rammed his shoulder into the crate to get it onto the ramp. It teetered dangerously to one side. Father Bergdahl's lips moved in silent prayer as the workmen maneuvered it to the ground, carried it to the shipping container, and disappeared inside. A bang sounded seconds later, followed by loud scraping. Father Bergdahl opened his mouth to weigh in, only to be silenced by a glare from Rattana. The priest's self-control was commendable given the situation.

The workers emerged. Rattana told them to wrap it up. They closed the container door, rotating the handles attached to the vertical locking rods until they engaged the cams and keepers. Then they swiveled the custom catches down and repeated the process on the other side. The colonel stepped forward to secure the lock box.

"Not yet," Father Bergdahl said, placing a hand on his arm.

Rattana's eyebrows rose as if to say, *There's more?*

"The director has a few other things she's sending over."

"Will you be needing these guys?" Rattana asked, angling his head toward the workers.

"No. She has her own crew. They can go."

Rattana said a few words in Thai and handed each worker an envelope. Then he instructed the driver to take the truck back out the way they came. He waited until they had driven away before turning back to the priest. "Are we done here?"

Father Bergdahl nodded.

"In that case I'll be going."

"I'll follow you out." He gave a wry shake of the head. "This place is a labyrinth. I don't know how you do it."

"A ball of string."

The priest shot him a confused look. Rattana didn't bother explaining. The men said their goodbyes and climbed into their respective cars. Their taillights disappeared into the darkness.

Rune jumped out of her hiding spot as soon as they were out of sight and made a beeline for the container. Her eyes moved over the doors. *Swivel the custom catches up, lift the door handles, twist to disengage the cams and keepers*, she said to herself as she performed each task from memory. *Now pull.* The door swung open.

Rune climbed inside the dark container, fished around for her phone, and switched on the flashlight. The interior was less than half full. She took a step forward and pointed her phone at one of the crates. The word FRAGILE was stamped on the wood in bright red majuscules. Large arrows indicated which way was up. She held her phone in the crook of her neck and tried to pry the crate open with her fingers.

"Ouch!" she cried out when she was rewarded with a massive splinter. She inspected her injured finger and gently sucked on the tip. Then she used her phone to scour the container for something to use as a tool. Several minutes elapsed and she still hadn't found anything useful. She was contemplating searching one of the nearby warehouses when she heard a stern voice coming from outside the container.

"What do you think you're doing?"

She froze.

"Give me one good reason not to arrest you right now."

She twisted her head slowly. She was expecting the worst, so it was almost a relief to find herself staring into the eyes of Colonel Rattana. He didn't look happy. In fact, he looked thoroughly pissed off. She opened her mouth to speak, but he cut her off before she could get a word in.

"Do you really think I didn't see you skulking around in the shadows? What kind of fool do you take me for?"

Rune sniffed. She took pride in her ability to blend into the background. Her livelihood depended on it. "Well, no one else saw me." She realized how childish she sounded the moment the words came out of her mouth.

"You're sure about that? What about that security guard you left for dead?"

Rune shook her head, confused. "How do you know?"

"Never mind how I know. Now answer the question. Why are you here?"

"I don't owe you an explanation."

"Really?"

She held her ground.

"Let me remind you that you were in serious trouble at the police station yesterday. I let you go, and this is how you repay me? By breaking into an international port? By stealing?"

"I'm not stealing anything."

"Then I'll ask you again, why are you here?"

"I followed your sorry ass!" Rune spat. Her words were barbed. So was the look she gave him.

"What?"

She let out a humorless laugh. "You're so full of it. You said you would help me. You pretended to listen, but the whole time you were lying to me."

"I haven't a clue what you mean."

"I saw you at Som's house with the priest. I told you they were up to something. I told you! And not once did you mention you knew them."

"I didn't say anything because it wasn't relevant. Som and Father Bergdahl have nothing to do with Madee's disappearance. They aren't human traffickers."

"Oh no? Then how do you explain all this?" She spread out her arms to gesture to the crates.

"Come on! Do you really think we're hiding girls in there?"

Rune knew he was right, but she was too upset to admit as much. She dug her heels in. "Open them," she demanded.

"You can't be serious."

"Open them."

"This is ridiculous."

"Ridiculous?"

"It's not what you think."

"Then open the goddamned crates!"

"Is that what it's going to take to get you to stop this craziness?"

Rune glared at him.

Rattana let out a frustrated sigh and jumped out of the container. He fetched a crowbar from the trunk of his car and held it out to her. "Be my guest."

Rune accepted it without saying a word and turned to the largest crate, the last one the workers loaded. Her fingers tightened around the metal tool as she attacked the wood, prying at it feverishly until a corner came loose. She bent down to tackle the bottom. Once that was done, she rushed to the other side. Within minutes, the slat was completely detached. She dropped the crowbar with a loud clang and tried to push the wood aside. It was clear she was struggling, but Colonel Rattana made no move to help. After a few hard shoves, it slid out of the way. Rune tore through the packaging material, pausing when she came face to face with the Bodhisattva Avalokiteshvara.

The four-armed statue was even more remarkable in real life than it was on Father Bergdahl's camera, but Rune didn't waste time admiring it. She moved on to a second crate, revealing the stone Buddha that was also part of the priest's collection. By the time she tackled the third crate, she was breathing heavily from exertion. She raised the crowbar.

"Enough," Rattana said, putting his hand on hers.

Rune lowered the crowbar, spent.

"It's okay, you can let go."

Her fingers loosened. He grabbed hold of the crowbar.

It was a long time before Rune found her voice again. She squeezed her eyes closed, but she couldn't shut out the disappointment. Not only had she not found Madee, but it seemed she had been on the wrong track the entire time. She had been so certain about Som and the priest, so sure they were doing something to the slum children. How could she have been so wrong? She shook her head as if to clear it. She expected Rattana to say I told you so, but when he spoke, his tone was soft and far more sympathetic than she anticipated.

"Come on, let's get you out of here," he said, putting a gentle hand on her elbow.

Rune allowed herself to be led to the door. They sat down, their feet dangling over the edge of the container. They stayed that way for quite a while, neither of them inclined to talk. It was Rune who finally broke the silence. "How long have you been trafficking art?" she asked, her voice now devoid of any emotion.

Rattana chafed at the words, like he didn't agree with her characterization of his work.

"We don't have to talk about it if you don't want to."

"It's hard in Bangkok," he said with a hint of defensiveness. "Even people with good jobs can't make ends meet. You don't understand. You're not from here."

"So I'm told."

He looked at her pensively.

Rune grew quiet again. She rubbed at the splinter on the tip of her finger and let her mind wander to Kit and Madee. It was funny how such a small thing could hurt so much. The pain was oddly reassuring, cutting through the sadness that enveloped her and threatened not to let go.

It was Rattana who spoke next. "I'm not a bad person, you know."

"I didn't say you were."

"No one's going to miss these," he added, gesturing to the crates. "The country is full of antiquities that no one cares about."

"You're sure about that?"

Rattana didn't answer.

"Where are they going?"

"Does it matter?"

"Not really. I'm just curious, I guess."

"Most of them are going to Europe, but some are earmarked for buyers in Asia and the Middle East."

"I take it Som is in on this?"

Rattana gave a slow nod. "The whole thing is her operation. She recruited me a few years ago, after learning that my son had run up some gambling debts." The muscles in his jaw tightened and loosened. "I handle checkpoints and customs. The priest cleans the money and stores everything in the church until it's ready to be moved. His cut goes to funding health and education programs in Khlong Toei. The poor get the help they need, and I get to help my son. What's the harm?"

"I'm not judging you, Colonel," Rune said. She wasn't. After all, what she and Kit did was not so different. At least some of the proceeds from Som's operation went to needy kids, which was more than she could say for hers.

"I wouldn't blame you if you did."

"How did I get into this mess?" Rune exclaimed suddenly. She rubbed her temples with her fingers and tried to make sense of what had happened. "I was so sure something was going on at the church. And at the Youth Center."

"You were right. It just wasn't what you thought it was."

"But Madee disappeared from the Youth Center, and other girls have gone missing from the slum. There's no denying that."

"You're right. It's been going on for years, and no one has been able to stop it. But we're talking about girls from very poor families—as poor as they come. Some are runaways. Others were probably married off or sent to work in factories by their own parents. There's no single explanation for all the disappearances. You've imagined a highly organized human trafficking ring, but that's just not what's happening here."

"Madee isn't poor. She didn't run away. And she wasn't married off or sold. She was taken in broad daylight by a man with a scar on his leg. I saw the video."

"She may simply have been unlucky. Crimes of opportunity happen all the time, especially in places like Khlong Toei."

"Is that supposed to make me feel better?"

"No, of course not." Rattana paused, unsure of what to say. He looked at her with deep concern. "Listen, you're clearly exhausted. Go home. Get some sleep. We can start fresh in the morning."

"I'm not going home until I have answers."

Sensing it was a losing battle, Rattana changed tack. "When's the last time you ate?"

Rune shrugged.

"If you're not going to rest, you should at least have something to eat. Let me take you somewhere."

She stared ahead blankly. Rattana was right. She was exhausted and hungry. She gave him a short nod then let her gaze drop away.

"Just give me a minute to put the container back together."

She nodded again.

"Did you really have to tear the crates apart like that?" he asked as he gathered the packaging materials.

Rune shot him a contrite look. He was right. It was like a tornado hit. She got up to lend a hand.

The mess had taken minutes to make, but they spent a long time cleaning it up. They worked side by side, their phones lighting the way. It was hot and airless inside the container, and it got worse the longer they worked. By the time they jumped out, they were red-faced and out of breath.

They were on their way to Rattana's car when they first heard the grumbling sound of an engine approaching. A truck came into view a few seconds later. It was a white lorry, exactly the kind Father Bergdahl had used to transport the statues. Rune shot Rattana a questioning look. He held out a hand telling her to hold still. The truck slowed to a stop. He pulled her behind a container and pressed his index finger to his lips. If Port Authority officials discovered her, she would be beyond his help.

Two men emerged from the truck's cab. Rune's eyes narrowed. Even from a distance, she could see that they weren't truck drivers or dock workers. For one thing, their clothes were far too clean. Both wore dark slacks and white dress shirts, like they were coming from the office. One had the long, lean body of a runner. The other, the older of the two, was about the same height, but much heftier in build. Each had a SIG Sauer P226 holstered at the hip. They exchanged words Rune couldn't make out before walking around to the back of the truck. The lanky man drew his weapon. The brawny one unlocked the cargo area. The door rolled up. Then out came a parade of petrified girls.

31

Port of Bangkok

At her best friend's funeral, when Rune was six years old, two men she had never seen before stood at the back of Immanuel Lutheran Church on the corner of East 88th Street and Lexington Avenue looking like they didn't belong. She noticed them as soon as her parents ushered her into the rusticated stone structure. It wasn't just that they were the only two Black people in the building—though that certainly made them stand out—it was their expressions. The men wore somber masks appropriate for the occasion, but they looked nothing like the dazed, heartbroken mourners filling the pews. They were alert.

Rune remembered nothing about the service, except that it seemed inordinately long for someone who had lived for such a short time. Her eyes were everywhere except on the child-sized coffin resting before the altar. That hit too close to home. She spent a lot of time staring at the ceiling. The open truss design reminded her of a barn, only prettier. She counted a total of ten stained glass windows, five on either side of the building. Mostly, she stole glances at the two outsiders behind her.

It would be several years before Rune found herself singled out by bullies, but even at the age of six, she understood that she shared something with the two strangers that she didn't with anyone else in the room, except her father. Otherness. Difference. Being betwixt and between. For as long as she could remember, she always had to choose between her sense of self and a sense of belonging, only to end up compromising both. The feeling was always with her, whether she was in New York or Bangkok or somewhere else in the world. There was no escaping it, not even in her dreams.

One of the strangers at the church was a giant man with kind eyes and a spray of freckles on his cheeks. He waved when he noticed her watching. Then he touched the tip of his nose with his tongue. She responded with a grimace of her own, stretching her mouth with her two index fingers and wagging her tongue up and down. They carried on like that until her mother put a stop to the shenanigans with a gentle squeeze to her thigh. Rune wasn't sure why that episode stuck with her. Maybe because it was terribly inappropriate, or because it was the only moment of levity in a day that was otherwise unrelentingly sad.

Rune's most vivid memory of the funeral was the strangled cry that rang out when the two outsiders escorted her friend's older brother out of the church immediately after the service. The whispering started straight away. She remembered asking her father why everyone was telling secrets. He told her that some things weren't meant for children's ears.

It wasn't until Rune was much older that she learned the truth about what happened. Her friend was strangled. Her killer? Her maladjusted, pimple-faced brother. The two outsiders were cops. Her friend's parents had pulled some strings to allow their son to attend the funeral before shipping him off to a treatment center. If that wasn't grotesque enough, the judge in charge of the case eventually set the brother free, because his bright future mattered more than the fact that he'd taken a life. The details of how he avoided prison were unclear, though his father did play squash with well-connected fixers.

All these years later, Rune understood why things went down the way they did. Parents were programed to protect their offspring at all costs. Call it instinct. Or survival of the species. Whatever the case, her friend's parents bent over backwards to shield their remaining child from the consequences of his actions. Her own parents also chose to insulate her from the ugly truth. In hindsight, she wished they hadn't been quite so protective. It wasn't right to fill children's heads with fairy tales without also telling them about the monsters. With ignorance came vulnerability. Rune learned that the hard way.

As she watched the steady stream of girls emerge from the back of the box truck—eyes sunken, cheeks hollow—she wondered if any of them had been warned about the particular dangers they faced simply because they were young and female. Rune quickly corrected herself. Young, *poor*, and female.

There were twenty in total. The youngest was the pigtailed nine-year-old who went missing after Father Bergdahl's English class. The oldest was a lissome beauty who looked like she was just on the other side of puberty. In between were girls of various ages, shapes, and sizes. Inclusivity, for stomach-turning reasons.

The men with the SIG Sauers lined the girls up against the shipping container. The heftier of the two pulled out his phone and started making videos. Rune was surprised at how methodical he was being, like a police officer holding a line-up. First the girls posed straight on, then came the profile views. Each girl was assigned a number and made to repeat it at the beginning and end of her video. The little one with the pigtails was number nine—a lucky number in Thailand. Clearly she was anything but.

Rune turned to Rattana with an accusatory look and whispered, "What do you know about this?"

"Nothing. I'm in the dark, just like you." His startled expression revealed he was telling the truth.

"We have to help them." Rune's voice had risen a notch. All she could think about was Madee being in a similar situation.

Rattana held up his hand to quiet her. "Just wait. I'll call for backup."

Rune kept her eyes glued to his while he spoke. There was an urgency in his voice as he described, in broad strokes, what was going on and where they were in the shipyard. The call ended.

"They're on their way," Rattana said. "You have to go. You'll be arrested if they find you here, and I won't be able to help you."

Rune nodded. It was a solid plan, save one important detail. She didn't just want to save the girls, she wanted to ask them about Madee. Once the cavalry arrived, the opportunity to question them would vanish. A look of grim determination crossed her face. She knew what she had to do. The muscles in her legs tensed. Her weight shifted forward. She shot Rattana an apologetic glance. *Sorry*, she mouthed before stepping out from behind the container.

Later, when all was said and done, there were some who praised her bravery. Others called it the height of stupidity. Pundits across Thailand went back and forth for weeks discussing the unusual foreigner who risked everything for a group of trafficked girls. But for Rune, the choice was clear as day. If you didn't like the hand you were dealt, you turned the table over. It was as simple as that.

32

Port of Bangkok

Rune did not have a concrete plan in mind when she stepped into the line of fire. All she knew was that she had to talk to the girls and that meant confronting the traffickers. They were bigger than her and they had guns, but she had no intention of making this a suicide mission. Her eyes searched the ground for something to use as a weapon. They landed on a piece of discarded mooring chain that was roughly three feet long. *This will do just fine*, she thought as she picked it up and wrapped it around her hand. She tightened her grip. The rusted metal felt rough against her skin.

She targeted the thinner of the two men, not just because it would be a fairer fight, but also because his weapon was already drawn. She had to get it out of his hand, otherwise this whole thing would be over before it even started. She glanced over at the burlier man. He was still busy shooting videos. "Front . . . left profile . . . right profile . . ." she heard him repeat as he made his way down the line of frightened girls. It was now or never. Rune approached slowly at first, careful not to attract attention. Then she ran straight at the lanky man, her eyes fierce, her weapon raised.

He must have sensed something was wrong, or she made noise without realizing it. Whatever the case, he turned his head just as she was about to strike. His mouth dropped at the sight of the chain whipping toward him at lightning speed. His body jerk back instinctively, but it was too late. The chain coiled around his forearm. Rune yanked with all her strength. She felt more than heard the bone snap. The gun fell to the ground. The man doubled over, cradling his broken arm while yowling in agony. She released her hold on the chain and dove for the gun. It was just out of reach when she came skidding to a stop.

By this time, the burly man had recovered from the shock and was reaching for his weapon. It was a race for who could get the first shot off. Rune stretched her arm out and curled her hand around the grip of the gun. Her finger found the trigger as she sprang up and aimed at the trafficker. She saw movement out of the corner of her eye just as she was about to take the shot. It was Colonel Rattana hurtling toward her mark. He hit the man mid-torso, but the blow didn't take him down. The two wrestled for the gun. Rattana grabbed the man's wrist. The gun pointed upward.

Bang! Bang!

Two deafening shots went off in quick succession. The sound reverberated across the shipping yard. The smell of gunpowder was everywhere. The girls cowered and cried out in fear. Rune screamed at them to run, but none of them moved.

Rune scrambled to her feet and took aim again. She was itching to pull the trigger, but Rattana and the trafficker were now hopelessly entwined. "Get out of the way, Colonel!" She squinted as she sought to get a clean shot. Her arm started to shake. Sweat poured down her brow.

Bang!

The trafficker's third shot went wild. The bullet ricocheted off a container and lodged itself in another. Cries sliced through the thick air.

"Goddammit Rattana, move!" Rune was in full panic mode now. Sweat stung at her eyes. Her vision was horribly blurry. She blinked long and hard. When that failed, she wiped the sweat away with the back of her hand. All that did was spread the grit into her eyes.

Those few seconds of inattention proved to be Rune's undoing. By the time she saw clearly again, everything had changed. The trafficker had somehow gotten the upper hand. Rattana was on the ground. His nose was bleeding. There was a deep gash on his forehead. His right hand was raised defensively. "Chuai yaa thaam," he cried out. *Please, don't.*

Bang!

The trafficker shot him at point-blank range.

"No!" Rune screamed. Enraged, she squeezed the trigger, but the man she hit with the chain materialized out of nowhere and swiped her arm aside. The bullet went astray. Worse, the move allowed the hefty man to take aim at her. She found herself staring down the barrel of his gun.

"Wang man long!" he shouted. *Drop it!*

"Don't shoot!"

"Wang man long!" he repeated.

"Okay, okay." Rune maintained eye contact with him as she slowly lowered her gun to the ground. The lanky man picked it up with his functioning hand and shuffled over to his partner. The two exchanged words. Rune strained to understand them while keeping her gaze trained on Rattana. He lay on the ground—eyes closed, limbs akimbo—a crimson stain forming an ugly bib across the front of his shirt. His fingers twitched. His chest moved up and down irregularly. He was still alive. *Hang in there,* Rune urged silently.

The two men came to some sort of agreement. "Khao!" the hefty one yelled, waving his gun at the distraught girls. *Get in!*

The girls exchanged terrified looks. Some started to beg. Others wept and held on to each other as they filed into the shipping container.

Rune soon found herself alone with the traffickers. Fear tightened like a noose around her neck. The hefty man grabbed her face and shoved her backward until her head smashed into the steel container. She whimpered and tried to pull away. His partner pointed his gun at Rattana's head. She stopped struggling. His meaning was plain as day.

The hefty man took a few steps back. Rune's eyes darted from side to side, certain he was about to kill her. She squeezed them shut. She didn't want this monster to be the last thing she saw before she died. The seconds dragged on. *Come on!* she thought desperately. *Just do it!* She choked back a sob. There was no way in hell she would give this man the satisfaction of seeing her cry.

"Open your eyes," he said in a nearly impenetrable accent.

Rune clenched them even tighter. He delivered a knife-like strike to her gut. Her eyes flew open. A loud wheeze passed through her lips.

"Stand up straight."

She forced herself to obey. Her breath caught when he reached out to wipe a smudge of dirt off her cheek. Then he backed away and raised his phone. Rune flinched at the camera's blinding flash.

"Turn to the left."

Another flash.

"Now to the right."

And that was the last.

The man prodded her with his gun and marched her to the front of the container. "Reo reo!" he said. *Faster!* He gave her a hard shove when she didn't move quickly enough.

Rune picked up the pace. The trafficker pointed at the door. Her body shuddered as she climbed inside.

"Safe travels, American girl," he said with a sinister smile. He tossed a plastic bucket at her. A large bottle of water hit her straight in the chest. He nodded to his partner. A shot rang out, piercing Rattana straight through the head.

"No!" Rune screamed. She rushed forward, but it was too late. The trafficker pushed her hard. She landed painfully on her backside. The door clanged shut. Then all that remained was the darkness.

DAY 4

33
The Gulf of Thailand

It was hot and rank inside the container. All hope of rescue had faded. Only a miracle could save them. The trouble was, Rune didn't believe in miracles.

A high-pitched whine followed by choked crying rose in the darkness. The sound stirred Rune from her thoughts. She couldn't see her hand in front of her face, but she knew it was the youngest of the group experiencing hunger pangs. The pigtailed girl had been rotating through stages of agitation and lethargy with increased frequency. She was so tiny. Her body had long burned through its carbohydrate stores and was now relying on fats for energy. Once those were depleted, it would move on to the proteins in her tissues. Then her cellular functions would break down. Death would not be far behind. Rune was afraid that if they weren't released from the container soon, that stage would come far too quickly.

"Come here," she called out softly. "Follow my voice." She heard the girl crawl across the floor, her shoes scraping against the hard metal. Then she felt the girl's weight press against her arm. Her breathing was rapid and shallow. She shook terribly, despite the stifling air. Her metabolism had slowed in response to caloric deprivation. Her body could no longer regulate its temperature. She was suffering. They all were, but you wouldn't know it. Aside from the little girl sitting next to her, there was no crying or carrying on. Everyone was calm inside the container. Then again, terror was easy to hide in the dark.

Rune reached for the bottle of water, unscrewed the cap, and brought it to the little girl's lips. She heard her pull from it greedily. Her own mouth was parched. She gave the plastic a light shake and guessed it was less than a quarter full. She put the cap back on without taking any. By her calculations, whatever their worth, the ship was somewhere in the middle of the Gulf of Thailand. Rattana had said the container was going to Europe, with pitstops in Asia and the Middle East. That probably meant they were headed to the Malacca Strait—the most direct route to Europe via the Suez Canal. Their first stop could be anywhere: Singapore, Malaysia, Indonesia. Wherever they were going, it could be days, perhaps longer, before they saw land again. Better to save what little water remained.

A wave of nausea rolled over Rune. She felt light-headed and dizzy. Her stomach seized up. The cramps had become more frequent in the last few hours. And more acute. She tried slowing her breathing. She felt horrible but, like the other girls, she chose not to say anything. What would be the point? It wasn't as if she could conjure food out of thin air. She drew her knees up and dropped her head on her folded arms. Her eyelids rose and fell heavily. No one liked to go hungry, but as an unabashed foodie, Rune was particularly ill-equipped to deal with the effects.

DAY 5

34

The Gulf of Thailand

The ship's gentle rocking kept lulling Rune to sleep. Either that, or she was simply too weak to stay awake. Her sleep was not so much restful as an alternative consciousness. Her dreams were vivid and episodic, not quite nightmares, but an unsettling montage of childhood flashbacks and Grand Guignol fantasies.

She woke with a start. It was still pitch black in the container. Her skin was hot and clammy. Her mouth felt like sandpaper. There was an incessant throbbing inside her head. She reached for her phone. The two traffickers had been in such a hurry to get rid of her that they hadn't bothered to confiscate it. She glanced down at the screen. Then she remembered that she had turned it off to save what little battery life remained.

The air was staler and more suffocating than ever. The smell of sweat mixed with feces and urine permeated the air, as did the stench of vomit. Some of the girls had been seasick in the early hours on the ship. She, too, would have thrown up if there had been anything inside her stomach to expel.

It felt like weeks, even months since they had been locked inside the container. Misery had a way of doing that. It distorted time, stretching it in all directions until it ceased to have any meaning.

The first moments of confinement had been utter chaos. Rune's memories of them were vague, like they happened to someone else. She and the girls had pounded on the walls of their steel prison to attract attention. They had yelled until their voices were hoarse, to no avail. She remembered the sudden jerk when their chassis was hitched to a truck. The droning of the engine drowned out their cries during the fifteen-minute journey to the dock. The humming of machinery grew louder the closer they got to the water. They heard a loud bang when the gantry crane's spreader locked onto the container. Then came the upward yank that sent them tumbling to the floor.

Rune had placed a frantic call to emergency services while they were suspended mid-air, only to be transferred to the notoriously unhelpful Tourist Police Bureau, a civilian agency that dealt almost exclusively with pickpocketing and fraud, with the occasional sex crime thrown into the mix. Her story of being held captive in a shipping container with twenty young girls was so unbelievable that the operator promptly hung up on her. She tried again, only to have profanities flung at her in two languages. Her phone lost its signal shortly thereafter.

For hours they had screamed. For hours they had clawed at the container walls and kicked at the door. Their efforts had redoubled when they felt the vibrations of the ship's engine somewhere far below. Then the ship began to sway, and they knew they were lost.

There was talking in the beginning. Names and ages were exchanged, as were hometowns. Most of the girls were from the Thai countryside, lured to Bangkok with the promise of jobs and nice homes. The rest had grown up in Khlong Toei. Their stories were heartbreakingly similar. They were poor. They wanted to help their families. They were duped by a priest with a melodious voice. They looked at Rune curiously. It was clear she was the odd one out.

She spoke of Madee in the first few hours. She even showed them pictures of her. She was so used to dead ends that she almost didn't believe the shy girl with the thick frame glasses who said she recognized her.

I saw Madee at the Youth Center. She was kissing some guy, the girl said.

What guy?

I don't know his name. Someone older. He was tall and skinny, with hair like a Samurai.

The girls grew quieter in the hours that followed.

By the second day, silence descended like a shutter.

Rune's stomach growled. She tried to ignore it by focusing on the little girl resting against her shoulder. The girl was still now. Her tiny chest rose and fell with rhythmic regularity. The sound of her breathing carried through the air. *In, out, in, out*, Rune repeated silently, grateful that the girl was asleep and not dead.

Rune very badly wanted to close her eyes and sleep, too, but she forced herself to stay awake. The longer they were in the container, the worse their chances of getting out alive. *Think, think,* she said to herself. Fighting through her malaise, she gently lowered the girl to the floor and got to her feet. She fished her phone out of her pocket and powered it on. There was no signal. The battery level was at fifteen percent. She turned on the flashlight. Her eyes swept the container in search of something—anything—that could help them escape.

The search only lasted a few minutes, until Rune spotted Rattana's crowbar tucked between two crates. Never in her life had she been more ecstatic to see a hand tool. She took the crowbar to the front of the container and started prying at the door. She worked for hours. She worked until blisters formed on the palms of her hands. And then she worked harder. Another girl took over when the crowbar finally slipped from her grasp. Then another. And on like that it went until everyone who could had taken a turn. They hardly made a dent.

This is useless, Rune thought miserably. It was all she could do not to break down and cry.

But feelings of hopelessness sometimes had unexpected effects. Their problem had no obvious solution, so maybe it was time to think outside the box. A crazy plan began to form in Rune's mind. It was a longshot—to say nothing of risky—but if it worked, it could solve everything. She turned to the oldest girl, the pretty one who was newly through puberty, and said, "Choo-ay dai mai?" *Will you help?*

The girl shot her a puzzled look.

Rune gestured to the crates.

The girl gave a trusting nod.

Together they used the crowbar to pry the front slat off the largest crate. It wasn't a particularly difficult task, but days without food and water made it nearly impossible. The two grunted from the effort until they finally pushed the slat out of the way. The girl stood back while Rune tore through the packaging material.

"An nii arai?" the girl asked when she saw the bronze Bodhisattva statue. *What is it?*

The others leaned in for a better view. Murmurs sounded all around.

Rune didn't stop to answer. She had to work fast, while she still had battery power. She pulled out her phone and took a picture of the sculpture. The flash exploded inside the dark container. She grabbed the papers in the plastic sleeve taped to the lid and scanned the contents. It took no time at all to find the information she was looking for and commit it to memory. She pointed to the next crate, the one she knew held the stone Buddha. The girl nodded and helped Rune open it.

Two should be enough, she thought as she snapped another photo.

The text message took only a moment to type. A few seconds more and the pictures were attached. Rune hesitated, knowing this was the equivalent of pouring water on an oil fire. Her thumb hovered over the Send button. *Do something, or do nothing? Take a swing, or lie down and die?* It was no choice at all. Her thumb descended. Her phone would keep trying to send the message until it found a signal or until the battery died.

The girl who helped open the crates grabbed Rune by the arm. Her eyes were full of questions. Rune shrugged and remained silent. It was a Hail Mary pass. Better not to get anyone's hopes up. She shuffled back to her spot next to the pigtailed girl and lowered herself to the floor. White spots floated in and out of her visual field. Her stomach churned angrily. She drew her knees up and lowered her head to them once again. Only time would tell if her plan had worked. For now, there was nothing to do but wait.

DAY 6

35

The Port of Singapore

Rune sensed the change in her surroundings even in her semiconscious state. The interminable humming of the ship's engine had stopped, as had the gentle swaying that signaled they were at sea. A metal chain clanged in the distance, but the sound was so faint—and Rune was so out of it—that she assumed she had imagined it. Shouts rang out nearby. Her eyes sprang open. They were at a port.

Rune pawed around in the darkness for the crowbar and crawled to the front of the container. She pressed her ear against the door. Twice she heard voices coming from close by. Twice they faded before she could catch their attention. She tried calling for help, but the words died at the back of her throat. The day before, the sound of the crowbar hitting the steel door had been deafening. Now Rune's body was so weak she had to use both hands just to slide it across the floor.

Tap. Tap. Tap.

"Please," she said inaudibly.

Tap. Tap. Tap.

She lost track of how long she kept at it. The sound became fainter with every passing hour. The pauses between each strike grew longer.

Rune felt impossibly ill. One minute she was sweating, the next she was shivering violently. She struggled to draw a breath, but her lungs felt like they were in a vise grip. She leaned her body against the door. Then she slid to the floor and curled into a ball to rest. *Just for a second*, she promised herself.

She closed her eyes and slept. In her dreams, she was back on the Ducati with her arms wrapped tightly around Kit's waist. She laughed gleefully as they sped through the colorful streets of Bangkok, the warm wind caressing her dewy skin. Then she was alone, wandering through the vast Pak Khlong Talat flower market. She inhaled deeply, savoring the sweet smell of wild jasmine. Garlands of marigolds caught her attention, the kind she and her father used to present as offerings to the spirits. She picked one up and brought it up to her nose, but the bright orange petals disintegrated in her hand. Kit reappeared. They were at the snake farm at the Queen Saovabha Memorial Institute. He leaned over an enclosure to get a better look at a venomous pit viper. Rune tried to warn him, but he leaned further and further until he dropped to the other side. *No!* she screamed. She tried to run to him, but her limbs wouldn't respond. Metal bars came down around her. The snake farm faded away. Now she was alone in a cage with nothing around her but darkness.

Rune woke with a jolt at the metallic sound of the door unlatching. She thought she was still dreaming until she felt a gust of fresh air on her face. She stretched her neck toward it and squinted against the morning light. A man stood in her line of vision. Her eyes moved from his shiny derby shoes, up the razor-sharp pleat of his trousers, to his perfectly pressed jacket. She blinked several times until his face came into focus. Her heart gave a sideways lurch. Her breath caught in her throat. Her plan had worked—Charles Lemaire had come to the rescue.

Rune awoke in an unfamiliar bed. Her skin felt clean and cool. There was an IV drip in her arm. She was wearing someone else's clothes. Whoever they belonged to was at least two sizes bigger than her.

The room was tastefully decorated with furniture that was modern but not sterile. The ash wood flooring was beautifully polished. A large TV was affixed to the wall directly across from the king-size bed. There was a door to the right. To the left were two leather accent chairs arranged around a metal strut table. A pair of sliding glass doors opened onto a narrow balcony. Beyond was a shimmering expanse of water.

Rune sat up slowly. Her head throbbed and her lips were parched. A bottle of water beckoned from the nightstand. She brought it to her lips and chugged it in one go. A fit of coughing ensued, making her eyes water and her lungs burn.

Rune waited for the fit to pass. Then she pulled the needle out of her arm with a grimace and swung her legs over the side of the bed. *Where the hell are my shoes?* she thought. She tried to stand, but her legs gave out, sending her crashing into the IV stand. She hit the floor with a hard thud. She was still trying to pick herself up when she heard the door open. Her eyes turned toward it.

"Tsk-tsk. You mustn't do that. You could hurt yourself," Lemaire said. He lifted her up like a ragdoll and put her back on the bed.

"Where are we? What is this place?" Rune asked in a croaky voice as she watched him smooth his jacket with his left hand. This was only their second meeting, but she already recognized the gesture for what it was—compulsive perfectionism.

Lemaire stopped worrying with his jacket long enough to fluff her pillow and pull the bedsheet over her body. He folded it neatly so that it grazed the top of her shoulders. Then he wiped up the water she had spilled with some tissues.

"Where are we?" Rune repeated.

"You're on my yacht," Lemaire said with a steely expression. "It's just you and me. And the crew."

"Shit."

"I believe what you mean to say is *thank you*. I saved your life."

"Thank you," Rune said in a wobbly voice.

"You have something that belongs to me," Lemaire said, cutting straight to the chase.

She nodded solemnly.

"I've already searched through your things. The rubies aren't there. Or anywhere in the abominable container I fished you out of."

The container! The horror of it came back in full force. "The girls I was with . . . where are they? Are they okay?"

"They're fine. They're in the custody of the Singapore police, which is where the ship was docked when I found you." Lemaire peered at her with something that resembled admiration. "It was very clever of you to send your boyfriend the container's tracking number. I never would have found you without it, or the sculptures you promised me. You were right. The pictures don't do them justice."

"They're yours, just as I promised. Keep them, and I'll keep the rubies."

Lemaire threw his head back and laughed. "Your message said I was getting both. The sculptures are just the interest. You still owe me the principal. Now tell me where my gemstones are."

Rune's heart rate jumped. This was it. What happened next would determine whether she lived or died. She took an unsteady breath. "I lost the rubies in Khlong Toei the same day I stole them. I looked everywhere. I think the rain washed them away. I think they're gone for good." She fell silent. Telling the truth was sometimes the only course of action, even if the truth could get you killed.

Lemaire's pale eyes went from bemused tolerance to overtly hostile. He leaned closer. His expression turned menacing. "What are you playing at?"

"I'm not playing at anything. The rubies are gone. You're holding Kit hostage. Don't you think I'd give them to you if I could?"

"I'm afraid we have problem then."

No kidding.

"The only reason I kept you and your boyfriend alive was so I could retrieve my property. You're useless to me now."

A crippling fear suddenly gripped Rune. Lemaire bought and sold illicit gemstones from Myanmar, one of the most repressive countries in the world. He had blood on his hands, and he wouldn't think twice about killing her and Kit. Her mind raced when she saw him make a move for the door. If he walked away now, she and Kit were as good as dead. "Wait!" she called out. "Don't go!"

"Give me one good reason why I shouldn't throw you overboard right now and be done with it."

"Hire me. I'm really good at what I do. I'm one of the best. We can make a lot of money together."

His eyes held hers. Her proposal had piqued his interest.

"You choose the marks and I'll do the rest. We can get rich together."

"I'm already rich."

"I'll make you richer. We can put your competitors out of business. We'll split the profits fifty-fifty. All you have to do is say yes."

Lemaire tugged on the bottom of his jacket and brushed a piece of lint only he could see off his sleeve. He looked to be on the cusp of making a decision. The tension dragged on while he contemplated his options.

"It's the smart choice. You know it is," Rune said, giving him a final push. "If you kill me, you get nothing—no rubies, no money. If you keep me alive, you can recoup your losses. It's a win-win situation."

Silence once again filled the room. It went on and on. It felt like it was never going to end. Finally, Lemaire broke into a tight smile and said, "This is your lucky day."

A wave of relief rushed over Rune.

"I happen to be in need of someone with your skill set."

She opened her mouth to say something, but he held up his hand to stop her.

"Before we go any further, let me make something perfectly clear. We won't be splitting profits. You'll work for me. For a small stipend."

"For how long?"

"Until I say so."

The look on Rune's face said she was unhappy with the terms, but her head moved up and down to indicate she understood. She was in no position to argue. "What about Kit? Will you let him go?"

"We can revisit that down the road."

It wasn't the answer Rune wanted, but now wasn't the time to test the man's limits. "And this job you're talking about, when would you need me to do it?"

"There's no time like the present."

Rune was afraid he was going to say that.

"Get dressed," he said, clapping his hands like a pair of cymbals. "You're going on a trip."

"Where to?" Her voice was filled with apprehension. She envisioned having to break into a sludgy mine in Myanmar, getting caught by the military police, and spending the rest of her days in a filthy prison. That couldn't happen. She wouldn't survive it. "Seriously. What is this job?"

Lemaire gave her another tight smile and pulled out his phone. His eyes bored into hers as he brought it to his ear. "It's me," he said when the person on the other end answered. "I want to book a flight."

There was a brief pause. Rune held her breath.

"From Singapore to New York."

DAY 7

36

Sotheby's, New York

Benicio Rivera flashed his ID badge at the bearded security guard stationed at 1334 York Avenue, a glass midrise in Manhattan's tony Lenox Hill neighborhood. A blast of cold air greeted him the instant he stepped through the revolving doors. For Benicio, just entering the building was like being transported to a different universe. The chronically delayed D train faded from his mind. The fickle AC in his parents' walk-up lost all importance. His working-class reality simply couldn't compete with the glamour and prestige of Sotheby's, auction house of international repute and broker of all things expensive. The time was 9:50 A.M.

Benicio was short in stature, with prominent cheekbones and earnest brown eyes that drooped at the corners. His face was perpetually serious, his wavy hair neatly trimmed. He wore an ill-fitting suit made of fabric that was entirely wrong for the season. He gave the lapels of his jacket a tug and fussed with his tie as he made his way to the bank of elevators. A feeling of nervous gratitude swelled inside him as he walked. With its subdued neutrals and high ceiling, the lobby of Sotheby's was exactly what one would expect from a corporation with annual earnings in the hundreds of millions of dollars. Cream-colored tiles shone beneath layers of polish. Famous artworks and sales announcements flashed on wraparound screens suspended beneath the mezzanine. The sweeping vista leading from the entrance, past the twin escalators, and into the exhibition spaces at the rear of the building never failed to impress.

Benicio took the elevator to the fourth floor, home to the auction house's recently revamped galleries. The hoards were about to arrive, but for the moment everything was quiet, and, for that, he was infinitely grateful. The serene, almost contemplative atmosphere was a welcome change after the chaotic week he'd had. Thousands of people had flocked to Sotheby's in recent days—art dealers, museum curators, private collectors, scholars, and students—all keen to view the collection of the reclusive Karl Kohl-Stromer, an American hotel magnate with exquisite taste in art. Kohl-Stromer's heirs were putting his estate up for sale, offering the public its first glimpse at his expansive collection. Visitors had been tripping over themselves fawning over the artworks, but all Benicio could do was fret. What if someone took an ax to a precious sculpture or threw acid on an irreplaceable painting? Worse, what if a maniac smuggled a bomb into the building and blew the place up? The Kohl-Stromer sale was going live that afternoon. The powers that be were expecting record-breaking crowds in the galleries. Benicio looked at the time. His right eye started twitching. His palms dampened with sweat. He wiped them on his nearly new pants and tried his best not to look anxious. At just nineteen years of age, he was the youngest member of the security team at Sotheby's. It was his seventh day on the job.

Benicio was desperate for things to work out at the auction house. It was his first real job—flipping burgers in high school didn't count—and despite the long commute, he was determined to make it through the three-month trial period. His base salary was $46,500, a fortune for a kid from a not-so-nice part of the Bronx. Sweetening the package were annual raises and ample opportunities for overtime and holiday pay. His mother cried when he told her about his 401(k). His father could barely contain himself as he leafed through the tome detailing his excellent health benefits.

The Kohl-Stromer auction was gearing up to be the biggest and most profitable sale in Sotheby's history. The collection comprised over a hundred objects ranging from ancient Roman sculptures to new media works. The galleries were installed in such a way as to showcase individual lots, while also highlighting the dialogue between them. *Sell them in pairs*, was the recurring mantra among senior staff. Large-scale works by a who's who of the modern and contemporary art world lined the walls of the central corridor, which functioned as the exhibit's organizing spine. Jackson Pollock's *Black and White Painting*, c. 1952, hung next to Gerhard Richter's *Abstraktes Bild*, 1985. The former was valued at $12 million. The latter was worth at least twice that. In the middle of the corridor were three-dimensional works by renowned modernist sculptors, including Constantin Brancusi, Claes Oldenburg, and Louise Bourgeois. The objects in the subsidiary galleries opening off the main corridor were sorted by department, highlighting the breadth of the Kohl-Stromer collection: Old Master Paintings, Impressionist Art, and Photographs were expected to be particular draws. Everything else was relegated to smaller rooms.

Benicio exchanged pleasantries with a colleague and then reported to his workstation at the junction of two diminutive galleries: Ancient Art and Jewelry. His supervisor, a corpulent man with a flaccid face and a smoker's rasp, told him it was an easy assignment. It was true that almost all the pieces under his purview were secured in tamper-proof display cases. The ones that weren't were made of heavy marble, making theft a physical impossibility. And although Benicio had nightmares about vandalism and terrorist attacks, deep down he knew that such acts were exceedingly improbable. He reckoned that he would spend most of the day scolding visitors who failed to maintain a safe distance from the artworks. It surprised him how many people chose to ignore the "Please Do Not Touch" signs displayed in every room. To him, it was a lot like initiating sex. No touching without permission. Nothing could be simpler. Then again, there were plenty of folks who couldn't get that straight either. He clucked his tongue in disapproval then looked at his watch again. It was ten o'clock. His heart jumped into his throat. The first rumble of visitors sounded in the distance. Before he knew it, the galleries were packed to capacity.

Benicio noticed the woman the moment she walked through the door, not because she stood out, but because he had a thing for brunettes. Her dark hair was pulled back in a ponytail that grazed the middle of her back. Her blunt bangs drew attention to her magnetic eyes. She was dressed stylishly in separates that looked like they belonged on the runway. High-waisted trousers draped her slender frame to perfection. The outline of her bra was visible through her silk blouse. Pretty ballet flats and red lipstick completed the package. Benicio watched out of the corner of his eye as she sashayed into the gallery and paused in front of a marble bust of the Roman emperor Lucius Verus. She tilted her head to one side and pressed her left hand to her chin, studying the sculpture as he imagined an expert would. *She must be a very serious art collector*, he thought when she pulled out a Moleskine notebook and started scribbling inside. It was then that he noticed the woman's peculiar hands. Her nails were painted with glossy black polish. She had a ring on every finger, even on her thumbs. Benicio fell head over heels right on the spot. He had no way of knowing that the dark-haired woman would cost the auction house a rich client. As the bottom man on the totem pole and a convenient scapegoat, the incident would in turn cost Benicio his job.

37

Sotheby's, New York

Rune made a show of sizing up the Lucius Verus bust. According to the catalog, it was a museum-quality piece with a low estimate of $700,000. The sculpture was in pristine condition, save a chip in the figure's nose and a minor crack along the front of his cuirass. The young emperor was shown in all his leonine majesty, but what really made the work great was its range of surface effects: the smoothness of the emperor's skin, the luxuriance of his curly locks, and the softness of the cloak fastened at his right shoulder. With his prominent brow and deeply drilled eyes, the figure was uncannily life-like, yet far too perfect to be real. Rune gazed at it with feigned admiration. She liked old stuff as much as the next person, but the truth of the matter was, she wasn't at Sotheby's for the antiquities. Her real interest lay in the adjacent gallery—in a state-of-the art display case in the middle of the room.

Rune walked past the guard without acknowledging his presence. She knew he was watching her, though he was trying his best not to show it. She entered the jewelry gallery and paused to survey it. The well-lit case at the center of the room beckoned. She felt an irrepressible urge to smash it, grab the contents, and run like hell.

Just do it! her inner voice screamed.

But of course, she didn't. Instead, she joined the crowd perusing the collection, moving from one display case to the next with uncharacteristic restraint. It was all a charade—a ruse she cooked up on the long flight from Singapore to conceal the fact that she was casing the place. Still, the professional in her couldn't help but admire some of the pieces on display, especially the vintage ones. A pendant watch with diamonds and calibré-cut sapphires caught her attention, as did an aquamarine and enamel broach in the form of a peacock. Most beautiful of all were the dangly Art Deco earrings made of emeralds and rock crystals. Rune wondered in passing if she might be able to swipe them alongside the piece Lemaire wanted. She smiled briefly at the prospect before scolding herself for losing focus. She shook her head in an effort to stay alert. Catnapping on the plane was no match for the twelve-hour jetlag.

Rune browsed the Kohl-Stromer jewelry collection for a few minutes. During that time, she counted two security cameras, one motion detector, and lockdown gates at the exits. The display cases themselves, made of impenetrable laminated glass, were equipped with pick-proof locks and vibration sensors to detect break-ins, both of which interfaced wirelessly with the auction house's external alarm center. None of this came as good news to Rune. She excelled at breaking and entering. Cracking safes was right up her alley. And though it wasn't her preference, in a pinch, she could fight her way in and out of most sticky situations. This Sotheby's job lay way outside her comfort zone, but it wasn't as if she had a choice in the matter. If there was one thing Lemaire had made clear, it was that failing wasn't an option. Kit's life depended on her success. *You can do this*, she said to herself, trying to muster the confidence to do what had to be done.

She approached the central display case with a mix of curiosity and trepidation. A crowd three deep had formed around it, but the wait looked worse than it was. Studies showed that the average museum goer only spends about thirty seconds in front of an artwork. As it turned out, the same could be said of people viewing gemstones.

The crowd thinned suddenly. Rune resisted the urge to adjust her wig as she inched closer to the display case. Before she knew it, a tanned man with big teeth and suspiciously thick hair was all that stood between her and her target. Her pulse quickened. She hated being under Lemaire's thumb, but there was no sense pretending that this job didn't excite her. She couldn't help it any more than Lemaire could help being a perfectionist. It wasn't their fault. It was in their nature.

The tanned man moved out of the way. Rune slipped into his spot and peered inside the display case. Her pupils widened with excitement. Heat rushed to her cheeks. Before her, in all its glory, was the world-famous Kohl-Stromer ring, a piece of jewelry as stunning as it was unique.

The ring featured a pigeon-blood ruby from the Mogok mines in Myanmar—the most magnificent Rune had ever laid eyes on. The cushion-cut gem was surrounded by ten round-cut diamonds and mounted on an eighteen-carat yellow gold band. The ruby was mesmerizing, with a vivid red hue and a natural fluorescence that made it appear internally illuminated. It was also huge. Whoever said size didn't matter was clearly not in the business of selling rubies. Large diamonds, emeralds, and sapphires regularly appeared on the auction block, but sizeable rubies were exceedingly rare, especially those originating from Myanmar. At just over sixteen carats, the Kohl-Stromer ruby was more unusual than a solar eclipse. The fact that it was surrounded by flawless diamonds just added to its beauty.

The low estimate for the ring was $15 million. The high estimate, $17 million. The former would still make it the most expensive pigeon blood ruby ever sold at auction in the United States, a record previously held by the Jubilee Ruby, which sold at Christie's New York in 2016 for $12.5 million, plus commissions and fees. There were whispers that the Kohl-Stromer ruby might even set a new per carat record, topping the Crimson Flame sold at Christie's Hong Kong in 2015 for an unprecedented $18 million. The mere thought was enough to set Rune's heart racing. She had handled her fair share of rubies, but none came remotely close to this one. She felt a familiar rush as she brought her face closer to the display case. The ruby gleamed tantalizingly under the light. She looked at the time. It was nearing eleven. For now, it was enough to admire it. By the end of the day, she was going to steal it. There was just one problem. She couldn't do it alone.

38

Upper East Side, New York

Bethesda Terrace in Central Park was a landmark in a city that was filled with them. Everyday locals and tourists descended upon the area in droves, snapping selfies from its twin staircases and lounging insouciantly by its famed circular fountain. The terrace offered unparalleled views of the Lake, the most scenic body of water in the city. Its bronze statue of the Angel of the Waters drew praise from people of all ages. With its graceful arcade and tree-lined borders, the terrace offered a welcome respite from the chaos of Manhattan, while also remaining integrally tied to its animated streetscape.

The charming allure of Bethesda Terrace was impossible to deny, but that wasn't why Rune chose it for her meeting that afternoon. Escapism held no interest for her. What she wanted was much harder to come by—anonymity. All criminals worth their salt knew that New York City was equipped with more than fifteen thousand CCTV cameras, each with a range of six hundred feet. Big Brother's all-seeing eyes monitored nearly every inch of the city, giving law enforcement an edge over miscreants of all ilk. Central Park was a notable exception. Although dozens of cameras lined the perimeter of the park, notably the four corners and the southern part of Fifth Avenue, the park itself was almost entirely free of surveillance equipment. Rune silently thanked Amnesty International for releasing a digital map of the city's security network as part of its Ban the Scan campaign, an effort to stop the NYPD from using CCTV footage in conjunction with facial recognition technology. The organization wanted denizens of the city to know that they were being watched, particularly communities of color, which were disproportionately targeted for surveillance and patrol.

Rune used Amnesty International's map to chart her route from Sotheby's to Central Park. After exiting the auction house, she headed south on York Avenue and turned right on East 70th Street, passing modest tenements and mid-century brick towers that looked every bit their age. The character of the neighborhood changed when she reached Park Avenue about fifteen minutes later. Gone was the eclectic mix of high- and low-rise buildings. In its place, as far as the eye could see, were stately prewars manned by a veritable army of uniformed doormen. Rune cast a glance in both directions and hurried across the intersection. The soles of her shoes tapped rhythmically against the pavement. The tip of her ponytail swung pendulum-like between her shoulder blades.

A red light at the corner of East 70th Street and Madison Avenue slowed Rune down long enough to notice her discomfort. New York summers were not nearly as bad as Thailand at any time of year, but that didn't mean they were tolerable. The two stylishly dressed women beside her seemed immune to the heat as they compared manicures and fresh blowouts. Another woman, this one in baby-blue hospital scrubs, stole longing glances at them as she tried to smooth the frizz from her hair. Rune sympathized. It was hard not to want things in a city that constantly reminded you of what you didn't have.

The pedestrian signal across the street started counting down. Rune drew closer to the edge of the sidewalk as she waited for the light to change. She recoiled when she heard rustling coming from the trashcan on the corner. It was a sound she knew all too well. A sound that could only signal one thing—rats. Every neighborhood had them, no matter how moneyed. It was one of the great equalizers in a city that was plagued by inequality.

The light turned green. Rune stepped off the sidewalk and went straight to the swanky boutique across the street. She didn't want to attend the auction in the clothes she wore to surveil the galleries. It wasn't just paranoia, it was nerves. Her slacks were sticking to her thighs. There were sweat stains under her arms. She normally didn't give much thought to what others thought about her appearance, but today was different. Today she cared.

She emerged from the shop looking prim and proper in a navy-blue dress with an A-line skirt that fell just below the knee. The top, while sleeveless, was just as conservative. The shop's attentive saleswoman had given her a bag to carry her other clothes. She couldn't have known that Rune would toss it into the trash at the first opportunity.

Central Park was visible up ahead. Rune approached knowing there was no way to get in without being caught on CCTV, short of jumping over a wall. She rejected the entrance at East 72nd Street, a major intersection covered by not one but two cameras, opting instead to enter the park at 69th Street. She kept her head down as she crossed Fifth Avenue so that no amount of zooming, panning, and tilting could capture a clear view of her face.

Vibrant cardinal flowers and chirping sparrows greeted her inside the park. The ambiance was so lovely that Rune was able to relax long enough to give herself a pep talk. *There's nothing to be nervous about. It's just a meeting*, she said to herself even though she knew it was a lot more than that.

Her budding feeling of well-being dissipated the further she walked. By the time she reached East Drive, it had entirely disappeared. She crossed the road, narrowly dodging a group of cyclists sporting gear fit for the Tour de France. Three runners in identical green singlets thumped passed just before she reached the other side. Her nose wrinkled at the ripe scent that lingered in their wake.

Rune made her way past the Naumburg Bandshell and veered onto the Mall. Mature American elms lined the picturesque walkway, providing a shady canopy for parkgoers on the benches below. Her eyes landed on a teenage couple that couldn't keep their hands off each other, then on a dogwalker with no fewer than ten designer pooches, none of whom were particularly well-behaved. Up ahead, Bethesda Terrace beckoned.

Rune descended the staircase to the terrace's lower level. She slowed under the gracious arcade beneath the 72nd Street crossroad. The tiled passageway was empty save a solitary violist playing Beethoven's Spring Sonata in F major. The music swelled inside the shadowy space, filling the air with crisp, upbeat notes. Rune reached into her pocket and dropped a five-dollar bill into the musician's open case. He acknowledged her contribution with a gallant tilt of his head.

The lower terrace was busy, but not excessively so. Rune hung back and scanned the area. A group of senior citizens stood by the fountain listening to a tour guide who looked like her day had already been too long. A nanny and her charge approached the edge of the Lake to feed a pair of ornery geese. Rune's eyes shifted from side to side until she found the person she was looking for.

The slight, black-haired man had his back to her as he gazed across the water. He wore tailored khakis and a short-sleeved button-down with a light plaid pattern. As Rune drew closer, she noticed that his shoulders were narrower than she remembered and that his hair was laced with white. *He looks frail*, she thought before correcting herself.

Not frail, older. She felt a pang of regret as she approached. The pang became more pronounced the closer she got. Her hand rose. He turned before she could speak.

"Hello Rune," he said.

She swallowed hard and tried to smile. Then, in a shaky voice, she said, "Hi Dad."

39

Central Park, New York

"I have to admit, I was surprised to hear from you," said Aran Sarasin. His English was unaccented save a slight inflection on the vowels.

Rune stared at him without speaking. He had the same high cheekbones and golden skin tone as her, but his eyes were smaller, darker, with deep lines at the corners. Gravity had begun tugging at the corners of his mouth. There were creases on his forehead that weren't there the last time she saw him.

Aran cleared his throat. He had a habit of doing that when he was ill at ease. "I didn't know you were in town."

"It was a last-minute thing."

"I see."

She averted her gaze. Her father's silent recrimination hung in the air. He had the uncanny ability to let her know he was disappointed in her without saying anything at all.

"You're welcome to stay at home."

"I already booked a room." Her reply came out a little too quickly. It had been years since she had slept under the same roof as her parents. Now was not the time to revisit that decision.

"Your mother misses you. You should come home."

Rune bristled. She knew he meant she should move back to New York. His words felt like a critique of every life decision she ever made. *This was a mistake*, she thought as she contemplated walking away.

"Thailand isn't a good place for you. You belong here, with us."

"I don't need a lecture, Dad." Rune regretted the words the instant they came out of her mouth. She and her father had never been good at communicating. Their relationship, such as it was before she was committed, revolved around his work. Her expression grew serious. His work was precisely why she had reached out to him. It was best to forget the chitchat and get on with it. "I called because I need your help."

"Oh?"

"Not here," she said when two park workers with rakes and pruning shears stopped within earshot. She led her father away from Bethesda Terrace, along a winding path bordering the Lake. Weeping willows kissed the surface of the water. The twin towers of the historic San Remo rose in the distance. She waited until she was sure they were alone before speaking again. "I'm working on something, and I need your expertise."

"I'm listening."

"The Kohl-Stromer ring is going up for auction today."

"Yes, I'm aware."

"I need information about it."

"Why?"

"That's not important."

Aran's face remained placid, but he spoke his next words carefully. "What is it you want to know?"

"You're still plugged into the high-end jewelry scene, right?"

"Yes."

"Do you happen to know who's on the market for the ring?"

"I wouldn't want to speculate."

"I'm asking you to."

The muscles around Aran's mouth twitched, like he was uncomfortable having to choose between disclosing sensitive information about his work and helping his daughter. He gave Rune a serious look. Then he cleared his throat again and said, "Rumor has it that Sarah Scofield is motivated."

"What can you tell me about her?"

He shrugged. "She's New York based. Comes from old money. She's been collecting colored gemstones for well over a decade. She bought a sapphire ring at Christie's Hong Kong for nearly $3 million a few years ago. Rectangular cut. Sixty-two carats. Very rare. She's quite knowledgeable." He seemed more relaxed now that they were on familiar ground.

"Have you had dealings with her?"

"Not personally, but B&B designed her daughter's engagement ring—a very nice pear-cut diamond." He was referring to his employers, a company in the Diamond District known for selling high-quality gemstones.

"Who else might be interested in the Kohl-Stromer ring?"

"The usual suspects—Bernard Turner, Vera Nielson, maybe Natalia Gomez." His voice trailed off.

"That's it?"

"It's a collector's piece. The market is small."

Rune nodded. Four potential buyers was manageable. She glanced at her watch. It was just past noon. The auction wasn't scheduled to start for another few hours. That gave her plenty of time to find out where the buyers lived and maybe learn something about their home security systems. She had already started digging into Sotheby's safety protocols—who they let into the saleroom, how they transferred lots to buyers, and so forth. Her posture relaxed somewhat until she heard her father's next words.

"I expect several anonymous buyers will also bid on the ring."

"Anonymous?" Rune echoed.

"The people I mentioned are locals. Some or all of them will be in the saleroom, but the ring will probably sell to an international buyer over the phone or online. Most gems of that size and quality are purchased anonymously, for obvious reasons."

"How can I find out who owns it if that happens?"

"You can't. That's the point."

"Right." Rune tried to keep the disappointment out of her voice. She must have failed because her father assumed a concerned expression.

"What's going on, Rune? You disappear for over a year and then you show up unannounced asking these strange questions."

"Nothing's going on."

The look on Aran's face suggested he wasn't buying it.

"I'm working for someone with an interest in the ring."

"A buyer?"

Rune weighed her next words carefully. Her father wasn't going to let this go. She didn't want to divulge information that might put him at risk, but for some reason, she wasn't prepared to lie to him either. She settled on being vague. "My employer is a gemstone dealer who's looking to grow his top-end customer base."

Aran's expression was openly skeptical now. He drew closer. His voice dropped to a whisper. "What have you gotten yourself into?"

"Nothing."

"Rune."

"Nothing. Really." She widened her eyes and shook her head for emphasis.

"You think I don't know when you're hiding something from me? You forget that I raised you."

"Mom did that. You were never around."

Aran looked confused and genuinely hurt. "That's not fair. What about all the afternoons we spent together?"

"You mean when I came to your office and watched you work?"

"I enjoyed our time together. I thought you did, too."

Rune couldn't stop herself from rolling her eyes. "I was ten, dad. It never occurred to you to take me to the park or out for ice cream like a normal parent?"

"You never said anything."

"Like I said, I was ten. I just wanted to spend time with you. And it's a good thing I did because you basically abandoned me after that."

His confusion deepened. "You were hospitalized. I'm not to blame for that."

Rune let out a long, frustrated breath.

"You pushed that girl. Her family wanted to press charges. You're lucky you ended up in a care facility and not juvenile detention."

Rune didn't bother defending herself. Her father hadn't believed her back then and he wasn't going to now. Still, hearing his words was like having an old wound ripped open. Grief flickered across her face. Being disbelieved by her parents was the single most damaging thing that had ever happened to her. Even worse than being locked up. Nothing her parents said or did after that could make up for it.

"Your mother and I did the best we could."

"Two years," Rune said before she could stop herself. "I spent two years in that place, and you didn't do anything about it."

Aran started to speak.

"I know, I know," she said, cutting him off with a wave of her hand. "It was that or juvie."

The two lapsed into an uncomfortable silence. Aran looked pained. Rune deeply regretted the turn the conversation had taken. After all these years, she knew better than to rehash the past. She had her truth, and her father had his—that was all there was to it. She searched for something to say, but the words wouldn't come. She had what she came for. It was time to cut her losses. "I have to get going," she said, making a studious effort to avoid his gaze.

"Rune . . ."

"Thanks for your help, Dad." Her mouth wavered between a grimace and a smile. She gave a half-hearted wave. She spun around and walked away before he could see the hot tears spill from her eyes.

40

Sotheby's, New York

The Kohl-Stromer sale went live at four o'clock that afternoon. Bidding proceeded at a brisk pace. The press office at Sotheby's had done a marvelous job of creating a buzz around the Kohl-Stromer collection over the past several months. Art lovers from around the world had flocked to the pre-auction viewings, oohing and aahing at the quality and scope of the lots on offer. And now, less than an hour into the first day of the sale, a number of big-ticket items had already smashed their estimates. The Richter sold to an anonymous collector who placed the winning $30 million bid by phone. The Pollock went for $1.5 million above its high estimate of $12 million, also to an anonymous buyer. But the surprise of the day was the Lucius Verus bust, which hammered down at a whopping $7 million, exactly ten times its low estimate. The buyer, a middle-aged woman who married well and divorced even better, was among the first to arrive at the auction house that afternoon, clearly preferring the excitement of the saleroom to the convenience and anonymity of bidding over the phone or online.

For a place that played host to the one percent, the seventh-floor saleroom at Sotheby's was surprisingly ordinary, with dove gray walls and exposed theater lights on the ceiling. A well-lit niche used to display lots dominated the front of the room. To the right was a lectern emblazoned with the company logo. Harold Stewart, a British-born auctioneer blessed with lustrous brown hair and piercing blue eyes, held court behind it. On either side of him was a veritable army of auction house employees tasked with handling telephone and online bidding. Behind them were screens displaying images of the lots, as well as the high and low estimates in a variety of currencies.

Unlike most people in the room, Rune did not hold a numbered paddle in her hand. She was not there to bid on a lot, she had something else in mind. She was unrecognizable in the navy-blue dress she had worn to meet her father just hours before. She had swapped her long dark ponytail for an auburn-colored wig slashed just below her jawline. A pair of tinted contact lenses toned down her striking hazel eyes. She looked good, but she didn't stand out, which was exactly the point as she observed the proceedings from the back of the room. She glanced at her catalog. The Kohl-Stromer ring was Lot 40—the last of the afternoon. They still had a way to go.

Rune's conversation with her father weighed heavily on her mind as the auction wore on. He seemed certain that the ring would sell anonymously. She sincerely hoped he was wrong. If not, stealing it would be next to impossible, and both she and Kit were sure to suffer the consequences. She flipped to the last page of the catalog and found the document she had made in preparation for this job. It consisted of photos and brief bios of all the collectors her father had mentioned, as well as their addresses and phone numbers.

Rune's current task was simple—to identify the buyer. The tricky business of finding out when, where, and how the ruby would come into their possession was a problem for later. Lemaire hadn't given her any instructions, but she was confident she could figure it out, so long as the ruby sold in the saleroom. It was what she did, after all.

Animated murmurs brought her attention back to the front of the room. The first of the Neo-Impressionist paintings was up for sale. Rune could barely see the display niche from where she was sitting, but she instantly understood what the fuss was about. Even from a distance, Paul Signac's *La Corne d'Or (Constantinople)*, 1907, was a sight to behold. The Turkish city and its recognizable landmarks looked positively ethereal as they floated in a miasma of pinks and yellows. With feathery brushstrokes and strategic highlights, the artist captured the frenetic movement of the modern metropolis, while also conjuring the glittering luminosity of its antique treasures.

"Ladies and Gentlemen, Lot number 21, a masterpiece by Signac," Harold said in an oh-so-posh British accent. He rubbed his hands together as if he were washing them. An excited smile crossed his lips. "I'm going to start the bidding at nineteen million dollars."

Rune lifted a brow in surprise. That was one million above the high estimate. The auctioneer had taken the temperature of the room and concluded that it was red hot. He obviously expected the painting to break records.

Harold deftly managed the crowd as bids flew at him from all directions, including from the staff handling distant bidding. The price went up in hundred-thousand-dollar increments until it reached $21.3 million. The bidding stalled. A silence fell over the crowd. Harold leaned forward, coaxing and cajoling the audience until the bids commenced again.

"We're at twenty-one point three million," he called out. "Do I hear twenty-one point four? We have twenty-one point four on the phone. Do I hear twenty-one point five?" And on like that it went until the hammer came down at $23 million. Like everyone else in the room, Rune was on the edge of her seat. Art auctions were all theater. And with stakes this high, nothing was more thrilling to watch.

The next hour flew by. Multimillion dollar auctions had that effect. By the time the Kohl-Stromer ring came up on the auction block, the atmosphere was positively electric. A picture of the ring flashed onto the screens. Murmurs rippled through the audience. People shifted in their chairs and craned their necks in anticipation. Although there wasn't much of a market for large, colored gemstones, when it came to blingy jewelry, everyone was a lookie-loo.

"Ladies and Gentlemen, Lot number 40," Harold announced from the lectern. He waited a few seconds for the room to settle, then launched into his well-rehearsed spiel. "At just over sixteen carats, the Kohl-Stromer ruby is one of the largest pigeon blood rubies ever to sell at auction—comparable only to the famed Jubilee Ruby and the equally famous Crimson Flame. Procured from the ancient mines of Myanmar's Mogok Valley, this premium-grade ruby is flawless in color, clarity, and cut. The ruby is mounted on a yellow gold band and surrounded by a halo of round-cut diamonds that lend the ring extraordinary cachet, while also adding tremendously to its value and beauty. Ladies and gentlemen, let's start the bidding at fifteen million dollars, shall we?"

A matronly blonde wearing all black and dripping with sapphires raised her paddle immediately. Rune glanced at her notes. It was Sarah Scofield, the New York–based collector her father told her about.

"Fifteen million," Harold said. "Do I hear fifteen point one?"

An attractive bald man with warm brown eyes and a neat goatee raised his paddle. Rune checked her notes again. It was Bernard Turner. She silently thanked her father for helping her out.

"We have fifteen point one, do I hear fifteen point two?"

An anonymous telephone bidder entered the mix.

"It's Genevieve's bidder at fifteen point two million dollars," Harold said, referring to a young Asian woman with a phone pressed to her ear. "Can we make it fifteen point three?"

The bidding went back and forth between the three buyers until they hit $16.4 million. A hushed silence descended on the room.

"I can sell to Genevieve's buyer at sixteen point four million dollars," the auctioneer said. He waited a beat. Then another. "Do you want to bid, madam?" he asked Sarah Scofield.

The woman kept her paddle firmly on her lap.

"And you, sir?"

Bernard Turner gave a disappointed shake of the head.

Rune's anxiety spiked. Her job would be next to impossible if the ring sold to the anonymous buyer. She willed someone in the room to place a bid, clenching her fists so tightly her nails left marks on her palms.

"It's still Genevieve's buyer at sixteen point four million dollars," Harold said. "Do I hear sixteen point five?"

The room remained silent. Harold raised both his arms. His keen blue eyes swept over the audience. Rune held her breath. It was over. She was out of luck.

"Sixteen point five," came a deep voice from the left-hand side of the room.

All heads turned sideways. There was a collective gasp. Rune sat up taller to get a better view, but she was too far back to see the man's face. *Who is he?* she thought as she flipped through her notes. Her father had only named one local male collector—Bernard Turner. The identity of this new bidder was a complete mystery.

"Sixteen point five million dollars," Harold declared in a tone that indicated an important buyer had entered the mix. He spun back toward the phones. "Do I hear sixteen point six, Genevieve?"

The Asian woman whispered into the phone and then raised her forefinger.

"Yes!" Harold exclaimed jubilantly. "Sixteen point six million dollars. It's with Genevieve's buyer. Can we make it sixteen point seven, sir?"

The mystery man lifted his paddle.

Smiling as widely as the Cheshire Cat, Harold prodded the buyers until the bidding reached $17.1 million. He leaned forward until his torso was practically hanging over the lectern. His voice crackled with energy. “Genevieve, the ball is in your court.”

She covered her mouth with her hand and exchanged words with her buyer. The conversation seemed to go on forever.

“Do I hear seventeen point two, Genevieve?” asked Harold. He waited a few seconds before adding, “Seventeen point two. Can you get us there, Genevieve?” A few more seconds passed. He raised both arms again. “The hammer is up.”

Genevieve locked eyes with him. The tension in her body was unmistakable. She whispered madly into the phone.

“The bid is seventeen point one million dollars. Fair warning. It’s not with you, Genevieve. It’s with the gentlemen at the front. Seventeen point one million for the Kohl-Stromer ring. Final call now.”

Crack!

The crowd gasped. Rune sprang to her feet. It was time to find out exactly who this mystery buyer was.

41

The Carlyle Hotel, New York

The mood was jovial at Bemelmans Bar on the ground floor of the Carlyle Hotel, where well-dressed patrons were celebrating summer in the city over strong cocktails and Kobe beef sliders. The Upper East Side venue was Old New York at its best—stodgy, exclusive, and staffed with experienced waiters in jaunty bowties and bright red jackets. Named after the Austrian-born author and illustrator, Ludwig Bemelmans, the candlelit bar boasted the only public display of Bemelmans's art anywhere in the world—a series of lampshades and, more important, a wraparound mural that paid tribute to Central Park. Bemelmans reputedly created the works in exchange for free accommodations at the hotel for a year and a half. His whimsical cast of characters, including dapper rabbits in suits, giraffes donning top hats, and a pipe-smoking dog, were a delight to locals and tourists alike.

Having drinks at Bemelmans was a longstanding tradition in New York's art circles, and it was easy to understand why. Around the corner was the Museum Mile and its world-class institutions—the Metropolitan Museum of Art, the Neue Galerie, the Solomon R. Guggenheim Museum, and the Cooper Hewitt Smithsonian Design

Museum, to name only a few. Two dozen art galleries could be found within a five-block radius of the bar, while the prestigious Institute of Fine Arts, the country's top graduate program in the history and conservation of art, occupied a nearby mansion. The Frick Collection, the Asia Society, and, of course, Sotheby's were only a short walk away. Given its location, the staff at Bemelmans was used to catering to a who's who of the art world. They witnessed celebrations of all kinds, including exhibition openings, newly minted degrees, and blockbuster sales. The bar charged a ten-dollar cover per person. A drink cost about twice that. Prices were steep, but expense accounts were made for exactly such occasions.

The art world was well represented at Bemelmans that evening. A group of senior staff from Sotheby's occupied the entire length of the banquette along the side of the room. Three curators from the Jewish Museum hosted a European colleague at a table near the piano. And at the bar was a mousy-looking graduate student having an animated discussion about Hegelian aesthetics with her bespectacled advisor. So focused were these individuals on their own narrow interests that they did not hear the elderly pianist's skilled rendition of *They Can't Take That Away from Me*, nor did they notice the caramel-skinned man seated alone by the entrance.

The man looked like a human Ken doll, if Ken were a seven out of ten. His sandy hair was thinning slightly on top but was otherwise well groomed. His teeth gleamed from hours in the dentist's chair. Nothing about his appearance hinted at the shrewdness that lay within. That his parents called him Dion—a name he shared with a tyrant from classical antiquity—was either a coincidence or a self-fulfilling prophecy.

Dion appeared relaxed with his rolled shirt sleeves and unbuttoned collar but, in reality, he was keenly aware of his surroundings. He was stone-cold sober, unlike everyone else at the bar. The expertly mixed negroni on the table in front of him did not present the slightest temptation. In truth, he had only ordered it to justify occupying a table. It was his job to be attentive. His salary was such that he never slacked off, but the stakes were higher than usual that night.

"I'd like to propose a toast," a man with a Germanic accent called out nearby.

Dion's head swiveled. The speaker was in his seventies with a large paunch and even larger jowls.

"To Karl Kohl-Stromer and raking in the commissions!" the man bellowed as he raised his martini glass and smiled like a demented clown. The people sharing his table cheered loudly enough to garner dirty looks from patrons seated nearby. Dion turned away from the bacchanalian celebration, judging the group to be obnoxious but ultimately harmless.

The sound of a glass shattering caught his attention. It came from a table on the far end of the room, where three young women laughed hysterically while a fourth tried to keep her espresso martini off her lap. A waiter hurried over to mop up the mess. Dion shook his head in disapproval. It was too early for people to be breaking things.

Quiet tittering drew his gaze to the table closest to him. One of the occupants was a fetching redhead whose face was in shadows. The other was a young man, the most important in the room as far as Dion was concerned. This was the man he was charged with protecting—a Herculean task, if ever there were one.

His name was Ioannis Dimitriou and he was impossible to miss. He looked like a Greek god, rakishly handsome, with a head of thick black hair and a strong jawline. His lips were full, his eyebrows enviably bushy. His musculature was so defined it made lesser men question their masculinity.

Ioannis moved through the world as if he owned it, and for all intents and purposes, he did. He was the son of a tobacco tycoon from Kalamata, a city in the Peloponnese in southern Greece. At twenty-three years of age, he had not yet found his calling—DJing in Ibiza was just a pastime—but he was fully committed to enjoying the fruits of his parents' labor. He had given higher education a try only to discover that the rigors of Oxford were not for him. His father had offered to show him the ropes of the family business on many occasions, but young Ioannis did not enjoy the inflexible hours. He was not a bad person, he was simply a dilettante, flitting about from one adventure to the next as only the superrich could. He took the same approach to dating. A playboy, the tabloids called him as they plastered his face across their papers with a different girl every week. A philandering heartbreaker.

The Dimitriou family owned a five-thousand-square-foot penthouse on Billionaires' Row just south of Central Park. The apartment boasted four bedrooms, five and a half baths, and a terrace with sweeping park views. Amenities included an athletic club, a saltwater swimming pool, a golf simulator, and a wine cellar. A star chef was slated to open a residents-only restaurant on the second floor. Celebrities and foreign investors occupied the neighboring units. Ioannis had access to all of this, yet he chose to stay at the Carlyle. The Upper East Side stalwart was stuffy for his taste. He would have preferred a boutique hotel in the Meatpacking District, the neighborhood of choice for the young and beautiful, but he was only in town for the night, and the Carlyle came strongly recommended by his contact at Sotheby's.

We work with them all the time, the sales rep said. *No hotel is better suited to our security protocols.*

Ioannis bought the Kohl-Stromer ring primarily to please his parents. They had been pressuring him to make something of his life for nearly a year, threatening to cut off his allowance if he didn't get his act together. Investing in gemstones was his latest passion project. The year before, he had opened a surfing school in a small Costa Rican town, only to be shut down by local authorities for not having the proper permits. Then he had tried his hand at organizing a music festival, a task that required no particular skills, but he didn't much care for the work. The gemstone idea came to him during an LSD-fueled night at the notoriously selective Berghain nightclub in Berlin. Red and green lights panned across the dance floor as he writhed to techno music inside the former powerplant. The colors were so luminescent, he swore he was looking at gems. The next day, he contacted sales associates in the jewelry departments at Sotheby's and Christie's to inquire about investment opportunities. It was then that he learned about the Kohl-Stromer ring. Bidding on it had been such a rush, he was certain he had found his calling. He couldn't wait to tell his parents.

The post sale team at Sotheby's was second to none. They had arranged to deliver the ring to his hotel room via armed courier within an hour of the auction's end. Even better, they had assigned a staff member to accompany him back to his suite.

White-glove service, the fetching redhead with the big eyes said as they climbed into the back of an Uber Black while Dion slid into the passenger seat. Her navy-blue dress was downright boring, but there was something about her cherry-red lips and coquettish smile that made Ioannis want to go to bed with her.

She called herself Effie. The two were now huddled in a dimly lit corner of Bemelmans, with Ioannis doing his best to cajole his way into her panties. He had a raging erection. The pianist was playing *When I Fall in Love*, at his request. He hoped the romantic gesture would seal the deal. As for the ring, it was securely tucked away in his in-room safe.

42

The Carlyle Hotel, New York

Rune knew the ring was hers the moment she laid eyes on Ioannis. There was an overconfident air about him, the kind that came naturally to the rich and attractive. She knew the type. She had watched guys like that from a distance her entire life. She meant to tell the waiter not to serve her any alcohol, but she conveniently forgot the moment she stepped into the bar. She was now on her second glass of Sancerre. Or was it her third? Ioannis's wandering hand crept higher up her thigh with every round. She let him have his way. She did it for Kit's sake, but it wasn't a huge imposition. Ioannis's touch was not unpleasant, or maybe it was simply better than she expected. Given the circumstances, the bar was pretty low.

Rune needed Ioannis drunk. So drunk he couldn't perform. So drunk he would pass out and stay that way for a very long time. The problem was, she was more than a little tipsy herself. She giggled as he nipped at her ear. She didn't pull away when his lips found her neck. She told herself it was all part of the play. And it was. But it didn't hurt that the guy looked like a *GQ* model.

"Do you want to join me upstairs?" Ioannis said as he ran his forefinger up and down her bare arm.

"What do you have in mind?"

"You, me, and some really good blow."

She pretended to mull it over. Then she made a face. "Coke gives me headaches. What else do you have?"

"Molly. Pot." He shot her a sly look. "And poppers, but only if you're into that kind of thing."

Rune's eyebrows rose. It seemed young Ioannis had quite a pair on him. She gave him a sultry nod. A smile unfurled on his face. He signed for the drinks. His hand found her buttocks as they left the bar with Dion following close behind.

"Take the night off," Ioannis said when they reached the elevator.

"Your parents wouldn't approve," replied Dion.

"But my parents aren't here now, are they?"

The elevator doors opened. Ioannis took Rune's hand and pulled her inside. Dion followed them with a scowl. Rune stuck her tongue down Ioannis's throat the moment the doors closed. She was embarrassed to do this in front of an audience, but it was the only way to avoid the security camera. Ioannis responded by caressing her breasts. His hands grew more insistent as the ride went on.

Hallelujah, Rune thought when the doors finally opened. They stepped off the cab and into a private landing on the twenty-sixth floor.

"Wait here," Dion said before disappearing into the suite.

Rune pulled away from Ioannis long enough to shoot him a questioning look.

"Security check," he said by way of explanation.

"You must be a very important man," Rune purred before finding his lips again. Her fingers ran through his lustrous hair. The minutes ticked away. *What the hell is taking so long?*

The door opened. Dion emerged. He gave Ioannis a brief nod and said, "I'll be downstairs if you need anything."

Ioannis waved him away and guided Rune into the suite. She let out a breathy "wow" before she could stop herself. It was a natural reaction. The suite was bigger than most New York City apartments, with a king-size bedroom, a full kitchen, and a separate living room complete with two couches and a grand piano. The muted décor, a tasteful blend of beiges and whites, was designed not to compete with the panoramic views of the Manhattan skyline visible through the floor-to-ceiling windows. Rune's eyes narrowed slightly once she recovered from the shock. The Kohl-Stromer ring was somewhere in the suite, but where?

Ioannis was on top of her in seconds. His hands were possessive, and they were everywhere. She took a firm hold of his groin. He froze long enough for her to untangle herself. Gentle petting was one thing, being manhandled was quite another.

"Why don't you pour us some drinks while I freshen up?" Rune said, keeping her voice low and sensual.

He grabbed her face with both hands and kissed her deeply. "Hurry back, Effie."

Rune went into the bathroom and locked it. Then she leaned her back against the door and brought her eyes to the ceiling. The room was bright—too bright after all that time at the bar. She walked over to the sink and splashed cold water on her face. "You can do this," she said, gazing at her reflection through her tinted contacts. She lowered her head and drank straight from the tap. Then she straightened her wig and strode back into the room.

Ioannis was waiting for her on the bed. Au naturel. Flag at full mast. He shot her a grin and patted the spot on the mattress next to him.

Good grief, Rune thought as she searched for an acceptable place for her eyes to land. She settled on his forehead. "Where's that drink?"

He retrieved two glasses filled with amber liquid from the nightstand and handed her one.

"What is it?"

"It's a surprise."

"Bottoms up," she said in an overly cheerful tone. She brought the glass to her lips but didn't drink. There was no way in hell she was ingesting whatever was in it.

Ioannis knocked his back in one go. Then he pulled himself off the bed and took the glass from her hand. He spun her around so that she faced the mirror hanging directly across from the bed. She let him unzip her demure dress. She even helped him slip it off her. She drew the line when he reached for her pretty lace bra.

"Slow down," she murmured, physically removing his hands from her breasts. "I have something in mind."

Ioannis didn't like waiting, but he was willing to play along. With coke coursing through his system, the payoff could be huge.

"Sit," she whispered in his ear.

He lowered himself onto the bed. Outside the window, the city glimmered beneath the inky sky.

"You taste good," she breathed as she straddled him and started grinding into his body.

"So do you, Effie."

She allowed his hands to explore her before grabbing a fistful of hair and yanking so hard his head snapped back. He inhaled sharply.

"You like that?" she asked, running a nail over his chest and nipping at his neck.

"Yes!" he hissed.

"Then you'll love what comes next. Close your eyes."

He acquiesced.

"Stay right where you are."

He groaned in disappointment when she pulled away. She fetched a sash from the curtains and used it to cover his eyes. He raised his hand reflexively.

"Nuh-uh," she said. "No peeking."

"Christ," he cried when their mouths met.

Rune tightened the sash behind his head and kissed him again. She smiled as she backed away to admire her handiwork.

"Where'd you go, sexy?" he asked after a few seconds.

She didn't respond.

"Effie?"

Whack!

One strike, and he was out cold.

43

The Carlyle Hotel, New York

Rune worked tirelessly while Ioannis lay unconscious on the king-size bed, his once rock-hard penis flopped ignominiously on his stomach. A trail of blood seeped from where the table lamp hit his head. He looked pale, but his breathing was steady, much to her relief. She couldn't help thinking that if she got caught, the charge would be assault and not murder. *Thank goodness for small favors*, she said silently.

The first order of business was locating the safe. Rune searched all the closets, no small feat in the giant suite. She then moved on to the furniture. She finally found it hidden inside a faux cabinet in the living room, right next to the bedroom door. *Success!*

Her elation faded almost immediately. The safe was a rather large AMSEC fire and burglary safe with a mechanical lock and a half-inch steel plate door. It figured. The AMSEC was far better quality than the flimsy lockboxes that passed for in-room safes in most hotels. Worse, she had no experience with this model. Her greatest wish was to pick it up and make a run for it, but it was made of fire-resistant material and weighed almost four hundred pounds. It was also bolted to the floor. What she needed more than anything was a forklift. What she had were her hands. Locksmiths and burglars relied on a plethora of techniques to crack safes—weak-point drilling, scoping, and x-rays, to name a few—but Rune was self-taught and as old school as they came. She did it by touch. Her method had one distinct advantage—she was never without her tools. The drawback—it was always a protracted affair. She lowered herself onto the rug and got comfortable, knowing she was in it for the long haul.

Thirty minutes flew by. Rune sat perfectly still with her cheek pressed to the steel door. She was listening to the tumblers inside the locking mechanism as they turned, measuring internal movements with the dial numbers. It was delicate work, especially with newer safes. Manufacturers were now crafting wheels from lightweight materials that reduced sensory feedback, making a difficult task nearly impossible. But for Rune, it wasn't a question of if she could crack the safe, it was a question of when. She just hoped Ioannis would stay down for the duration.

Rune's shoulders were aching by the end of the hour. Her fingers were numb from repeating the same movements. All she had to show for her painstaking work was the first number of a three-part combination. She sprang to her feet, pacing the room and shaking her hands to coax blood back into her limbs. When that failed to perk her up, she reached for her phone.

A pizza arrived soon after. Rune grabbed a slice and bit into it as she carried the box into the living room and set it on the coffee table. The crust was a bit soggy and the sauce was sweeter than she cared for, but the options were limited in this neighborhood. She wolfed down three slices, dusted the crumbs off her dress, and got back to work.

Another half hour came and went with no progress whatsoever. "Focus," Rune said out loud as she fought through her fatigue. She cracked her fingers and massaged her palms. She thought of making herself a pot of coffee but quickly nixed the idea. For this kind of work, a steady hand was key.

Her body stiffened when she heard a pained grunt from the other room. She turned just as Ioannis was lifting his head off the bed. The curtain sash had slipped off his face. His eyes were wide open. He was staring straight at her. "Is that you, Effie?" he asked, his speech low and slurred.

"Go back to sleep, baby," she called out.

His head dropped back onto the pillow as if he'd been shot.

For several seconds, Rune didn't dare breathe. Only when she heard Ioannis snoring softly did she get back to the task at hand.

The close call must have flipped a switch in her mind, because the second number of the three-part sequence came only moments later. Encouraged, she redoubled her efforts. She was working against the clock now. Ioannis could wake up at any moment. There was also Dion to consider. The crabby bodyguard had thrown all kinds of shade her way when they were at Bemelmans, not to mention that he looked like the kind of person who never slept. She threw a glance over her shoulder. Ioannis was still out, but he wouldn't stay that way indefinitely. *Breathe,* she said silently. She closed her eyes and let her fingers move the dial one millimeter at a time.

Rune knew the moment she had it. It was a feeling more than a sound. Somewhere between a click and a pop. She spun the dial a few times to clear the lock and then entered the combination: 7-3-9. The drive cam notches lined up. The fence dropped. "YESSSSS," she hissed triumphantly. She gave the handle a gentle pull and opened the door, revealing the Kohl-Stromer ring in all its glory.

The ring sat in a velvet-lined box that was a deep shade of blue. Ioannis had left it open, like it was on display in a jewelry store rather than tucked away in his hotel safe. Rune barely gave it a glance as she plucked it out of the box and slipped it into her pocket. She stopped herself mid-gesture. The last time she put gemstones in her pocket, things didn't turn out so well. She slid the ring onto the fourth finger of her left hand without a second thought. Time was running short. She closed the safe and gave the dial a quick spin, watching as the numbers blurred into a hazy white ring. After it stopped turning, she grabbed a towel from the bathroom and systematically wiped every surface she had touched. A few minutes was all it took for the room to look spick and span. She reached into the pizza box and stuck a slice in her mouth. It tasted better cold. She made her way to the door, paused, then doubled back and scrawled the word "thanks!" in cherry red lipstick on the bedroom mirror. Satisfied, she exited the room and quietly shut the door.

44

The Carlyle Hotel, New York

Rune kept a firm grip on her pizza box as she stood in the elevator landing and punched the call button. "Come on, come on, come on," she said under her breath as she watched the numbers light up. The doors chimed open. She stepped inside. She kept her head low and angled away from the camera as she rode down to the lobby.

Her face was flushed. Her eyes were bright with excitement. This was the biggest job she had ever attempted, on the fly no less. Pulling it off left her feeling euphoric. It didn't matter that she was working for Lemaire. She wasn't at all interested in keeping or selling the ring. It was the feeling she was after. That, and freeing Kit.

The elevator doors dinged open. Rune glanced furtively in both directions before exiting. The lobby was deserted, even the reception desk. The black marble floor was so shiny she could see her reflection in it. She dropped the pizza box in an unattended room service cart. All she had to do now was make it through the revolving doors and she was home free.

A crowd loitering on the sidewalk in front of the hotel stopped Rune dead in her tracks. Evidently Bemelmans Bar was a popular choice that night. There were dozens of people milling about, all of them pleasantly drunk. The air smelled of booze and expensive perfume mixed with cigarette smoke. Rune coughed as she wove her way through their midst. She had almost reached the other side when she felt a hand on her arm. *Ioannis!* She spun around, ready for a fight. Her face softened when she saw a young woman with a low-cut top and too much makeup waving her phone at her.

"Hi! Sorry to bother you, but would you mind taking our picture?" the woman asked, tilting her head to one side like a curious puppy. Her accent was full of South Carolina twang.

"Um," Rune said.

"It won't take a second."

"Okay. Sure."

The woman wrapped her arms around a much older man who looked to be in the throes of a midlife crisis. His shirt was unbuttoned a bit too far. His pants were tight and equipped with too many pockets and zippers.

"Ready?" Rune said.

The man looked pained.

"One, two, three, say cheese!"

The woman flashed a huge smile, revealing a smear of fuchsia lipstick on her teeth.

"Here you go," Rune said, handing back the phone.

"Thanks! We just got engaged!"

"Congratulations."

She giggled and did what all newly engaged women did—she stuck out her hand to show off her ring.

"It's very beautiful," Rune said automatically. It took her all of two seconds to appraise the ring. Tiffany solitaire. Round brilliant cut. Diamond-encrusted platinum band. As unimaginative as it was over-priced. She silently chastised the man for putting so little thought into his fiancée's engagement ring. He was probably the type who bought red roses on Valentine's Day, too.

"Oh my gaaawd!" the woman exclaimed, grabbing Rune's hand and drawing it up to her face. "Your ring is incredible!"

Rune tried to pull back, but the woman's grip was unexpectedly firm.

"Hon, come take a look at her ring!"

The sugar daddy obliged with some reluctance. Rune shifted her weight from one foot to the other.

"I don't think I've ever seen a ruby that size! Have you?" The woman's voice was so loud people around them were starting to stare.

"It's just a cocktail ring," Rune blurted out. She wanted the conversation to end immediately.

The woman let out an embarrassed laugh. Her fiancé looked relieved not to have been outdone by a stranger.

"I picked it up at a flea market," Rune added for good measure.

"Well, bless your heart. You certainly had me fooled." The woman gave her a pitying look and released her hand.

Relieved, Rune congratulated the happy couple again and bid them good night. She dropped her eyes as she turned away.

A flash of the ruby. That was all she saw, but it was enough to make her look more closely. She raised her hand and angled it so that the gem caught the light spilling out of the hotel lobby. Her reaction was visceral. Her skin turned white. A visible tremor ran through her body.

"Are you okay, hon?" the woman asked.

Her drawl pierced through the fog in Rune's brain. She locked eyes with her. She opened her mouth to speak, but no words would come out.

"Do you want us to call someone for you?"

Rune shook her head. Her face was stricken, her eyes were wild. "It's not possible," she finally whispered.

The Kohl-Stromer ring was a fake.

Perhaps it was professional pride. Or maybe just necessity. Whatever the reason. Rune was able to collect herself and convince the newly engaged couple that she wasn't having a stroke. She took off the ring and brought it close to her face the instant she parted ways with them. There was no question. It was not the ring she saw in the gallery at Sotheby's that morning. For one thing, the central stone was darker and duller than the genuine ruby. She ran her thumbnail back and forth across the top a few times, leaving a slight scratch on the surface. *A worthless composite*, she thought with an incredulous look. The ring might have fooled the average person, but not her. She had her father to thank for that.

Once again in full possession of her faculties, Rune's mind raced to make sense of what had happened. It didn't take long for her to come up with two likely scenarios. Either someone at Sotheby's had swapped the rings, or the switch happened when the ring was in transit from the auction house to the hotel. Although Rune could not discount the first possibility outright, she instinctively knew that the likelihood of a breach happening at Sotheby's was slim, at best. The building had a top-of-the-line security system. Not only that, but all the employees went through rigorous background checks before they were hired. The second scenario seemed more plausible. Rune thought about the security company that transported the ring from the auction house to the Carlyle. *Maybe it was one of the drivers*, she said to herself. She rejected the idea almost as soon as it entered her mind. She hadn't noticed anything amiss when the transfer occurred, and she had been right by Ioannis's side the entire time. Her confusion grew. No one else had the means or opportunity to make the swap. Dion went so far as to make her wait at the bar while he and Ioannis took the ring upstairs and locked it in the safe.

Dion. The realization hit Rune like a battering ram. Dion had spent a long time alone in the room before allowing her and Ioannis to enter. A security check, Ioannis had said. But was it? It seemed impossible, but the more Rune thought about it, the more certain she became. The thief was not a Sotheby's employee or a clever outsider from the transport company. The thief was none other than Dion.

45

The Carlyle Hotel, New York

Rune stormed back into the hotel with fire in her belly and her face set in a look of pure determination. She hadn't gone to all this trouble only to have someone steal the ring right out from under her. What was she supposed to tell Lemaire? That the ring was gone? That she got there too late? There wasn't a chance in hell he would believe her. She was going to get that ring even if it required facing a hundred Dions. She had the right attitude. If the last few days had taught her anything, it was that bigtime criminals were rampant in the high-priced gemstone trade.

The reception desk was still unmanned, and that was a good thing. Rune went straight to the staff computer and jiggled the mouse. The screen lit up. She typed Dion's name into the search box hoping to find his room number. Her search yielded zero results. She tried typing Ioannis's name, but the only room that popped up was the Presidential Suite on the twenty-sixth floor—the one she was in only minutes before. She paused to think for a moment, then she clicked on SHOW ALL. A list of every guest in the hotel appeared on the screen. Her eyes found the SORT BY tab. Dion would have checked in at the same time as Ioannis. She selected DATE and started scrolling.

"Can I help you?" a voice called out from across the lobby.

Rune looked up. The speaker was the concierge, a clean-shaven man wearing a pinstriped suit and a no-nonsense expression. Despite his playful koala-themed tie, Rune knew right away that he was not the kind of person who could be sweet talked into doing her bidding. If she walked away now, she would never get what she needed. She dropped her gaze to the screen and went back to scrolling.

"Excuse me, ma'am, but you can't be back there."

Rune heard him move toward her. She didn't budge.

"Ma'am, step away from the computer or I'll have you escorted out."

Still she kept scrolling.

"Security!"

A uniformed guard with dark eyes and an ironic mustache showed up out of nowhere. He grabbed Rune by the arm, pulled her out from behind the desk, and marched her to the door. She didn't apologize or try to explain herself. There was no point. It wasn't as if she would ever see these people again.

The guard pushed Rune onto the sidewalk with both hands. She fell hard on her backside. The crowd had thinned somewhat in the minutes she had spent inside, but there were still a dozen or so merrymakers by the front door. They gawked as the guard flung a series of vulgar epithets at her, but she didn't care. All that mattered was getting back inside and finding Dion and the ring. She rose to her feet. Her mind raced, searching for an alternate way in. She gazed up at the hotel as if one would somehow appear.

A ladder did not descend from the sky, nor did a magical beanstalk sprout from the earth, but something just as unlikely occurred—Dion emerged from the hotel. He had traded his button-down for a dark t-shirt. A Yankees baseball cap covered his sandy hair. There was no mistaking him, despite the change in attire. He walked right past Rune, so distracted by his phone that he failed to notice her.

The encounter left Rune too stunned to react. Then she got a hold of herself and scrambled after him, darting through the crowd until there was no one left between them. She followed him down the street, keeping a safe distance until he turned on East 75th Street. She peeked around the corner and saw him duck into a parking garage midway down the block. *Follow or wait*? she asked herself. The garage would be empty at this hour. There was every chance he would see her. She lingered in the shadow of a building across the street hoping he would exit from the same side.

Nearly ten minutes elapsed before Rune saw the nose of a black sedan climb the parking ramp. She squinted, hoping to see inside the dark interior. It had to be him. No one else had entered the garage. The car inched forward until it reached the street. The dome light came on. The driver's back was in full view as he reached for something in the glove box. His torso twisted back around. The light went out, but not before Rune caught a glimpse of his face. It was Dion alright. She was sure of it.

He took a right on East 75th Street followed by another right onto Madison Avenue. Only when his taillights disappeared did Rune start running. She was panting heavily when she reached the end of the street. Her head whipped from one side to the other. A yellow cab was stopped at the intersection. Two tanned blondes in short skirts and strappy sandals were walking toward it. One had her arm extended. It was clear she was reaching for the door handle.

"Move! I have an emergency!" Rune said as she jostled her way passed them. She slid into the backseat and slammed the door before they even knew what was happening.

"Hey!" one of them exclaimed.

Rune slapped the lock with her palm.

"Seriously?" hollered the other.

The light turned green.

"Where to, ma'am?" the driver asked, unfazed by the commotion.

"Follow that car," she said, pointing at the sedan.

The cabbie eyed her warily from the rearview mirror.

She thrust a fifty-dollar bill through the acrylic shield and yelled, "Go!"

He took off the way only a New York City cabbie motivated by a big fare could, accelerating so fast Rune slammed back into her seat. She saw the sedan take a left turn on East 79th Street. The cab followed, pulling to a stop directly behind it at the corner of Fifth Avenue. Rune leaned forward and placed her hands on the partition. Her eyes were locked on Dion's car. Her temple pulsed as she willed the streetlight to change. The wait dragged on so long she jumped when it finally turned green.

The sedan went straight through the intersection to the transverse road through Central Park. The cab followed, but not too closely. They drove under a bridge and then another until they hit a red light in front of the central office of the FDNY. The cab slowed, but Dion blew right through it. Her driver shot her a questioning look as if to ask if he should follow.

"Just wait," Rune said. The road went straight through the park. There were no turn-offs, no places to lose a tail. Better to play catch up than risk tipping her hand.

The gamble paid off. A few minutes later, she spotted the sedan idling at the intersection of the transverse road and Central Park West, signaling a right turn. The cab pulled up behind it. The light changed almost right away.

The two cars stayed on Central Park West until they reached the traffic circle marking the entrance into Harlem. They sped north, passing an unsightly mix of crumbling brick tenements and expensive new condos built by developers with too much money and not enough good taste. They soon reached the edge of Sugar Hill—a neighborhood most New Yorkers didn't know existed. Dion took a left turn. The cab driver followed suit, slowing to a stop when he saw the sedan parallel park on a deserted side street. He looked at Rune with worry. This was not the sort of neighborhood to frequent alone at night. Rune shared his concern, but it didn't stop her from springing out of the cab. It wasn't bravery driving her. Simply a lack of options.

Rune spotted Dion heading toward the 155th Street viaduct. She followed until she found herself beneath the soaring metal structure. On one side loomed the Polo Grounds Towers, a densely packed housing complex built to house the city's poor. On the other side were shuttered businesses, including a tiny bodega and a rundown auto service shop. Graffiti tarnished just about every building on the block.

Dion stopped in front of a two-story warehouse. He grabbed the padlock securing the steel shutter and yanked, cursing when it remained closed. Out came his phone. The conversation that followed was short and intense. Rune strained to hear Dion's side, but the cars speeding along the overpass drowned out the sound.

What the hell is he doing here? she wondered after he hung up and started pacing in front of the warehouse. He lit a cigarette. It glowed every time he took a drag—a faint sign of life on the otherwise dark block.

Rune didn't know what to do. She didn't even know if the Kohl-Stromer ring was still in Dion's possession. She tried to come up with a plan as she watched Dion puff on his cigarette. He had seemed so calm and self-assured in Ioannis's presence. To see him pace with agitated energy did not fit with the image she had of him.

Rune jumped when a black Audi with custom rims pulled up not long after. She was so surprised that she barely had time to flatten herself against one of the viaduct's piers before the engine stopped.

What she saw when she dared look around the corner was intriguing, to put it mildly. A tall man in a tailored suit emerged from behind the wheel. His skin glowed like burnished copper against his white t-shirt. On his feet were expensive Air Jordans. The man twirled his keys on his index finger as he sauntered to the back of the car. He popped open the trunk. Out came a large duffle bag with a Ralph Lauren logo on the side. The fabric bulged at the center, straining against the contents. The man slung the bag over his shoulder and went to the passenger side to open the door for a stunning woman wearing a purple dress so tight it looked to be painted on. They walked toward the warehouse. The man shook Dion's hand and unlocked the gate. The shutter rolled up. Into the building they went.

What are they up to? Rune thought after they vanished from view. She crept a little closer to try to see inside. When that failed, she hurried across the street and pressed her ear to the door. With the cars roaring overhead, it was an exercise in futility. Rune's posture sank. A reluctant expression clouded her features. The last thing she wanted was to get mixed up in whatever was going on between Dion and his visitors but, once again, what she wanted really didn't matter.

46

Upper Manhattan

The sound of the door unlatching. The squeak of a hinge. The scraping of soles on the hard floor. The silence of the hour seemed to amplify every sound, but Rune was undeterred. Her need to get her hands on the Kohl-Stromer ring overshadowed all other thoughts, including self-preservation. She was worried, but not overly so. From the looks of the warehouse, it would be easy to find a place to hide.

The ground floor was equipped with floor to ceiling shelves coated with years of dust and grime. The space was lit by a single exposed bulb that hung from a rafter with visible signs of rot. Wood pallets lay discarded on the concrete flooring, alongside hand trucks with busted wheels and a rusted forklift that was missing some of its parts. It was clear that the warehouse had been out of use for a good long time.

Rune heard voices coming from the second floor, but the sound was too faint to make out any words. She approached the steel staircase with the utmost caution. She didn't have a clue what was waiting for her upstairs, but she knew it was sketchy and almost certainly dangerous. She placed her foot on the first step. She was about to transfer her weight when her phone vibrated in the pocket of her dress. She froze.

The conversation upstairs stopped. She heard footsteps directly above her head. Her body tensed as she prepared to bolt.

Five . . . four . . . three . . . two . . . one . . .

"It's nothing," said the unknown man just as she was about to take flight. "Probably just rats."

"Gross," came the woman's voice.

Gross is right, Rune thought. There was more shuffling upstairs. The sound receded. She let out a breath and then pulled out her phone to see who had texted.

Do you have it?

It was Lemaire asking for an update on the ring. She wanted to fling her phone across the room. Instead she typed, *Working on it.*

The response came almost immediately. *You'd better be.*

Rune hit the middle finger emoji, paused, then deleted it. Antagonizing Lemaire was not in her or Kit's best interest. She replaced it with a thumbs up, silenced the phone, and slid it back into her pocket.

The voices coming from the second floor grew more audible as Rune climbed the staircase. She managed to get midway up before stepping on a busted tread. It clanked under her weight. She froze again and listened for signs that she had given herself away. Hearing none, she continued her ascent.

The second level was nothing like the ground floor. It was brighter. Cleaner. It did not look like it had been abandoned last century. It also lacked the shelves of the lower level. In their place were metal lockers of varying sizes, including units large enough to store furniture. The warehouse was being used as a storage facility, but for what?

Rune followed the voices coming from behind a row of lockers. She stopped when she was sure they were just around the corner. She crouched slightly and stole a look. What she saw made her want to run away and never look back.

The man in the suit had opened several lockers, revealing enough weaponry to equip a small army. He was laying different kinds of guns on a metal table—revolvers, semi-automatic pistols, assault rifles—handling them with something approaching reverence. A new fear took hold of Rune. Gemstone trafficking was one thing, guns were quite another. She was in open water now.

"This is everything?" Dion asked. He was eager to close the deal, but he didn't want to give that away. Information was power in any negotiation, and he was determined to maintain the upper hand.

"Not quite."

Dion watched as the arms dealer lifted his duffel bag onto the table. The woman in the purple dress busied herself with her phone. Her long, bejeweled nails clicked against the screen while she typed.

"If untraceable is what you're after, nothing beats ghost gun kits."

"How do they work?" Dion asked.

"Let me show you." The dealer unzipped the bag, revealing small plastic boxes with no markings of any kind. He pulled one out. "These just came in from Virginia."

"The iron pipeline?"

"Uh-huh."

The woman interrupted her typing long enough to ask, "How much longer is this going to take?"

The dealer continued as if she hadn't spoken. "This kit is for a polymer pistol. It's basically a knockoff of a Glock 19. They're in high demand."

"Hmmm." Dion's interest was piqued.

"This is the frame," the dealer explained as he pulled the lower receiver out of the box and held it up.

Dion leaned in to get a better look.

"Each kit also comes with a slide, a barrel, and a trigger mechanism. All you have to do is put them together."

"And you said the guns are untraceable?"

"Completely. You can order legit kits online and bring them in from other states, but the Feds are cracking down." He placed his hand on his duffel bag and added, "My guns don't have serial numbers. Plus, you get to skip the background check and mandatory waiting period."

"How easy are they to assemble?"

"A kid could do it." The dealer snapped the pieces together with practiced hands. In no time, he had a functioning gun. "Legal kits require drilling and filing, plus extra parts. These are the IKEA of kits. Everything is included—frame, pins, springs—everything."

"How do I know they work?"

The dealer's brow flicked up. "Are you calling me a liar?"

"No. I'm protecting my investment."

"These kits are top-notch. No one has ever complained." The dealer sauntered over to a nearby locker and punched in a four-digit code. The door popped open with a soft click. He pulled out a box of 9mm ammunition and loaded a few rounds into the ghost gun's magazine. The slide clicked when he pulled it back to chamber a bullet. He aimed at Dion.

"Get that out of my face."

The dealer smirked and pointed the gun to the back of the room.

Bang!

Dion flinched in spite of himself. So did the woman in purple.

"You want to give it a try?" the dealer asked with a sly grin.

"That won't be necessary."

"Suit yourself." He placed the gun on the table.

Dion gazed at it, impressed.

"There are fifty kits in here," the dealer said as he zipped up the duffel bag. "My supplier can deliver that many every month. Are you interested in working with him?"

"Very."

"I'll make it happen."

Dion gave a curt nod. His backers would be pleased. He relaxed somewhat and patted himself on the back, not just for closing the deal, but for being in a position to do so at all. It was sheer luck that brought him together with the Dimitriou family. Although babysitting Ioannis had been tiresome, it put him in contact with powerful people—the kind with deep pockets and no scruples. Finally, after nearly two years of maneuvering, he was about to take over a lucrative gun-running business that would make him one of the most powerful men on the East Coast. The Kohl-Stromer ring was the final piece of the puzzle—the one thing he hadn't planned on, but that made the deal possible. He didn't understand its appeal. Then again, he didn't have to.

"Are you still with me?" the dealer asked, as if sensing that Dion's mind had strayed.

"I'm with you."

"Everyone is onboard—suppliers, runners, buyers. Even my police contacts. My business is now your business."

"That settles it, then."

"Not quite." The dealer gave Dion a thin smile. "I showed you mine. Now it's your turn."

Dion hesitated briefly before reaching into his pocket and handing over the Kohl-Stromer ring.

The dealer held it up to the light and let out a long, low whistle. "There she is."

The woman in purple stopped typing.

"A piece like that isn't easy to move," Dion remarked.

"You let me worry about that." The dealer pocketed the ring. The woman looked disappointed that he didn't put it on her finger.

"We have a deal then," said Dion.

"We have a deal."

They're leaving! Rune realized as she watched the two men shake hands. She couldn't let that happen—she couldn't lose the ring a second time. Her alarm grew as the man in the suit started packing up the weapons. One gun after another disappeared inside the lockers. Soon all that remained was the newly assembled ghost gun. The man reached for it. The woman in purple made a move for the staircase. Rune didn't think. She just acted, striding out from behind the lockers with confidence she was far from feeling. "Wait!" she called out. Her voice was loud and unnaturally high. All eyes swung toward her.

"You!" exclaimed Dion.

Rune ignored him and kept her focus on her mark. She scrambled for what to say next.

"Who the hell are you?" the dealer demanded.

"I'm the person saving you from making the biggest mistake of your life."

The man scoffed.

"Dion is scamming you. You can't trust him."

Another scoff.

"I'm telling you the truth. The ring he gave you—it's a fake."

"She's full of shit," said Dion.

A glimmer of doubt passed over the man's face. He picked the ghost gun off the table.

"You don't believe me? Check my pocket." Rune saw the man's doubt grow. He was mistrustful by nature. Her words had tapped into his suspicions. She angled her body closer to him. "Go on. See for yourself."

The man pointed his gun at her and patted her down with his free hand. His features hardened when he felt the ring. He reached into her pocket and pulled it out. He looked at it for a moment. His eyes moved from Rune to Dion. "One of you better tell me what the hell is going on."

Dion's mouth hung open slightly, like he couldn't quite believe what was happening. When he finally spoke, he did so quickly and without taking a breath. "She's lying. She's a hustler. A con artist. My dimwitted employer picked her up at Sotheby's."

"He's the con," Rune spat back. "He had a replica made of the ring and gave it to you thinking you wouldn't know the difference. He thinks you're stupid. He's making a fool out of you."

The genuine Kohl-Stromer ring came out of the man's pocket. He now had both rings in his hand.

"Look at the ring he gave you," Rune said, the words rushing out as fast as she could form them. "It's a darker color. That's a sign that it's fake. Real pigeon blood rubies are lighter red."

The man drew the rings closer to his face and squinted.

"You can't believe a word she says," sputtered Dion, realizing for the first time that he was in trouble.

"Hold his ring up to the light," Rune continued. "You can see the imperfections. Do you think a place like Sotheby's could sell a flawed gemstone for $17 million? Dion swapped them. He gave you a piece of junk—a cheap composite." Rune's entire body was tight. She blinked rapidly. Her mind flashed to her early childhood lesson: *Truth doesn't matter. People only see what they want to see, especially those with something to lose. Everyone has something to lose.*

"She's a liar," Dion said. "Don't fall for it."

The man's eyes became slits of anger. He pointed his gun at Dion. Then he swung it back toward Rune. Back and forth he went until Rune was sure she would die of terror.

Bang!

The sound was sudden. Deafening. It happened so fast Rune wasn't sure if she had been shot. She looked down at her body fully expecting to see a bullet wound. A dull thunk directed her attention to the floor.

"Jesus Christ," she whispered.

Dion lay on his back in a growing pool of blood. The bullet had entered his chest just below the left clavicle, shattering one of his ribs. He was still alert when he hit the ground, but only for a second. He was gone before Rune could react.

"Wait for me in the car," the man said to the woman in purple.

She didn't move. She looked petrified.

"I said go to the car!"

The woman gave Rune a look that bordered on apologetic before scurrying away. It was all Rune could do not to scream for her to stop. The man approached once they were alone. It was only after he invaded her personal space that she noticed the minute drops of blood on his white shirt. She stared at them, imagining it was her blood splattered all over the place and her body crumpled on the floor. *Please don't shoot me, please don't shoot me*, she repeated silently.

The man leaned in until his face almost touched hers. It was a grotesque distortion of her first encounter with Kit. His next words drew a faint cry from her. "Don't think you're off the hook. I'm going to kill you, too."

Rune whimpered softly. The man's breath felt like fire against her skin. She couldn't stop herself from shaking.

"But before I do, you and I are going to have a little talk."

"I'll tell you anything you want to know. Just don't kill me. Please don't kill me."

Rune recoiled when he bared his teeth at her. She gasped when he spun her around and wrapped a muscular arm around her neck. Her hands flew up to relieve the pressure. She clawed at his wrists, but that only made him squeeze harder. Her face turned purple. A strangled sound came out of her mouth. She felt herself start to slip away. *No!* she screamed internally, but there was nothing to be done. First her vision became clouded. Then she blacked out.

“Get it together. You’re not finished yet,” Kit said. He placed his hands on her shoulders and gave her a firm shake.

Rune wanted more than anything for that to be true, but every part of her body felt bruised, like it had been tumble-dried for an hour. Blood dripped from a deep gash on her cheek. Her left eye was swollen shut. She gazed at her opponent across the boxing ring with her good eye. The woman looked huge under the arena’s bright lights. She was built like a tank, with a crop top and twin French braids that were incongruously girlish given her size and musculature. Her name was Prim Thongchai and she was a three-time winner of the IFMA World Muay Thai Championships. Rune didn’t understand why she was in the ring with this woman. Her Muay Thai skills, while passable, were no match for an elite fighter. They weren’t even in the same weight class. They had already gone two rounds, but Prim didn’t have a mark on her. In fact, she had barely broken a sweat.

“Focus,” Kit said, snapping her back to attention.

Rune’s unsteady gaze found his.

“Use your legs.”

She nodded vigorously.

“Speed is key. Go after her and don’t let up, understand?”

She nodded again.

The bell dinged. Cheers rang out from the packed stands.

“Now get in there!”

The two women met in the middle of the ring. Prim towered over her. Her biceps were more than twice the size of Rune’s. Her legs were lean and strong. Rune immediately brought her gloved hands up into a defensive position. She tried to hold Prim back with a couple of jabs. The woman responded with a push kick followed by a right hook that sent electric shocks through Rune’s jaw. She shook her head to clear it and threw a straight punch, but Prim dodged it easily. Rune didn't even see the knee strike coming. She felt a rib crack. She fell to the floor. The audience roared.

"Get up!" Kit yelled over the din of the crowd.

She turned toward him and gave a slight shake of her head.

"Come on, Rune! Get on your feet and fight!"

She could hear the audience jeering. She closed her eyes, trying to summon the strength to stand.

"Get up!" Kit shouted.

She sniffed loudly and wobbled to her feet.

The referee stood between her and Prim. He asked if she could continue. She gave a terse nod. He stepped out of the way. Prim sprang forward.

"Offense! Offense!" Kit screamed.

Prim closed in.

Rune blocked a couple of strikes with her gloved hands before moving into a rapid jab-jab-cross sequence. To her surprise, her fist connected with Prim's nose. A spray of blood painted the air scarlet. The crowd went wild. Rune was elated, but the feeling was short-lived. Prim recovered quickly. She wiped the blood from her face with the back of her arm and set her sights on Rune's aching ribs, unleashing three quick body hooks that left her gasping for air. Rune doubled over, cradling her stomach. The referee stepped in again.

"Get back in there, Rune! You can do it!" Kit yelled.

The audience booed when she remained hunched over. It was a ploy to run down the clock and everyone knew it. The referee issued a warning. Prim smirked from across the ring. She knew it was just a matter of time before the match was hers. She lifted her arms as though she had already won, sending the crowd into a frenzy.

The goading reenergized Rune. Her back straightened. She pounded her gloves together and took an assertive step toward Prim, moving in for a devastating knee-elbow sequence that made her opponent's head snap back at a wicked angle. Groans erupted from the stands. Rune's expression was one of unbreakable resolve. For the first time since the match began, she felt hopeful. She unleashed a series of powerful kicks that sent Prim stumbling back into the ropes.

"That's it, Rune! Don't stop!" Kit shouted.

She took her eyes off Prim for a split second to acknowledge Kit. That was all it took. The woman recovered her footing and charged toward Rune. The next few seconds felt like they happened in slow motion. Prim leapt in the air, elbow raised. A primeval cry rose from her throat as she brought her entire weight down on the side of Rune's head. A flash of light erupted. Rune's body went limp. After that, everything went dark.

47

Upper Manhattan

"Open your eyes, lady."

The familiar voice sliced through the cottony darkness, but Rune wasn't prepared to obey. It was blissful here. There was no pain. No beast trying to kill her. No crowd giddy to see it happen.

"Wake up."

She felt someone shake her shoulders. *Just five more minutes.*

"I said wake up!"

Rune's eyes drifted open. She blinked slowly. It took her a few seconds to realize she was about as far away from a Muay Thai ring as she could get. She was inside a storage unit that would have terrified even the bravest of souls. A table covered with random metal scraps and rusty hand tools lined one of the walls. On the opposite side was what looked like a serial killer's starter kit, complete with tarps, bottles of bleach, and zip ties. It smelled bad inside the unit, like body odor and rotten meat. Rune's ribs throbbed, just as they did in her dream. She turned her head, sending a bolt of pain through her temple.

"There you are."

Rune's skin turned ashen at the sight of the arms dealer. The man had killed Dion without a moment's hesitation. Nothing was stopping him from doing the same thing to her. Worse, the storage unit contained everything he needed to make it a torturous death.

"You've been out for a while," the man said.

Rune tried to stand, but she understood instantly that she was tied to a chair. Her arms were stretched tightly behind her back, cutting off her circulation. Her legs were immobilized at the ankles. Wholesale panic ensued. She went to war with her restraints.

"Save your energy. You're going to need it."

"Where are we?" Rune's words came out hoarsely. Her throat hurt from being choked. A metallic taste coated the inside of her mouth.

"We're still in my warehouse, in my special storage unit. I keep it to deal with people like you."

"People like me?"

"People who need a bit of convincing to tell the truth."

The man pulled up a chair and sat down across from her. The legs squeaked under his weight. He reached over to brush matted strands from her auburn wig off her cheek. The gesture was gentle and uncomfortably intimate.

"Don't touch me," Rune snapped, jerking her head away.

The man laughed in her face. She lunged at him, nearly toppling her seat over. He was on her in an instant. His hands found her throat. He squeezed until all she could do was gurgle.

"Take it easy, okay?" he said. He tightened his grip and gave her a firm shake when she continued to struggle. "Are you going to take it easy?"

She blinked rapidly.

"Good." He released her neck.

She heaved and took big gulps of air.

"I make it a point to know what's going on around me, so imagine my surprise when you showed up at my warehouse unannounced."

Rune didn't respond.

"Now you're going to tell me who you are and why you're meddling in my affairs."

Still nothing.

"Are you sure that's how you want to play it?"

Her body trembled, but she kept her mouth shut. She knew she was dead the moment she answered his questions.

"Don't say I didn't warn you," he said as he rose to his feet.

Rune didn't see the blow coming. She didn't know if that made it better or worse. The impact of his fist against her jaw sent her head snapping sideways.

"It's going to get a lot worse," the man said, his mouth forming a shallow smile. "Start talking and it will be over quickly. Trust me, you don't want me to take my time."

"Go to hell."

Her words wiped the smile from his face. His cheeks flushed. His entire body grew taut. He drew his fist back and swung again. Rune tucked her chin to protect her face. His fist caught the top of her head. It was better than her jaw, but it still hurt like hell.

"You're going to regret that," the man growled, flexing his sore hand.

She fought to keep the tears from her eyes. She spat at him defiantly. He struck her again, this time in the temple. Stars exploded inside her skull. Then came another punch, and another. Survival instinct kicked in.

"Stop!" she blubbered. "I'll tell you what you want to know. Just please stop!"

He lowered his arm, momentarily appeased.

"Untie me," she begged. "I promise I'll tell you everything if you untie me."

The man relaxed. He reached out to stroke Rune's hair.

She whimpered like a scared animal.

"Shh," he said in a soothing voice. "It's almost over, okay?"

She gave him a desperate nod.

He spoke his next words slowly, like each one was its own sentence. "Now tell me, what brought you to my warehouse?"

"I followed Dion. I came to warn you. I knew he was trying to rip you off."

"Liar."

"I'm not lying."

His fist landed on her jaw again, drawing an involuntary groan from her lips.

"Tell me why you're here."

"I just told you."

He knocked her chair over with his foot. With her hands tied behind her back, she had no way to break her fall. Her head hit the floor with a thud. She let out a loud grunt when he kicked her in the stomach. He kicked her again and again until sweat formed on his brow. He kicked her until she was screaming.

"Stop it!"

Her face was contorted in pain. Blood seeped out of the corner of her mouth, from her nostrils, and from a deep cut on the side of her head. The man reached for the handkerchief in his jacket pocket and wiped the sweat off his brow. "You're going to tell me the truth now, you hear me?"

Rune bobbed her head. She would have agreed to anything at that moment. She trembled when he reached for her, but all he did was hoist her chair back up.

"What are you doing here?"

"I followed Dion. I knew he was planning to rip you off. I wanted to stop him." She cowered in anticipation of the next strike, but it never came.

The man cocked his head as if he was hearing her for the first time. Part of him must have believed what she said because his tone changed suddenly. "Why would you want to help me?"

"I thought we could make a deal. Dion was stupid and careless. He wasn't fit to run your business. I am. I can turn what you've built into an empire."

The man frowned, like he didn't quite believe her. He grew more suspicious as the seconds ticked away. "This is a set-up, isn't it?"

"What?" His sudden about-face terrified Rune.

"Who's listening to us right now? The cops?"

"No one's listening. This isn't a set up."

The man's eyes bulged. He grabbed the collar of her dress and yanked until it tore. Seeing she wasn't wired calmed him down somewhat. Rune saw the opening and took it.

"I could have let Dion screw you over, but instead I came here to warn you. I knew I was risking my life. Would I have done that if I wasn't serious about making a deal?"

"What kind of deal are you talking about?"

"The same deal you made with Dion. Your business in exchange for the Kohl-Stromer ring. The real one." She paused. The pain in her jaw was making it hard to speak. "You want out of the arms trade, right? That was the point of your deal with Dion? You can still have that—with me."

"I have his money and the ring. I don't need you. The business can die for all I care."

Those were not the words Rune hoped to hear. Part of her knew it was useless, but she tried once more to sway him. "Are you really willing to let everything you've worked for disappear? Everyone in the business knows and respects you. Why risk your legacy when you don't have to? Just let me go. Leave your business to me."

The man looked to be considering her words. Rune kept her eyes on him as he started pacing inside the storage unit. Being at a madman's mercy with no way out was like living out her worst nightmare. The pain of his beating was more ferocious than anything she had ever experienced, but it paled next to the fear that was now engulfing her. The man shot Dion without thinking twice. In front of witnesses, no less. Never before had she been more frightened, not even when she was bobbing in the Gulf of Thailand in that vile container. Every part of her body hurt. She didn't want to die, but she didn't want to live through whatever horrible things he would do to her, either.

The pacing stopped. The man approached Rune.

Please not again!

He didn't hit her. Instead, he grabbed her chin with one hand and raised it toward him. His touch was firm. Possessive. It left no question about who was in charge. Rune closed her eyes and imagined she was in the Muay Thai ring of her dream, only he was her opponent, and she was kicking his ass. She was more skillful in her imagination than she was in her sleep, capable of impossible jumps and spins.

The hand on her chin disappeared. Her eyes flew open. She could see the change in his countenance, and it didn't bode well for her. She started to shiver—a violent, uncontrollable shiver that amplified the pain in her body. She nearly threw up when she heard his next words.

"No deal." His face was impassive, as if his decision was entirely inconsequential.

"Wait! Hear me out!" she cried. It couldn't end this way. She wouldn't let it.

The man reached into his pocket. "This is yours," he said, tossing a ring at her feet. It clinked when it hit the ground. His tone turned smug. "I'll keep the real one. Thanks for giving it to me."

He was gone before Rune could respond. The shutter came down on the storage unit. The padlock clicked into place. Rune wondered why he had bothered. She was tied to a chair. It wasn't as if she was going anywhere. Even so, her eyes searched for a way out. The overhead light flicked off, but not before she caught a glimpse of the ring on the floor.

Even in her current state, she knew it was the Kohl-Stromer ring—the real one, not Dion's worthless replica.

"Seriously?" she whispered. A soft laugh came out of her mouth. It was followed by another and another until she dissolved in gales of hysterical laughter. She laughed so hard her shoulders shook. It went on so long her stomach hurt.

Her laughter eventually ebbed. In time it came to a stop. Silence descended upon the storage unit. Rune grew serious and still. She knew where Madee was, and she finally had what she needed to save Kit. Now all she had to do was get out of this room.

48
Upper Manhattan

Ten thousand and eighty minutes. A hundred and sixty-eight hours. Seven measly days. That was all it took for Rune's life to derail.

Seven days ago, she sped through the sweltering streets of Bangkok on the back of a vintage Ducati Scrambler, her arms wrapped tightly around the man of her dreams. Seven days ago, she lived for the next exciting job. Madee was safe at home.

It was fitting that she should end up this way—in a locked room at the mercy of an arms dealer. She had spent her whole life playing with fire. Spying as a child. Delinquency as a teen. Stealing as an adult. She had moved to Bangkok to start over. But you couldn't outrun your past. Now she wondered if she had been running toward it all along.

Rune lost track of how long she had been stuck inside this miserable storage unit. Her arms ached from being pulled so tautly behind her back. Her face throbbed from the thrashing she had received. Come to think of it, there was hardly a spot on her body that didn't hurt. It was no wonder given the week she'd had.

It was the creaking that sent her imagination running. A twinge of panic jabbed at her. *No*, she pleaded silently when she felt it swell inside her chest. She had to keep her wits about her, otherwise she would never get out of this room. She squeezed her eyes shut and counted down slowly.

Five . . . four . . . three . . . two . . . one . . .

Her eyes sprang open. The measured ritual did not have its usual calming effect. Instead, it made her hyperaware of the passing time.

Another creak hoisted Rune's head straight up. Her heart rammed against her ribcage. She took an unsteady breath to force it back into a normal rhythm. Her cheeks puffed when she let the air out. The movement dislodged the auburn strands plastered against her cheek. She wanted to scream when they settled at the base of her neck. Fear magnified every sensation—the scratchiness of her wig, the gritty film coating her tinted contacts, the starched cotton of her torn navy-blue dress.

A bead of sweat rolled off her brow, snaking its way down her temple until it reached the tip of her earlobe. It slithered past the jade studs her father gave her, dangling perilously for a moment before dripping onto her neck. It was the smallest of things, but it was the proverbial last straw. A feral growl emerged from her lips as her willpower faltered and slipped away. She bucked ferociously against her bindings, twisting her feet against them so violently she cried out from the pain. But pain didn't deter her. No. Pain cut through the fear. She wanted to feel every bit of it.

Rune fought madly against her restraints. She fought until she was spent. Silence filled the room. Her panic built up. Then the creaking returned, prompting her to fight again. So went the cycle until she was drained of all energy. With nothing left to give, she resumed her compulsive counting.

Five . . . four . . . three . . . two . . . one . . . Five . . . four . . . three . . . two . . . one . . .

She counted down methodically. Obsessively. Bodily autonomy was no longer hers, but she still had her mind. That no one could ever take from her.

The signs of trouble were faint at first. An acrid smell. A strange sound. The room was suffocating.

It's all in your head, Rune chastised herself silently. She had almost convinced herself when a whiff of smoke crept into her nostrils. Then her eyes started to burn, and it wasn't the wretched contacts.

"No!" she croaked. The realization of what he had done came crashing down on her. All the creaking wasn't him pacing outside the door. It was the sound of wood being transformed—at a molecular level—by heat. The warehouse was on fire, and there was no way out. "Help!" she called out, even though there was no one around to hear her. "Somebody! Please, help me!" She redoubled her efforts to free herself, roaring with fear and rage as smoke poured into the storage unit. She didn't want to die this way—alone in the dark. She didn't want to die at all. A fit of coughing wracked her body, but still Rune struggled, thrashing so wildly she shredded her skin and sprained her own wrist. "Let me out!" she screamed, kicking and pulling as she sought to escape her fate.

The smoke thickened. Rune's fear turned to terror. She gasped for air knowing that soon, there would be none left to breathe.

The walls rumbled like distant thunder. A crash rang out from somewhere nearby. Rune knew instantly that part of the warehouse's framework had collapsed. When old buildings went, they went fast.

Facing certain death—and an excruciating one at that—there were some who would have closed their eyes and let the smoke take them. Rune was not among them. She knew that her efforts were futile. Even if she managed to break free of her bindings, she would still have to get through the locked door. None of that mattered. She had to fight. Kit and Madee were depending on her. She would fight until there was not an ounce of fight left in her.

The smoke was everywhere. It swirled around her, caressing her body and seeping into her orifices. Her eyes burned. Her lungs ached. A feeling of nausea swept over her. Still she willed herself to keep going.

"Help me!" she screamed over and over again. She choked back a sob when her pleas went unanswered. The cost of her failures filled her with profound sadness. The feeling washed over her. It blotted out fear. It blotted out everything.

Her movements slowed as her energy began to wane. "You can do this . . . you can do this . . ." she intoned before breaking into a fit of coughing. She tried to keep fighting, but she couldn't summon the strength to continue. Her senses grew foggy. Her eyelids fluttered. She began hearing voices inside her mind—Kit declaring his love, Madee's carefree laugh. Her body stilled as she felt herself start to let go.

Going up.

Her breathing slowed.

All clear.

The darkness called out to her.

Door.

Her eyes cracked open. "I'm in here," she whispered when she realized the voice was real. When her own voice failed her, she used what little energy she had to pound her foot against the floor.

I hear something! Taking action!

There was a moment of terrifying silence, followed by a resounding crash.

"Please," Rune whimpered.

The metal door rolled up. In stepped a giant holding a flat head axe. "What the hell?" he said when he saw her strapped to the chair. He quickly untied her. She slid to the floor, pawing around in the darkness until her fingers curled around the Kohl-Stromer ring. He scooped her into his arms and carried her out of the burning building.

Rune woke up on a gurney in the middle of the street with a brace around her neck and an oxygen mask on her face. Two EMTs with concerned expressions were wheeling her toward a waiting ambulance.

"Stop," Rune said before they could load her in. She tried to remove the mask, but her arms were strapped in place. She rocked frantically from side to side trying to break free.

"It's okay. You're safe now," said the EMT by her head.

The gurney stopped moving. His face came into focus. It was odd seeing him from this angle. The perspective distorted his features, amplifying his nostrils and chin dimple. She relaxed when she saw his eyes. They were black. They were kind. They reminded her of Kit's.

"My name is Zaf. I'm going to help you. Can you tell me your name?"

"Where are you taking me?" The words came out as a throaty rasp.

"New York Presbyterian in Washington Heights. Don't worry. The doctors there will take good care of you."

Rune pulled at her straps again.

"Those are for your safety."

"I know what they're for," she said between labored breaths. "Now get them off me."

Zaf and his partner exchanged worried looks but obliged.

Rune sat up with difficulty. She removed the mask. "This too," she said, indicating the neck brace.

"It's not safe. You could have a spinal injury."

"I was tied to a chair, not pushed off a building."

Zaf eyed her uncertainly.

"I promise not to sue you."

He tore the Velcro loose.

Rune swung her legs over the side of the gurney and turned toward the warehouse she had just escaped. It was engulfed in flames. The brave men and women of the FDNY were fighting to contain it. The plaintive wail of sirens pierced the air. Red and black plumes ascended into the dark sky. Rune turned to Zaf, her eyes full of questions. "How did the firemen know I was in there?"

"Whoever called to report the fire told them."

Who could that have been?

"You're lucky the firemen knew where to look for you. It could have turned out very differently."

Rune twisted her torso and scanned the crowd that had gathered to gawk at the fire. People had risen from their beds to see what was happening. She couldn't say she blamed them. Rubbernecking was human nature. There was a grandfather in checkered pajamas, a woman with foam rollers in her hair, and a boy who looked too old to be sucking his thumb. Rune thought she spotted a familiar figure in the midst of the chaos. She squinted through the haze of smoke. The man's short-sleeved shirt was neatly pressed. His black hair was shot with white.

"Dad?" she called out.

He was too far away to hear her clearly, but he raised his hand in response.

"Dad!"

He ducked under the yellow tape. A police officer with a moon round face and a sensible ponytail tried to stop him. There was some back and forth. The conversation grew animated. Finally, the officer let him pass.

"Oh my god, Dad!" Rune cried when he drew nearer. She jumped off the gurney and promptly fell to the ground. He was by her side in seconds, grabbing her arm and helping her to her feet. She clung to him like she did when she was a little girl, before she was disbelieved and sent away.

"You're alright, Rune. Everything is alright."

"How did you find me?" she sobbed.

"I saw you at Sotheby's. I knew you were going to try to steal the ring. I followed you to Bemelmans and then here."

"Why didn't you say something?"

"Would you have listened to me if I had?"

Rune stayed silent. He had a point.

"I assume there's a good reason you did all this."

She wanted to tell him everything—about Kit and Madee and Lemaire—but old wounds were hard to heal, and trust couldn't be rebuilt in a day.

"Did you at least get what you came for?"

"I did," she conceded, knowing he was referring to the ring. Her father had saved her life. He deserved to know at least that.

"The police are going to want to talk to you."

"I know."

"It's not a good idea, given the circumstances."

"I know," she repeated. She saw his gaze move past her and knew instantly that the cops were approaching.

"Is she okay to answer a few questions?" came a husky voice from behind. The speaker was a statuesque brunette with flawless olive skin and perceptive brown eyes. She was blessed with naturally serious features that criminals feared and victims found comforting.

"I can talk," Rune said before breaking into a fit of hacking.

"I'm Detective Alejandra Vega from the 32nd precinct. What's your name, please?"

"Effie. Effie Davis." As a matter of principle, Rune never gave cops her real name, not unless she had to.

"Are you alright, Effie? Can you tell me what happened to you?"

Rune exchanged looks with her father. She couldn't very well admit what had happened. Her shoulders rose and fell.

"You don't remember?" Vega said, filling in the blanks.

"It's fuzzy. One minute I was having drinks with a friend. The next thing I remember is waking up in a storage unit. The man who took me there hit me. He wouldn't stop." Her eyes welled up. It wasn't the complete truth, but it was close enough.

"Do you know who this man is?"

"I've never seen him before."

"Can you describe him?"

"It was dark."

Vega's brow creased, like she knew Rune was deliberately being uncooperative. That didn't stop her from trying again. "The FDNY pulled a man's body out of the warehouse. He'd been shot in the chest. Do you know anything about that?"

Rune shook her head.

"They also found weapons, a lot of them. Can you tell me anything about them?"

The detective's questions were getting uncomfortable. It was clear she wasn't going to let up. Apparently, her father shared her opinion because he chose that moment to step in.

"Excuse me, Detective. This woman need go to hospital."

Rune broke into another coughing fit, but it wasn't because of the smoke in her lungs. Her father—a man who spoke English with only a hint of an accent—sounded like he had just gotten off a plane from the Thai countryside. She caught his eye. There was a look in it that she had never seen before—somewhere between steely purpose and mischief.

Detective Vega turned her back to Rune to address Aran. "And who are you, sir?"

"Just bystander."

"This is a restricted area. You're going to have to wait behind the yellow tape."

He held up his hands in mock surrender. "I only try to help."

"I understand, sir, but I need you to move back. It's not safe here."

"Who I tell about man?"

Vega's attention spiked. Cooperative witnesses were hard to come by, and this one had fallen onto her lap. She gave the man her full attention. "Am I understanding you correctly, sir? You saw someone near the warehouse?"

He gave an emphatic nod.

Vega couldn't believe her good fortune. She had just applied for a promotion. Solving a big gun-running case was sure to land her the job. She pulled her notebook out of her jacket pocket and flipped to a clean page. "I'm listening, sir."

"I saw man outside warehouse. Then big fire." He raised his arms to indicate towering flames.

"Can you provide a description?"

His expression turned blank, like he didn't understand what she meant.

"What did this man look like? Was he old? Young?"

"Young. Maybe twenty-five . . . thirty. Short hair."

"Do you remember what he was wearing?"

"Dark pants. Black shirt. No sleeves."

"And about how tall was he?"

A shrug indicated he didn't know.

"Was he taller or shorter than me?"

"Same."

Detective Vega was thrilled. This man's memory was better than most. With any luck, his information would help crack the case and she would finally get the recognition she deserved. For years she had watched from the sidelines while less talented colleagues got promoted. For years she had pretended to be happy for them. It was her turn now. A nervous excitement ran through her as she once again addressed her witness. "This is very important, sir. Did you see where the man went after leaving the warehouse?"

"That way," he said, pointing toward the Polo Grounds Towers.

It was all Vega could do not to pump her fist in the air. "This is very helpful," she said with a broad smile. "Now I just need your name and contact information."

"There's more."

"Oh?" Vega's eyes widened. This night could not get any better.

"The man—he was not alone."

"Who was he with?"

"Not who. What."

Vega tilted her head, intrigued.

"A Bichon. Bolognese. Smaller than Bichon Frisé. Very nice dogs."

Vega's face fell. She snapped her notebook shut. This man hadn't witnessed anything except a random guy walking his dog. Her disappointment was so acute she thought she might choke on it. She wanted to tell the man to get lost. She wanted to scream a bunch of expletives at him. Then she remembered what she had learned in the community outreach training course she had taken the previous month, the one she was told would help her get a promotion. "Thanks very much for coming forward, sir," she said with only the slightest trace of frustration in her voice. "You've been a big help. You can go now."

"Happy to help."

Vega managed a tight smile, but inside, she was cursing like a sailor. She had a complicated case to solve, and this man had just wasted precious minutes of her time. She stewed for a moment, then she shook off her anger and swallowed her disappointment. With a calming breath, she turned back to her victim.

The woman was gone.

EPILOGUE

Central Bangkok

Rune started sweating the moment she stepped out of the airport and onto Bangkok's steamy streets. For once, she didn't mind the heat. She angled her face toward the sun and inhaled deeply as its rays stroked her skin. The waistband of her jeans pressed uncomfortably against her tender stomach. Her sprained wrist throbbed beneath its bandage. Cuts and bruises crisscrossed her face. Despite her injuries, Rune felt rejuvenated. No. She felt alive. For the first time in more than a week, she was in control.

Rune hailed a tuk-tuk with her uninjured hand and slid onto the leather seat. She hesitated for a moment before telling the driver her destination. He smirked at her accent. The slight rolled right off her back.

They drove to a neighborhood called Thong Lor, which literally translates to *molten gold*. Until recently, it was a no-go area known primarily for its car dealerships and gaudy wedding showrooms. Its transformation happened at warp speed, like everything else in the booming Thai capital. Young creative types moved into the neighbor-hood, bringing with them street art, funky eateries, and an unbeatable nightlife. What Thong Lor lacked in temples and historic sites, it made up for in sheer energy. Housing options were diverse. It was well connected to public transportation. It also happened to be a stone's throw from the notorious Khlong Toei slum.

The hum of traffic dimmed as soon as the tuk-tuk took a right off Thong Lor Road. They passed an international middle school. It was deserted. Rune's brow furrowed. Then she remembered that school was already out for the day.

The gated entrance to SOI 55 appeared on the right. Rune knew the Michelin-rated restaurant well. Kit had taken her there to celebrate after their very first heist. They had dined on rainy season bamboo, a deconstructed pomelo salad, and several other dishes that came in portions so small Rune was hangry by the fourth course. Kit had promptly paid the five-hundred-dollar tab and whisked her away to Saphan Lueng, one of the city's top destinations for street food. Once there, they devoured Thai porridge with seabass, a spicy cockle salad, and a heap of noodles so tall passersby stopped to take pictures. The memory drew a smile from her.

The tuk-tuk rattled to a stop. Rune paid the driver and stepped out. A group of young skateboarders shouted "We love you" from across the street. Rune had to laugh at their benign attempt at catcalling. She turned toward a derelict apartment block with a low wall enclosing an unkempt yard. She stepped inside the unattended lobby, called for the elevator, and took it to the sixth floor.

Florescent lights illuminated the hallway. The smell of wet dog and dirty carpet filled the air. Rune counted the apartment numbers inside her head: *602, 604, 606*. She stopped in front of apartment 608.

The distinctive sound of video game gunfire filtered through the door. Rune raised her hand and rasped her knuckles against the wood. The apartment went quiet. She sensed movement behind the door.

"Open up. I know you're in there," she called out.

Silence.

"I can see your eye." She knocked harder now. The sound cut through the silence of the hallway, drawing a curious neighbor from her home. Rune waved her away. "I'm not going anywhere, so you might as well let me in."

The deadbolt clicked. The door opened a crack. Rune pushed it so hard it banged the startled occupant in the face. Her eyes turned to narrow slits.

Standing in front of her wearing nothing but a wrinkled t-shirt and boxer shorts was Thanu, the lanky young man in charge of security at the Khlong Toei Youth Center. His arms were as skinny as she remembered. An S-shaped scar marred his left calf. His long hair was swept up in his usual man-bun. Rune's face darkened as she thought back to a conversation she had with a desperate young girl trapped inside a shipping container.

I saw Madee at the Youth Center. She was kissing some guy.

What guy?

I don't know his name. Someone older. He was tall and skinny, with hair like a Samurai.

"Remember me?" asked Rune.

Thanu nodded nervously.

"Where is she?"

"What are you talking about?"

"Cut the crap."

"There's no one here."

"Bullshit." Rune brushed past Thanu and strode into the living room. Dirty laundry was strewn across a blue velvet couch that had seen better days. The pale linoleum flooring was cracked and peeling up at the edges. Rune's eyes landed on a pair of Xbox controllers on the coffee table. "Madee!" she called out. She didn't wait for a response before stalking into the miniscule kitchen. It was empty. She glanced at the heap of dishes in the sink with distaste. "Madee!" she called again, rushing into the bedroom. The girl was nowhere in sight.

"I told you I was alone."

Rune's eyes flashed. She got within inches of Thanu's face. "If you did something to her, I'll kill you," she seethed.

Thanu watched in stunned silence as she stormed out of his apartment.

Rune waited for him across the street, behind a stumpy palm tree with a clear view of his building. It took all of ten minutes for him to appear. He adjusted his bun and set off at a brisk pace. She followed him to the Skytrain.

They rode six stops to Siam Station. Thanu kept his eyes on his phone the entire time. He was so absorbed that he didn't notice Rune sitting just a few feet away from him.

They transferred to the number 79 bus heading west. It was packed. Staying out of sight was cakewalk.

The ride was long. It took them past the Democracy Monument and into Banglamphu—the oldest part of the city. The bus slowed, its progress hindered by one of Bangkok's legendary traffic jams. The journey across the Phra Pinklao Bridge was never-ending.

Rune frowned when Thanu buzzed for his stop some time later. She knew the neighborhood well. It was minutes from the small house she shared with Kit and Madee. Her stomach tightened.

She could almost explain away the first two turns Thanu took after he got off the bus, but by the third, his destination was clear as day. Home was at the end of the street—on a quiet canal with a flowering rain tree growing on the opposite bank. Still, she could hardly believe it when he marched right up to her house and rang the doorbell. She held her breath. The door swung open.

And there she was. Standing in the late-afternoon sun, her hair coiled in playful space buns. Madee. Precocious, gap-toothed Madee. She had been right there all along. Rune stumbled forward. She wanted to shake the girl until her teeth rattled. She wanted to ground her for the rest of her days. Instead, she rushed past Thanu and drew her close. "Thank god you're okay," she whispered, her arms tightening around the teen's pliant body.

"Where were you?" Madee asked the moment Rune let her go.

"Where was *I*?"

"You've been MIA forever. What the hell?"

"I was out looking for *you*. What happened?"

"Nothing happened. Thanu picked me up after school last week. I stayed with him for a few of days. You guys weren't home when I got back."

"Why didn't you call me?"

"My bag was stolen. My phone was inside."

"You couldn't borrow one?"

Madee rolled her eyes as only a teenager could. "Like I know your number. It's programmed into my phone. I called Kit a billion times. He never picked up. He's not with you?"

"I'm meeting him later."

Madee bobbed her head, blissfully unaware of the danger Kit was in and the upheaval she had caused. Rune gently asked her to step inside. Then she turned her attention to Thanu.

"Why on earth didn't you tell me where she was?"

"I didn't know who you were. Why would I tell you anything?"

"Because I told you she was missing!"

"Well, I asked her to call you. She said she didn't know how to reach you."

Right, Rune thought. *No phone number.*

Rune poked her head inside the house after sending Thanu home. Madee was in the living room listening to music and painting her fingernails bright turquoise. She looked up when she noticed Rune and said, "Thanu left?"

"Yup."

"Where are you meeting Kit?"

"At the Mandarin Oriental."

"The bar?"

"The Riverside Terrace."

"Can I come?"

"It's better if you don't."

Madee blew on her nails.

"We'll be home in a couple of hours. It's really important that you wait for us here."

"Why?"

"Just promise me, okay?"

"Okay," Madee said with a shrug. She peered at Rune. Her nose crinkled. "No offense, but you look terrible. You should drink more water."

Rune started to respond, but then thought better of it. The mouthiness. The lying. The stealing. Those were conversations for another day. She gave Madee a long hug and walked out of the house.

A shadow fell across her face as soon as she stepped outside. She looked up briefly. The sun had disappeared behind an angry black cloud.

Soon the sky would open and release buckets of water onto the city. Rune wasn't worried. *This too shall pass*, she said silently.

She set off for her rendezvous with Lemaire. They had arranged an exchange—the Kohl-Stromer ruby for Kit. She would still be in his debt, but she would worry about that later. She glanced at her watch. She had a bit of time before their meeting. *Good*, she thought. There was something she had to take care of first.

The Mandarin Oriental, Bangkok

They were meeting at the Mandarin Oriental. Rune was not the least bit nervous about the venue, despite having wreaked havoc at the hotel the previous week. She looked the part in a white one-shoulder jumpsuit and lips the color of Bing cherries. Artfully applied makeup covered all her cuts and bruises. Barely-there sandals showed off her fresh pedicure. Tonight was about a lot of things, but practicality was not among them. She stepped inside the marble lobby and gazed at the floral arrangement that hung from the center of the coffered ceiling like a chandelier. Her eyes dropped to the fountain filled with pink lotus flowers directly below. She turned slowly. There were no outward signs of the damage she had caused—no broken furniture, no chips in the floor, no shattered windows.

They had a reservation at the Riverside Terrace at the back of the hotel. Rune brought her palms together and bowed at the smiling maître d' who greeted her at the entrance. He led her to a table right by the water and pulled out her chair. Rune lowered herself into it gingerly, careful to protect her battered body.

The view called out to her. It was so exquisite that for a split second, she forgot about her pain. The sun was sliding down on the horizon, streaking the sky in orange and purple. The mighty Chao Phraya gleamed ephemerally under the dwindling light. Rune found herself suddenly grateful for her adopted city and all its offerings.

She felt Lemaire's presence as soon as he entered the restaurant. She stood when she saw him approach. He was dressed impeccably, as usual. The pleat in his trousers was razor-sharp, the matching jacket perfectly tailored. His eyes looked paler than ever against his cornflower blue shirt. She extended her hand, determined not to be intimidated by him. They were business partners after all, albeit unequal ones.

"Good evening, Rune." His handshake was firm and confident. His skin surprisingly cool and dry.

She bobbed her head once in response.

"You look well," he said after they took their seats.

"As do you."

A waiter in a black suit approached and hovered over them. Lemaire dismissed him with a curt wave of his hand. "I take it New York went off without a hitch?"

Rune nearly laughed in his face. If only he knew. "Everything went fine."

"Give it to me."

"Not until you let Kit go."

"If I let him go, I lose my leverage."

"If I give you the ruby, I lose *my* leverage."

"We seem to be at an impasse."

"It looks like we'll just have to trust each other."

Lemaire smiled, like he admired Rune's nerve.

"Why don't we split the difference?" she said, keeping her tone even. "I'll give you the ring after you prove to me that Kit is alive."

Lemaire gave her a thoughtful look and pulled out his phone. He spoke into it quietly. Then he gestured to the back of the restaurant.

A jolt of emotion coursed through Rune when she saw Kit by the bar. He looked worn out, but uninjured. Standing beside him were the two men who had chased them through the Omni—Lemaire's hired guns. Rune turned her attention back to him.

"I've fulfilled my part of the deal. Now where's my ring?" he asked.

Rune pulled her necklace out from the top of her jumpsuit. The Kohl-Stromer ring hung from the end, dazzling as ever. She unclasped the chain and placed the ring on the table.

Lemaire picked it up to inspect it. A satisfied expression crossed his face. He had been in the business long enough to know the real thing when he saw it. He tucked the ring in his jacket pocket and rose to his feet. "This has been a most fruitful evening," he said as he extended his hand again.

Rune looked at him with a tinge of distrust before standing and accepting his handshake.

"I'll be in touch shortly with your next assignment," he added. He made a move to leave.

"Wait! How long will I have to work for you?"

"Until I say so."

Rune's face darkened.

"And in case you get any funny ideas, just remember that I can get to you and the people you care about no matter where you go. Nowhere is out of reach." Lemaire paused to see if his words provoked a response, but Rune kept her expression neutral. He gave her a final look before turning and walking away.

Rune followed him with her eyes, watching as he squeezed through a group of boisterous diners by the entrance, bumping into a teenager more focused on his phone than on the people around him. Her attention shifted to the bar. Relief washed over her when she saw

Kit standing alone, no goons in sight. He raised his hand. She took a tentative step forward. Then she ran to him and fell into his arms. Her hands found his face and chest and neck. She couldn't stop touching him, his realness, his thereness.

"She's safe, Kit. Madee is safe," she said, choking back a sob.

"I knew you'd find her," he replied, his voice full of emotion.

Rune felt her chin start to wobble. All the stress and fear of the last seven days were finally catching up to her. The floodgates opened. She closed her eyes as hot tears spilled down her cheeks.

"Don't cry, Rune," Kit said. He cupped her face with both hands and stroked it tenderly.

"Lemaire. He owns me now. He owns you."

"It's okay, you hear me? We're okay. The two of us, we can get through anything."

"We'll never be free. He'll never let us go."

"We'll figure out a way. I promise. It won't be forever."

Rune's next words rushed out so fast they were barely coherent. "It's not just Lemaire, Kit. Something terrible is happening in Khlong Toei. The director of the Youth Center is trafficking girls. The priest is in on it. They killed the policeman who was helping me and locked me in a shipping container. And my dad—he saved me from a fire. I got away and . . ."

"Shh. Slow down, my love. You're not making any sense."

Rune's shoulders shook as she wept quietly.

Kit leaned in and pressed his nose against hers, like he did the first time they met. It calmed Rune instantly. Her body stilled. He kissed her lips softly. Then he pulled back and looked deeply into her eyes. "Madee is okay," he said. "We're both okay. That's all that matters. Everything else we can figure out."

Rune nodded and wiped her wet face with her fingers.

"What do you say we get out of here?"

Another nod.

He took her hand and squeezed it tightly.

She held on like she would never let go.

They left the restaurant and found their way back to the lobby. They stepped outside. The air smelled of sweet jasmine. The city was a constellation of lights. Kit raised his arm to hail a tuk-tuk.

"No," Rune said. "This way." Her voice was steady now. Her eyes were clear. Her moment of fragility had passed.

"Where are we going?"

"Not far." She shot him a faint smile and led him around the corner to an alley lined with towering fan palms. The breeze picked up, sending drops of rainwater rolling from the massive leaves.

Kit spotted the vintage Ducati Scrambler parked under a streetlight instantly. He turned to face Rune and said, "For me?"

Her smile broadened.

He circled it slowly, running his hand over the yellow and black frame.

"Do you like it?"

"Do I like it?" he repeated incredulously.

"What are you waiting for, then?" called a voice from behind.

Rune and Kit spun around, squinting through the darkness.

"Madee?" Kit said.

The girl stepped into the light. She looked older than her fifteen years in a strapless black minidress and full makeup. Her dark eyes twinkled impishly. Her glossy black hair grazed the small of her back.

"I thought I told you to stay home," said Rune, suddenly wishing she hadn't told Madee where she was meeting Kit.

"Yeah, but I didn't want to miss out on all the fun."

Rune and Kit exchanged concerned looks. Kit opened his mouth to say something, but the sound of screeching tires followed by a chorus of agitated voices interrupted him. The commotion was coming from the entrance to the Mandarin Oriental. The voices grew louder and more numerous. A lump formed in Rune's throat when she realized it was Lemaire and his men.

"I think they're looking for this," said Madee, holding out her hand.

Rune lowered her gaze. There, in Madee's outstretched palm, was the glittering Kohl-Stromer ring. She froze. The crowd outside the Riverside Terrace. The distracted teenager who bumped into Lemaire. Madee had used the moment to steal the ring. She felt Kit's eyes boring into her. "Don't look at me," she said with a vigorous shake of her head. "This isn't my fault."

"Whose fault is it, then?"

"I'm the one who fixed everything!"

"Uh, you guys," Madee interjected. She angled her head toward the street.

Rune turned. Two security guards from the Mandarin Oriental had materialized at the end of the alley. One had a cellphone glued to his ear. The other was staring at them with undisguised suspicion. She locked eyes with him.

"Thang nan!" he shouted. *Over there!*

A rush of adrenaline flooded her body. Her senses sharpened. Her heart did a somersault inside her chest. She breathed deeply, savoring the familiar feeling.

"Let's go," Kit said, barging in on the moment.

"Oh, yes!" Rune replied.

He threw his leg over the bike. Rune and Madee scrambled on behind him. The Ducati hummed to life. And in an instant, they were gone.

THE END

Acknowledgments

I want to thank my editor, Luisa Smith, whose incisive feedback and eye for detail made this book the best it could possibly be. I owe a debt of gratitude to Otto Penzler, Charles Perry, Julia O'Connell, Will Luckman, and the entire team at Mysterious Press and Mysterious Bookshop for their steadfast commitment to this project. I thank Liza Fleissig, literary agent extraordinaire, and her business partner, Ginger Harris-Dontzin, for their unwavering support of my writing and career. My sincere thanks also go to Erin Mitchell for tirelessly championing this book.

The road to publication was full of ups and downs. I want to thank my family for their love and optimism on this journey: Kim and Christiane Doquang, Doan Doquang, Mathis and Jonathan Strasser, Ralph and Mary Selby, and the extended Selby and Wolever clan. A special thank you to my sister, Kimchi, for being my sounding board and always having something positive to say, even on early drafts. I also am grateful to Jennifer Udell, Daniel Newsome, and Anne Hrychuk Kontokosta for a lifetime of friendship, and to the many friends and relatives, at home and abroad, who inspired and supported me while I wrote this book. Finally, I thank my husband, Don Selby, for his encouragement, his advice, and the pleasure of his company around the world and back again.